The Write Way to Die

HUT 22
BOOKS

For Tanya.
With best wishes.

The Write Way to Die

Jo Bavington-Jones

The Write Way to Die

2nd edition published by Hut 22 Books in the United Kingdom 2025

1st edition (ISBN 978-1-913567-90-3) published by The Conrad Press in the United Kingdom in 2021

Tel: +44(0)7921 887519

www.hut22books.com

jo@hut22books.com

Print book ISBN 978-1-0683088-6-4

eBook ISBN 9781839787829

Typesetting and Cover Design by: Charlotte Mouncey, www.bookstyle.co.uk

Printed and bound in Great Britain by Clays Ltd, Elcograf S.p.A.

Also in this series

Bang to Rights

The Wipeout Round

The Wrong Mind Murders

Other books by Jo Bavington-Jones

Lucy Shaw's Not Sure

Lucy Shaw Wants More

A Giraffe Thing

The Bonfire Buddleia

For Sam. Always for Sam.

It takes two to make a murder. There are born victims, born to have their throats cut, as the cut-throats are born to be hanged.

Aldous Huxley

CHAPTER 1

One door closes

It was my last week working at the vet's, and I couldn't wait for it to be over. It was almost exactly a year since I'd started, foolishly believing it would be my dream job of cuddling puppies and cooing over kittens. With a little bit of admin and phone-answering thrown in. And there had been puppies. And kittens. There had been some amazing, heart-warming moments. But many more awful, heart-wrenching ones.

I think back to my interview when they asked how I would feel about assisting the vet with the 'occasional euthanasia'? I'd said I thought I'd be okay as I'd been through it with my own pets in the past, and felt I could handle myself well in that situation. 'Professional, but empathetic' were the words I used, if I remember rightly. They obviously believed me, because I got the job, and I really needed a job at that particular time in my life.

It was two years since my marriage had ended and I'd muddled along on my savings and part-time income until I had to admit that I needed more money coming in. When I saw the advert for the Veterinary Receptionist job, I didn't hesitate to apply. As I filled out the application, I took stock of myself and my life. Amy Archer, age fifty-one, divorced, no children (it had just never happened for us... I think that's what destroyed us in the end), shared custody of an Old English Sheepdog called Dexter, and a gnawing feeling that life was passing me by.

I'm sitting behind my desk in the reception area of one of the branch surgeries, leaning back in my rather ancient swivel chair, which feels as if it could give way at any moment, and twirling my long brown hair around my fingers. This branch is very much the poor relation of the group and is furnished with stuff that wasn't good enough for the others. The client chairs in reception are a prime example, having been cast out like unwanted kittens, their un-wipeable fabric covers making them wholly unfit for purpose. Personally I wouldn't sit in them, and regularly sprayed them with flea-killer. The young vet, Cameron, is not as squeamish and is sitting in one of the client chairs opposite me, eating a Magnum Ice Cream and, in between bites, telling me about the disastrous date he went on the previous night. We have no appointments booked in for another hour or so and are enjoying the peace. Cameron is the newest of our team of vets and as camp as a row of tents. I adore him. He's a drama queen of RADA standards and makes me laugh just by walking into the room. I do love being on shift with him, and he's without doubt one of the reasons I *will* be sad to go.

But there are so many more reasons to leave: the awful split shifts, the minimum wage, the abusive clients, and the endless heartbreak and pain. I'm sure there are many more greys threaded through my hair now, and there are definitely more lines around my green eyes, and deeper furrows between my brows. One thing they hadn't mentioned at my interview, was that most new receptionists lasted less than a month. I could feel proud I'd lasted a year then.

I stick my hand in the bag of sweets on the desk in front of me, pulling out a Colin the Caterpillar and biting his head off.

That was another thing about the job – we all seemed to run on sugar and caffeine. My five feet eight, size twelve frame had more curves than it had done twelve months ago. My muffin top was exactly that. Cameron finishes his ice cream and holds out a hand for a sweet. I throw one over to him and he chucks it in whole, while spinning his legs around and putting them up on the chair next to him. I follow suit and put my feet up on my desk, silently praying that the chair survives the manoeuver and no one walks in off the street to catch us. We feel like we've earned the right to this time out after a stressful clinic earlier in the day.

'That's it! I'm joining the gym,' Cameron exclaims, pulling his dark green veterinary top down over his belly, which can be seen protruding over his waistband.

'I'll believe it when I see it. You've been saying it every day since you started here. Proof's in the pudding,' I say, breathing in as I munch on another jelly sweet.

'Pudding's in my belly,' Cameron groans. 'I'm such a pig.'

I reach into my bag underneath the desk and pull out a packet of Percy Pigs, tearing it open and holding one out to him. 'You are what you eat,' I grin at him.

'You wicked temptress, you!' he says in his best West End voice, but holding out his hand for the sweet anyway.

'I know, but someone has to save me from myself, and it might as well be you. You're so easily led. Anyway, you only have to put up with me for another few days.'

Cameron sticks out his bottom lip. 'God! It won't be the same without you here. I really wish you weren't leaving. You're the best receptionist we have, and you bring sweeties. And you make me laugh.' His bottom lip protrudes even further.

'I'm sorry. I'll miss you too, but it's time. I'm done. And we can keep in touch. I still owe you a trip to the pub to introduce you to the gorgeous gay landlord.'

Cameron claps his hands together like a small child. A girl child. I do so love him. 'Yay!' he says, his bottom lip forced to partake in an open smile.

I smile back. 'If I'd had a son, I would've been very happy if he'd been just like you.'

'What? Short, tubby and gay?'

'You know what I mean. You have a good heart, young Cameron Clarke. Never change. Apart from out of that scrub top. It is *way* too small and your wee belly is peeping out!' I've slipped into a Scots accent for some reason. Cameron's name may be Scottish, but he's very much Home Counties, like me.

'Well, you know you're my surrogate mama. Even if you are abandoning me.' The bottom lip is back in play, and he turns his head away with the back of his hand drawn across his darkly bearded face in feigned distress.

'Muppet. If you ever give up being a vet, you should be on the stage.'

'I know, dahlink, I missed my calling.'

'You certainly did,' I agree, just as the phone rings.

'Rude,' Cameron says huffily.

'I know! Do they think we're here to work?' I answer the call as professionally as I can with a half-chewed caterpillar in my mouth and a grin on my face.

It's the finance officer from the main branch, asking for Cameron. I pull a face at him and mime cutting my throat. He doesn't need to be told who it is as I pass the handset to him. Never was a person more aptly named than Mona. She usually phones at least once a day to tell one of us off. Today is Cameron's turn. He's probably used a paperclip inappropriately or stapled something at the wrong angle. I try to put him off with my best moany Mona facial expressions. Naturally, I'm mid face-pull, and Cameron silently mouthing obscenities down the phone, when the door from the street opens.

CHAPTER 2

Another door opens

I recognise the client coming through the door straightaway, even though her head is down as she focuses her attention on manoeuvring her slim frame and the cat buggy through the doorway. It's the bright pink hair that's the giveaway.

I wait until she's in and closing the door behind her before I greet her.

'Hello,' I say brightly. 'And hello, Marmite,' I add, trying to peer inside the cat carrier on top of the buggy. 'Have a seat, you're all booked in.'

Cameron had made himself scarce as soon as the front door opened, closing the inner door between reception and the consulting room as he tried to pacify Mona. At least he now had an excuse to end the call quickly.

'Sorry I'm a bit early,' pink-hair lady says, looking up at me through her black-framed glasses.

She is *very* early. 'No problem. Luckily we're not too busy, so you should be able to get in and see the vet a bit earlier. How's Marmite been?' Marmite is a new rescue cat, and pink-hair lady is a very committed pet owner.

'She's been okay until now. Very nervous still though. Won't come downstairs. I have to feed her in the bedroom. She's just got a mucky eye today,' pink-hair lady says quietly. She always seems anxious somehow, and never very animated.

I smile reassuringly, thinking for a second that Marmite and her owner are well-suited. 'Well, we'll get Cameron to take a look. Hopefully it's nothing to worry about and a few days of ointment will do the trick.'

Pink-hair lady smiles back. I can't keep calling her pink-hair lady. Her name is actually Jenny Jones. She's been a regular visitor to the surgery while I've been working here, and sadly we had to put her previous cat to sleep not so long ago. Jenny Jones is one of those people you form impressions of quickly. Quiet, quirky and shy. Unassuming, and maybe a little socially awkward. She adores her cats, though, and is dedicated to their well-being. She's the perfect client, really. When I first met her, and on all the subsequent visits, it never occurred to me that we could possibly have anything in common. Apart from a love of cats.

'I probably won't see you again, I'm afraid,' I say to her as we wait for Cameron. 'I'm leaving to write my third novel.' (I know, I've kept that quiet, but that's what I did after my marriage broke up. I wrote two books.)

'Oh! I'm a writer too,' Jenny's face registers surprise at my revelation, just before mine does the same.

'No? Really?'

We're both suddenly animated, and I think to myself that you should never judge a head by its pink hair and shyness.

'I'm sorry that you're leaving though. You're such a good receptionist, and you were amazing when I had to have Gizmo put to sleep.'

'Oh, thank you! I'm sad in some ways, and I will miss the vets, and my regular clients, but I'm never going to make it as a writer if I'm not writing. What sort of thing do you write?'

'Oh, all sorts, articles, blogs, short stories – I'm a freelancer.

There's a local book festival happening next month; I could try and get you a spot there if you're interested?'

'Really? That would be amazing. Yes, please.'

'If you give me your email address I'll put you in touch with the organiser.'

I jot down my details on a Post-It Note and hand them to Jenny, bending down to make high-pitched kissing noises to Marmite, where she crouches anxiously in her basket. 'With Marmite's anxiety, it's still early days,' I say. 'What you could try doing is gradually moving her food bowl out of the bedroom and down the stairs. She'll get there, I'm sure. Just got to persevere.'

At that moment, Cameron pops his head out of the consult room and beams his best smile at Jenny. 'Have you got Marmite? Come on in.'

I can hear the conversation from the reception area. Cameron quickly assesses Marmite's eye and dispenses the necessary ointment, spending the rest of the consultation time offering general advice and reassurance.

Jenny looks much more relaxed when she comes out, now she knows it's nothing serious. I remember her heartbreak when she lost Gizmo. I always remember.

'All sorted?' I say, smiling, already knowing the answer.

Jenny settles the bill, and Marmite's carrier back onto the buggy. 'I'll let you know about the book event,' she says as she prepares to leave.

'Great! Thank you so much. Hopefully I'll see you there too?'

'Yes, definitely, see you there.'

We exchange goodbyes and, once the street door is closed, Cameron joins me in reception once more, pulling open the top drawer of my desk in search of the sweets.

'She's a writer,' I tell him, still a little bit surprised myself.

'Who? Pink-hair lady? No! Really? Well, who'd a thunk it?'

'I know, right. If I hadn't told her I was leaving to write a book, we'd never have known we were both writers. And now she's going to see about getting me a table at a book festival in the town. How mad is that?'

'It's fate, my darling, fate.'

CHAPTER 3

Bloodbath

My last days at the vet's are largely uneventful and spent mainly at the quiet branch surgery that I have made my own. I will miss the tatty old place, even though it's a tatty old place. The vets say it's where dreams go to die. I tried to change that; I tried to love it, and I succeeded to a degree. When asked to name one good thing about the place, two of the vets said, 'Amy'. That made me pretty damn happy. I did worry that no one would love it after I left though.

But it's time.

My last shift is spent with Cameron, and he brings in sweet treats for us to share: my favourite pain au chocolat, and almond croissants. Thankfully, we only have three clients booked in for routine things: two cat vaccinations and a claw clip on a Jack Russell. Actually, that one could get bloody. It was a wriggler with dark quicks, and it was entirely possible that I would be greeted by a bloodbath when I went into the consult room to clear up. I thought about my own dog, Dexter, who had to be sedated and sat on to have his claws clipped. He was an abuse case rescued from Ireland and he had issues. I'm reminded once more about the saying that pets take after their owners.

It's while one of the cats is in having its jab that I get the call about the road traffic accident. A tearful woman tells me that a dog ran out in front of her car. Between sobs, she asks if she can bring it to us.

'Yes, of course, come straight down. Do you know where we are?'

'Yes, by the chip shop.'

'That's right. How far away are you?'

'Just up the road. Two minutes.'

'Okay, we'll see you very soon.' I think about adding, 'drive carefully', but stop myself just in time. I haven't asked for too many details as I don't want to delay the woman getting to us. It could be time-critical.

As soon as the cat and its owner come out of the consult room, I ask them if they can please wait one moment and quietly give Cameron the heads-up about the dog being brought in. My smile is back on my face as I return to my desk and take payment from the cat owner and see them out, hoping they depart before the car pulls up outside with the injured dog.

Cameron is waiting by the door when the car arrives a couple of minutes later, and he goes out to help carry the dog in. We've already laid out some towels on the consult table and Cameron has raided the dangerous drugs safe for anything he might need.

I can see that it's a tan-coloured Staffie – Staffordshire Bull Terrier – in his arms, and that it has what looks like a serious head wound. I shut the pair of them in the consult room so that I can take details from the driver. I calm her down and hand her tissues first though. She's absolutely distraught.

'I… I… couldn't avoid it… it just appeared out of nowhere from between two parked cars,' she sobs.

'It's not your fault, really it isn't. There's nothing you could have done. The main thing is that you didn't just drive off – you did the right thing and you brought it to us. We will do everything we can to save it, but whatever happens, we won't let it suffer.'

The driver nods and blows her nose on the handful of tissues I've passed her. I pull some fresh ones from the box.

'Sorry,' she says, 'you must think I'm pathetic.'

'No! I'd be in exactly the same state, trust me! But it wasn't your fault, you must believe that. It could've happened to anyone. I'm sorry it happened to you.'

I take down her details, and where the accident happened. She says she doesn't know the dog, even though she lives just around the corner from where she hit it. I'm not that surprised. The town is full of Staffies and it's a breed that for some reason is often walked off the lead; I don't know if that has more to do with the type of owner or the breed itself. We see more Staffs than any other breed at the branch. That said, they are a gentle, loving dog unless they fall into the wrong hands.

Although I don't want to rush her, I'm anxious to get into the consult room with Cameron and the injured dog to see if I can help in any way.

'Will you be alright?' I ask her, putting my hand on her arm. 'You can sit here as long as you need to. Is there anyone at home? Maybe someone that can come and drive you? You're bound to be shaken up for a while.'

She sniffs and nods. 'My husband. I'll phone him. He can walk down and pick me up.'

I squeeze her arm. 'I need to go and help the vet now. Just remember that this wasn't your fault, and you did the right thing. Okay? Take care.' I smile at her and head to the consult room; one look at the dog and Cameron's face tells me everything I need to know.

'Catastrophic head trauma. Nothing we could do,' my young vet says sadly.

'Collar and tag? Chipped?' I ask, thinking of the awful phone call one of us will have to make if it is.

Cameron shakes his head. 'Nope. No collar, no microchip.'

'Bugger. Okay.'

Usually in cases like this, social media brings forth results, and we will be posting in various Facebook groups to try and trace the dog's owner. In the meantime, the poor thing will be bagged in a heavy-duty black sack and tagged with a description before being placed in the chest freezer in the back room. If the owner cannot be tracked down, the dog will eventually be taken for general cremation.

As there's nothing I can do for the dog, I pop my head back round the door to reception, but the woman driver is gone. I help Cameron clear up, bag up and lift the body into the freezer. It's another aspect of the job I will not miss. If I had any doubts that I was doing the right thing by leaving, they evaporated now.

They'd said when I started that I'd get used to the euthanasia. I was quite sure I wouldn't. And I didn't want to get used to it. I didn't want to stop being sad, and having a bit of a cry when I got home at night. But they were right. I did get used to it. Instead of shedding tears when I got home after a difficult day, I'd crack open a bottle of beer and drink a toast to whatever had gone in the freezer that day. I'm not saying I'd become hardened to it… it was just somehow easier. I didn't feel the owners' pain as acutely, or find it as disturbing to lower the lifeless bodies into the black sacks. I was still professional and empathetic, but it didn't hurt as much.

They tell me I hold the record for the most euthanasia-assists by a receptionist. Not sure that's a record to be proud of, but I hope I have earned it by being sensitive and supportive to vet, owner and pet alike. It's a bizarre fact that we got more thank you cards and gifts for putting animals to sleep than for anything else. I don't think it will be long before Hallmark announce a new range of 'Thank you for killing my pet so nicely' cards.

We've just finished removing all trace of the emergency when the Jack Russell arrives for its claw clip. It's a lively, barky little dog. They're all mouth these small breeds. It's the big ones that sit quietly quaking in the corner, wedging themselves between their owner's legs and trying to make themselves invisible. And the little ones who announce their presence vigorously and stop you from being able to hear what the person on the other end of the phone is saying. The person on the end of the phone on this occasion is the husband of the woman driver, asking what the outcome was for the Staff.

It puts me in a tricky position as we don't like to talk about death in front of clients. I ask the man if I can call him back in a few minutes, and wait until Cameron has taken barking Buster into the consult room before calling back.

'Hello,' the male voice says.

'Hello. It's Amy from the vets. Sorry about that, I was just dealing with a client.'

'No problem. My wife just wants to know what happened to the dog. She's so upset.'

'I'm afraid the dog didn't survive. I'm sorry. But the main thing is that it isn't suffering. Please reassure your wife that it wasn't her fault, and she did the right thing afterwards. That's all anyone could have asked.'

There's a moment of silence. 'Okay, thank you for your help. Do you know who owns it? Did it have a microchip?'

'Sadly not, but we will do our best to trace the owner. If you're able to ask around where you live that would be a big help.'

'Yes, yes, of course. What will happen if nobody comes forward?'

'We will take care of the cremation. His ashes will be spread on the rose garden at the pet crematorium.'

'Right, okay, thanks. Thanks for everything.'

'You're welcome. Take care.'

We say goodbye and I hang up the phone with a sigh, thinking of the anonymous body in the freezer, waiting for someone to claim it, knowing that it might never happen. My thoughts are interrupted by Cameron sticking his head out of the consult room, and rolling his eyes at me.

'Can you give me a hand?'

I can't help smiling as I get up and go in to hold the wriggliest little dog ever, who's determined not to have his claws cut. It never ceases to amaze me the power of these little dogs. They're solid muscle and doggedly determined. By the time we've done the claws on one foot, I'm covered in wiry white hairs and starting to perspire.

The owner is tittering behind us, and making helpful comments. 'He's so good at home. I can do anything with him.'

Cameron's eyes meet mine. We both know what the other one's thinking: if he's so ruddy well behaved at home, why don't you clip his claws yourself? But we smile sweetly, grit our teeth and start on paw number two. By some miracle, Cameron manages not to clip a quick and we don't have to rename the dog Buster Blood Vessel.

Buster is my last ever patient. We have nothing else booked in for the final half an hour of my shift. I can't cash up until we officially close at six, so Cameron joins me in reception one last time.

'Are you okay to post on Facebook?' I ask him, referring to the deceased dog.

'Yep. Doing it now. Fingers crossed we'll get a result.'

'I take it you're not putting a photo up?' I grimace.

'No, siree, but I did photograph it for formal identification if necessary.'

I grimace again.

'Don't worry – I took it from his best side.'

That's another thing you get from working at a vets, along with scratches, bites, and Type 2 Diabetes, you get a dark sense of humour. I think it's a kind of coping mechanism. It's also a very British thing, isn't it? You only have to look at the jokes and memes that arise almost instantly following some tragedy or other. It's what we do best. Trying to heft the deadweight of a St. Bernard dog up into a chest freezer is extremely unfunny, until you're actually doing it.

'One day I'm going to write a sitcom about a vet's practice,' I announce to Cameron as he taps away on his iPhone. 'Did I ever tell you about the locum who injected right through a cat and into my thumb? Or the time I was holding a particularly vicious cat to get bloods from its jugular, and it went to bite the vet, whose hand recoiled and punched me on the nose?'

He doesn't look up from what he's doing, but his reaction is enthusiastic. 'Oh my God! Yes! You must. And I can be in it! I can be in it? Can't I?' He stops typing and looks up at me, making puppy dog eyes. And not ones that have been recently hit by a car. (Sorry, that was inappropriate. I rest my case.)

I laugh. 'Of course you can be in it. Starring role, naturally.'

'Yesss!' He returns his gaze to his phone and finishes off the appeal to find the poor Staffie's owner.

I sit and think about the mixed emotions of my last day as it draws to a close. I do feel wistful. I like to think I've made a difference. There are a couple of clients in particular that I feel bad about leaving and, right on cue, one of them walks through the door. Mrs Reed. Oh, Mrs Reed! She and her dog, Kiki, both give me beaming smiles as they come in, and Mrs Reed drops Kiki's lead so that the little dog can run to me. I pull Kiki up onto my lap where she continues to beam at me. She is the only dog I know who genuinely smiles and I love her to bits. I feel like I'm letting her down by leaving.

Kiki rarely needs to see the vet, but Mrs Reed has been the most frequent visitor to the surgery in my time there. She has dementia and has been known to come in up to three times a day, often to ask the same questions over and again. I seem to be the only staff member who has the patience for her, and will make time to talk with her and answer those same questions time and again. Although she does sometimes try even my patience, I am genuinely fond of her and I know that she will miss coming in to see me. The other receptionists tell me that she sometimes pops her head in to see who's on duty but, when she sees it's not me, she says she'll come back when the 'nice receptionist' is on duty. Oh, Mrs Reed.

The way I look at it, that could be my mum wandering round, just looking for a kind word or a bit of company, one day. There but for the grace of God and all that. Anyway, I always have a smile for her and today is no different.

She's remembered that it's my last day and has come to say goodbye. I'm still fussing over Kiki when she passes something across the desk to me.

'I thought you might like this, as you're a writer,' she beams at me.

I reach out and take the offering. It's a word search puzzle book. I'm so touched that tears are pricking the corners of my eyes.

'I've written you a message inside the cover too. Have a look.'

I open the cover and read: To dear Amy, thank you for being our friend. We will miss you. Love from Christine and Kiki xx

I also notice that the first puzzle has been started. Smile and tears threaten to meet somewhere around the middle of my cheeks.

I catch Cameron's eye and can see that he's welling up too, while simultaneously stifling a giggle.

I put Kiki down and go round the desk to give her owner a hug. 'Thank you so much, both of you. I will miss you, but Cameron will still be here to look after Kiki and let me know how you're both doing. You must promise to look after yourself.'

Mrs Reed just stands there grinning at me. 'I started some of the word searches, but I didn't really like them.'

I can see Cameron trying not to laugh, but we both know that there couldn't be a more perfect way to end my final shift at the vet's.

CHAPTER 4

The smell of death

As I close and lock the door to the surgery for the last time, I pause for a moment. It's the end of an era. A short one, admittedly, but it has been a mass of memories and emotions. Friendships made, lessons learned and experiences stored away in my memory bank for future writings.

It's six thirty on a dark mid-November evening and I pull my coat around me as the chill air tries to insinuate itself underneath. I shiver involuntarily and have a momentary flashback to the dog that died and is now being freshly frozen, like a joint of meat for a Sunday roast. It will be stiff from the icy temperatures before rigor mortis has a chance to set in. As I walk the short distance to my car, I think about Cameron's attempts to locate the owner. I hope they'll be successful, otherwise the dog will just be an anonymous body in a deep freeze. It deserved better than that.

Reaching my car, I get in quickly and start the engine, pressing the heated seat button, and settling myself for the drive home. It's only a twenty-minute journey, and the roads are pretty clear as the main rush hour is over. I'm looking forward to a soak in the bath with a bottle of beer to toast the Staffie, and curling up on the sofa with a book.

I realise as I'm driving that I'm hungry, in spite of all the caterpillars, and I decide to stop off at the chippy near my house for cod and chips. I eat them out of the paper sitting at the kitchen table, still wearing my coat. The house is warm as the heating was left on a timer, but I'm feeling chilly this evening. I think maybe the relief of finishing work is hitting me and my body is reacting to the release of a lot of built-up stress. It's like a huge sigh of relief in a walk-in fridge.

With the leftover chips and fish skin in the food recycling caddy, and the paper in the kitchen bin, I wash my hands and head into the hall where I shrug off my coat and remove my boots. Grabbing a bottle of Beck's from the fridge, I plod up the stairs, closing curtains as I go. I get the bath running, adding a good glug of Molton Brown Pink Pepperpod Bathing Oil to the water. The flowery scent quickly fills the room, a welcome change for my nostrils after the smell of death earlier. There were some smells that stayed with you long after their release. Checking the temperature of the rising water, I head to my bedroom, closing the curtains before I shed my work polo shirt for the last time and chuck it in the laundry hamper. I'll have to wash it and return it to the main branch on Monday, along with my keys.

While I'm waiting for the bath to fill, I check for emails on my phone and I'm pleasantly surprised to see one from Jenny Jones, pink-hair cat lady. When people take your email address and say they'll be in touch, you never really know if they mean it, until you either do or don't receive a message. But Jenny was true to her word, and I clicked on the message to open it. It said that she'd been in touch with her friend who was organising the book festival event, and I could have a table there. She'd shared my email address with them and included theirs for me. I quickly typed a thank you reply and said I looked forward to seeing Jenny there, and that I hoped Marmite was alright after her trip to the vet, before jumping up to turn off the bath taps. The bathroom was now steamy and fragrant and I sighed contentedly as I sank into the bubbles, my legs quickly turning lobster-pink in the hot water.

Not even one day into 'retirement' and I already had a new contact in the local writing community and an opportunity to not only sell some books, but meet other local authors into the bargain. The universe apparently approved of my decision and was letting me know. It was good to have a sign that I'd done the right thing in giving up work to write full-time, because it was a daunting prospect and money was going to be tighter than the waistband of my jeans after a year of bad eating.

'Here's to you, poor no-name Staffie,' I say, lifting my beer in a toast. 'I hope somebody comes to claim you and sheds a tear over your death. Rest in peace.' I take a swig and lean my head back once more, the bubbles rising around my shoulders and into my hair which is fixed loosely up.

Closing my eyes, I let my thoughts drift and try to pin down the jumble of things popping around my head like the bubbles in the bath. Today has brought forth a myriad of emotions; too many to feel at once, but I seem to be managing to do so. I think the overwhelming feeling is one of relief that I've left the job. The stress and the drain on my emotions had made it untenable as a long-term position and I'd had more than enough. I didn't regret the past twelve months, but I'd had it. Tagging on relief's coattails, and playing catch-up, were both anxiety and excitement, making an interesting trio.

'What *have* you done, Amy Archer?' my rational side asked.

The irrational side just shrugged, and pulled a face.

'It's all very well pulling faces, but how are you going to pay the bills?'

'Er...' My irrational side was not the most eloquent, clearly.

Rational just rolled her eyes and tutted.

'Sell some books?' Irrational countered, raising her eyebrows hopefully.

'Sell... some... books...' Rational repeated slowly. 'Great plan.'

'Well, it's a start. I haven't really thought any further ahead than that...'

'No, you never do.'

I mentally tell Little Miss Perfect to bugger off and have a swig of beer. Something will turn up. It always does. All I know is I needed to leave the job and I want to give writing a proper go, for as long as I can.

My first two novels had been published by a small local firm and, while I was immensely proud of this, I wasn't making much money from them. Unless I got a break into the mainstream, that was unlikely to change. There was a limit to how much money I could throw at a marketing campaign, when the paperbacks were overpriced compared to similar titles on the market, and they were not available to buy 'at all good bookshops'. Unless I was prepared to schlep around the country and beg each book shop owner to stock my titles, they would continue only to be available to buy on Amazon or from the publisher. Not for the first time, I wondered if my choice of genre was the right one, as women's fiction is terribly overcrowded. Non-fiction is apparently easier to make money from, but I had no idea what I would write about. They say write what you know. Well, mainly I know about being a woman.

Putting the fear of destitution aside, I'm excited to be returning to writing. The horrid split shifts at the vet's, with their early start and late finish had not been conducive to writing, and I had penned nothing in twelve months. I had some ideas mooching about in my brain, but had yet to decide on my next project. And I had an event to plan for, which made me nervous and exhilarated all at once.

Another thing I was looking forward to now was having more time with my dog, Dexter. He spent most of his time with my ex and his new partner as she didn't work. I missed his company and a reason to go out walking. I was actually thinking about asking to have him full-time for security reasons too. I'd always felt very safe on my own in my little house until there'd been an attempted break-in last summer. So, there was plenty to look forward to, and I was feeling warm both inside and out as I climbed out of the bath a little while later. Life was mine for the taking.

CHAPTER 5

Amy Archer: Author

The book festival event was taking place on Saturday the fourteenth of December, so I had a month to prepare and also to try and get my head around marketing and selling my first and second novels. I had a couple of hundred copies of the books stashed around the house. Self-promotion was not something that came easily to me, but I knew I was going to have to overcome this if I was ever going to have any success.

Planning my book stall was relatively easy as Christmas would be just around the corner, and all I had to do was get hold of a tablecloth, raid my boxes of decorations, and buy a tub of Celebrations to attract people to my table if my book covers alone weren't enough of a draw. Simple. Marketing strategies. Not so simple.

The next few weeks were a busy blur of reigniting my author page on Facebook and attempting the occasional Tweet and Instagram post. I'd also started building a website, in spite of having zero idea what I was doing. I watched many a YouTube 'how to' video. They seemed to use a lot of acronyms and I spent more time looking these up and trying to understand them than anything else. But I didn't give up. Well, I did, many times, but I kept coming back to it until I finally had a very basic site.

Dexter was now staying with me most of the time, and it was nice to have company while I beavered away at my otherwise solitary occupation. I did miss my colleagues at the vet's, especially Cameron, but I knew this was the right thing for me now. Do or die, but at least I'd've given it my best shot. When I needed to clear my head, I'd wrap up warm and head out for a walk with Dexter. Sometimes we'd jump in the car and venture further afield, and we'd stumbled across a pig farm on our travels. Dex's nose went into overdrive as the aromas assaulted his senses. It made me think of some of the awful smells at the surgery. I certainly didn't miss them.

I'd started to write a third book, but wasn't really sure where I was going with it, so I was glad when the day of the event finally arrived to distract me. I packed up the car with plenty of copies of both books and the necessary accoutrements for my table, dropped Dexter off at my ex's house and headed to the venue. It was a clear, crisp Saturday, so I hoped plenty of people would attend, and was cautiously optimistic about selling a few copies of my novels. I'd decided to do a buy-one-get-one-free offer, just to try and get the books out there. It meant I wouldn't do much more than break even, but I just wanted readers and hopefully, down the line, reviewers. I was looking forward to seeing Jenny again too, and maybe talking to her some more about her own writing.

The hall was filling up nicely when I arrived, and I quickly bagsied a table and started to set up. I must admit to being nervous. It had recently been pointed out to me that my Twitter bio still said 'aspiring' writer, even though I'd had two novels published. I'd removed the offending word and was trying to think of myself as an *actual* writer. I knew it was going to take time to adjust my thinking. At the moment when people asked me what I did for a living I still said 'I'm not working at the moment, but…' I needed to start believing in myself if I wanted other people to. My name's Amy Archer and I'm an author. Easy. Pah!

It didn't take long to make my table look festive and, hopefully, appealing. I took a couple of photographs and posted them on my Facebook page, made myself known to the lady organiser and was sitting nervously waiting for the public to start arriving. I looked around at the other stalls and was surprised to see that most of them simply bore copies of the books for sale. Well, hopefully that just meant that my stand would… well… stand out. I even had orange and cinnamon essential oils wafting up from pine cones on the table. I was new to this and beginning to wonder if I was trying too hard? I'd started on the Celebrations. There would probably be no Malteser ones left by the time I had a customer. I offered the lady on the stall next to me one – she wisely chose a Mars Bar – and we got chatting about our books. She'd actually gone down the self-publishing route and had written four books, to date. As we chatted I realised I had one crucial ingredient missing from my life if I wanted to write full-time: a wealthy husband. Damn.

At two o'clock the doors opened and people started to arrive. I took a deep breath and stuck a smile on my face, hoping I didn't look as nervous as I felt. I still hadn't mastered the 'I'm Amy Archer and I'm a writer' thing yet, and was better at giving my books away than asking people to pay for them. It felt kind of arrogant to think I could have written something that people would pay to read. I had to get past that. Somehow.

People drifted around the room, some walked straight past

without even looking in my direction, others stopped to look, and a few picked up the books and turned them over to read the blurb on the back. I was delighted at how many people said how nice my table looked though. I offered them the tub of Celebrations. 'Sorry there aren't any Malteser ones left.' I was thrilled when I made my first sale and popped a ten pound note into the teapot I was using as a cash box.

'Thank you so much. If you enjoy the books, perhaps you could leave a review on Amazon? I'd be so grateful. If you don't enjoy them, perhaps you could still leave a review. Just lie,' I said with a smile. I think they thought I was joking.

I actually started to enjoy myself and to relax into my role. I was still a way off it not being a role, an act, but it was a great start. People seemed genuinely interested in talking to me about my books and the writing and publishing processes, and I began to believe that I deserved to be here.

I'd sold three BOGOFs when a familiar pink head appeared.

'Hello, Jenny! Glad you made it.'

'Hello, Amy. Your stall looks nice. Smells good too.'

'Thank you! Have a chocolate,' I say, passing the tub.

'Ooh, thanks,' she replies, rummaging around amongst the wrapped sweets. 'Can't seem to find any Malteser ones.'

'Oh! They never put enough Malteser ones in, do they? And double up on the Bountys.'

Jenny shrugs and pulls out a Galaxy instead.

'Thanks so much for getting me an introduction to this.'

'You're welcome. I'm just glad you told me you're a writer. All those months we never knew that about each other,' Jenny shakes her head.

'I know! Mad,' I agree.

'I wanted to ask you if you'd like to join a writing group I'm starting up?'

'Really? I'd love to – thank you.' I smile warmly at her.

'I'll send you details and pick you up on Facebook too,' Jenny tells me.

'Okay, great. The group sounds really exciting. I've never belonged to a writing group before.'

'What? But you've written two novels?' Jenny seems surprised by my admission.

'I know, but I just hid away at home and did that. Groping around in the dark, with no idea what I was actually doing,' I say with a shrug.

'I've started loads of writing groups. If I don't like the local group, I just start my own.'

'That's brilliant.' I must say that mild-mannered Jenny Jones is turning into something of a revelation. I pick up a copy of each of my novels and hand them to her. 'To say thank you.'

Jenny looks really pleased. 'Oh! Thank you. I look forward to reading them. And I'll do you some reviews, of course.'

'Would you? That would be fantastic,' I beam at her.

'And another thing I wanted to ask you, could I interview you sometime for my blog?'

She wants to interview me. I'm beyond thrilled. 'Yes, of course, I'd be delighted.' *I'm Amy Archer and I'm an author* pops into my head. Maybe I really am. If other people believe it, maybe I can too.

Jenny says her goodbyes and heads off to speak to one of the other writers she knows, with promises to be in touch about the group soon. And I know that she will be true to her word.

By the time the event draws to a close, I have sold six sets of books. It doesn't sound like many, but the lady next to me only sold two, so I'm actually really happy with my six. I'm not worried for her as she has her wealthy husband to look after her. To me, however, sixty pounds is not to be sniffed at. And I still have a good many Celebrations to take home with me. Admittedly there are a lot of Bountys, but all in all it's been a good day, and it's a contented Amy Archer: Author who's heading home tonight.

CHAPTER 6

Getting there

That night at home I'm feeling better about life than I have in a while, and daring to dream that maybe I really can be a 'proper writer'. I've left Dexter with my ex overnight and am happily catching up with social media and listening to Harry Styles' new album *Fine Line* (Harry is my guilty pleasure, but if you tell anyone I'll deny it) while enjoying a beer. I raise a toast, 'To a good day'. As an afterthought I add, 'And to not killing anything, ever again'.

When I log onto Facebook I find the promised friend request from Jenny, and I readily accept it. I have a quick nosy on her page and find lots of photos of her cats along with an assortment of writing-related posts. She's also sent me an invitation to join her new writing group 'Write Time, Write Place'. I eagerly click on the link:

The writing group for procrastinators!

A totally informal fortnightly writing session - no introductions, no homework, no sharing or reading out work (although there are plenty of tables, so if you do want to go off to another table and share your work or get some feedback/advice, feel free) - just writers getting out of the house to work on our own projects in the company of other writers. Bring yourself, your laptop or pen and paper and stay as long or as little as you like.*

**formal introductions, I mean. You are of course allowed to say hello to everyone.*

Jenny goes on to explain that we will meet fortnightly on a Monday from ten a.m. until midday, starting on January 13, 2020. The place she has chosen is the local Wetherspoons which is in an old Salem Chapel and we are to meet upstairs. I eagerly accept the invitation and mark the first meeting on my calendar. I know I'll be nervous about going on the day, but I'm not going to worry about that yet. I'm enjoying the warm glow of optimism too much.

I actually know the Wetherspoons we'll be meeting at. Funnily enough, it features in my first novel. I haven't been there in years and it will certainly be interesting going back, and for a very different reason. I'll be drinking coffee instead of vodka, for one thing.

The weeks leading up to the first writing group are uneventful and Christmas isn't even worth mentioning, so ignore this sentence. When Monday January thirteenth finally arrives, I'm actually looking forward to getting out of the house and meeting people again. I could very easily become a recluse if I'm not careful.

I pack up my laptop, adding pad and pen to the bag, and head off, arriving at the Wetherspoons just before ten. I'm shocked by how many people are already drinking pints of lager this early in the day, and head to the bar to order a coffee. I'm delighted to find that for just one pound thirty-five, I can get a bottomless tea or coffee. This is certainly the right venue for an impoverished writer. I work out the machine and am soon climbing the decorative black wrought iron staircase to the upper level, careful not to spill my flat white coffee. Memories are flooding back of the last time I ascended these stairs: I was wearing very different footwear then and probably clutching a bottle of Smirnoff Ice. I try and work out how many years ago this would've been. It must be twenty years.

Like so many Wetherspoons, the interior of the building is stunning. The ceiling is painted with frescos of brilliant blue sky and fluffy white clouds, and there are decorative carvings all around. At the far end, a set of organ pipes remains. The wood-panelled walls are adorned with prints and texts about famous people who lived in or visited the area, including H.G.Wells and Charles Dickens. I make a mental note to stop and read the one about H.G.Wells sometime as I've just reread *The Time Machine*. I chuckle to myself as I try to imagine ever having the kind of success and recognition these great men enjoyed, and having my own picture on the wall. 'Renowned local author, Amy Archer, got pissed here on many an occasion in the late 1990s' it would probably say.

As I reach the upper level, I look around, wondering what to do. I won't know anybody except Jenny. Most of the seating areas are enclosed two-bench affairs, with high-sided wooden panels between them. It's impossible to see if anyone is seated in one until you are right up next to it. I'm saved any more agonising, however, as the now familiar pink head bobs into view on the staircase.

Jenny smiles when she looks up and sees me, having safely made the ascent carrying a steaming mug. I'm relieved that she didn't go for the lager option. 'Hello, Amy. Glad you made it.'

'Hello. Me too. It's actually nice to get out of the house. I've become something of a hermit since leaving the vet's.'

'I hear you. Writing can become a bit lonely if you're not careful. That's why I do groups like this.'

I follow Jenny round to the left of the stairs and she leads the way to the last booth, just by the organ pipes. We each shuffle along opposite benches and settle ourselves into opposing corners.

'Brings back a lot of memories, being here,' I tell her. 'I used to come and drink in here before heading down the Old High Street to Club Indigo on the seafront. Seems like another lifetime… It was I suppose.'

'Really? I don't remember seeing that club and I've lived down here a couple of years now.'

'It's not there anymore. They demolished pretty much everything on that section of the seafront years ago.'

Jenny's reply is interrupted by the arrival of another lady, clearly here for the writing group. She looks to be about the same age as me, with blonde bob-length hair and half-frame glasses. She makes me think of the adjectives 'warm' and 'busy'. I quickly realise from their greeting that she and Jenny know each other well. I smile at the newcomer as she slides in next to Jenny, removing her hat and coat as she does so.

'Hello,' I say, extending my smile. 'I'm Amy.'

'Hello, Amy, I'm Pippa, Parsons, lovely to meet you,' she says warmly.

'Likewise,' I agree.

Jenny joins in, 'Sorry, I'm rubbish at introductions,' she says, shrugging.

I laugh, 'That's okay, we're all grown-ups and more than capable of introducing ourselves. On a good day, anyway,' I add, with a hint to my anxiety issues and tendency towards reclusiveness. 'Besides, the blurb for the group did specify "no introductions".'

Pippa and Jenny both laugh.

‘I met Amy at the vet’s. She helped kill my cat,’ Jenny informs Pippa.

‘Okay…’ Pippa says slowly, clearly a little flummoxed.

‘She did it really nicely,’ Jenny assures.

‘Oh… er… good…’ Pippa’s still not sure what the correct response is here.

I decide to put her out of her misery. Not literally. I’m still done with euthanasia. ‘We sadly had to put Jenny’s old cat Gizmo to sleep a while back,’ I say, pulling an appropriate face.

‘Ah!’ Pippa says, nodding.

‘On her last day at the vet’s she told me that she was leaving to write her third novel and we discovered that we’re both writers. Except that Amy’s had two novels published,’ Jenny continues by way of explanation.

Pippa looks suitably impressed and I cringe.

‘Wow! That’s impressive,’ Pippa says. ‘How exciting! A proper writer in our midst, eh?’

I’m Amy Archer and I’m a writer. It’s no good, I can’t do it. ‘Well, trying to be, not making any money from it yet, but…’ I tail off, wondering how I can change the subject. ‘So, what do you write, Pippa?’

Pippa makes a pfft noise and pulls a face. ‘Nothing really. Sort of blog a bit, the odd short story…’

I grab onto her words, ‘Short stories? Now that takes real skill. I can’t write short stories to save my life.’

Before we can talk more a fourth face appears by our booth. This time the face belongs to a man. He’s tall, probably about six feet, with wispy grey hair and silver-framed glasses pushed onto his large nose. I guesstimate his age to be around seventy.

'Hullo, all,' he says, pushing some stray wisps back off his face.

'Hi, Tom,' Jenny and Pippa chorus.

I just smile as I wait hopefully for an introduction. Ever the optimist.

Tom reaches over with his hand extended. 'Tom Taylor at your service, young lady,' he says, giving the impression of an old-fashioned gent.

'Amy Archer, very nice to meet you, Tom Taylor,' I say, shaking his hand and smiling. I haven't been called 'young lady' for a very long time.

Tom removes his coat and scarf and puts them on the last remaining seat at the table, next to me. 'Anybody need a drink, or a refill?' he asks. We all shake our heads as we're still nursing our first drinks, and Tom heads back down the stairs to get his own beverage. I'm pretty confident it won't be beer. I think how sweet it was to come and see if we needed a drink before getting his own, even though it meant double the stairs.

While Tom's gone, I ask Jenny how many people she's invited to join the group.

'About ten so far, I think. I expect people will drop in and out.'

'So, do you all know each other from the writing scene here?' I ask.

Jenny nods. 'Yes, there's a really active writing community here. Everyone knows everyone really.'

I feel a little bit of an outsider as it sounds as though I might be the only out of towner, but I push the worry to one side. If it doesn't bother them, I won't let it bother me. Besides, *I'm Amy Archer and I'm a novelist.* Nope. Still can't do it.

Tom arrives back at the table with his drink and as he sits

down he addresses Jenny. 'So, how did you get on with my book? What did you think of the storyline?'

It turns out that Jenny has been proofreading Tom's first novel, which is science fiction.

'Well, it's hard to focus on the story when you're looking for mistakes,' Jenny says. 'And there were a lot of mistakes.'

One thing I'm learning about Jenny is she just says it how it is. Not in a bad way. She's a very literal person. If something needs saying she just says it. Not to hurt or offend. She's intriguing actually, and I find myself wondering if maybe she has Asperger's or something. She's clearly very intelligent though, and she gets things done.

Tom's looking a little downcast at hearing how many mistakes Jenny found in his manuscript and I busy myself with firing up my laptop as they continue to discuss the matter across the table. I feel for Tom. I remember how I felt when I had to let someone read my first draft novel. It makes you feel very exposed and strangely vulnerable. I'm relieved when the discussion moves to another table so that Jenny can talk Tom through her findings.

It also gives me a chance to find out a bit more about Pippa, and I soon learn that she's extremely happily married, has two dogs, and is very active in the charity sector, especially working with the elderly. She very much lives up to my first impressions of her.

No one else turned up to that first meeting and, in a way, I was grateful for a gentle introduction. Although the others seemed impressed by my author status, I still felt like the beginner in a way. I had heard tales of them reading their stories aloud and entering writing competitions; of poetry and short stories galore; of blogging and article-writing. I was so glad that Jenny had invited me along, and that I'd had the courage to go. We parted about midday with promises to be back in two weeks, and an order for one of my books from Pippa. As I walked back to my car with my coat flapping open, I was oblivious to the cold. *I'm Amy Archer and I'm getting there.*

CHAPTER 7

Amy Archer: Pantser

For the next two weeks I labour half-heartedly on my third novel. As is my way, I have no real plan, but rather a vague idea for a story that will hopefully evolve as I write. At the moment, the book has no idea what it is and could as easily become a Young Adult novel as it could something even Barbara Cartland would've chucked in the bin.

I haven't felt quite so isolated in my work since meeting Jenny though, and the writing group members often post online and share ideas and writing competitions. It's so good to feel part of something again. The camaraderie was the main thing I missed since giving up work, and 'Write Time, Write Place' filled that gap nicely.

Jenny and I also chatted outside the group and I was learning a lot from her. I'd read some of her blogs and had come to realise that she's a really great writer. I can't understand why she hasn't written a novel, but she insists she's no good at fiction. Jenny has a lot more formal training than me and I have no doubt that she will be a valuable resource as I muddle along with my own writing. She's asked if she can interview me for her blog at the next writing group and I'm looking forward to it. I just hope I have something interesting and entertaining to say in response to her questions. She's also promised to write reviews for my books, and include them in the article.

The second group takes place on the twenty-seventh of

January and I'm less nervous as I park the car and walk the short distance to the pub, pushing open the big saloon-style door and avoiding the eyes of the early morning drinkers as they look up from their pints to see who's coming in. I can't help wondering what has brought them to this place. No, not the beer. You know what I mean. Life. What's happened to make them need beer before ten o'clock in the morning? I get my mug from the bar, fill it with milky coffee and head upstairs, making a beeline for the table we used last time. Jenny is already there, with a mug of tea and an open laptop.

'Morning,' I say, and she smiles in greeting.

We sit and chat about general stuff, how mild the weather is for January, how her cats are, as we wait to see who else turns up. Jenny says she's expecting Pippa and Tom, and possibly another friend called John who's said he'll try and pop in.

'I thought once everyone's here and we've said hello, we could go and sit at another table and do the interview?' Jenny says.

'Okey dokey, sounds like a plan,' I agree, nodding.

Just then, Pippa and Tom arrive together. Pippa sits next to me this time and Tom slips in beside Jenny. We're obviously going to be the core members of the group. Just behind them comes a rather distinguished-looking chap, with a very neat grey moustache and beard. He's not overly tall, and a little portly, but is an elegant fellow. I reckon him to be in his late fifties. He's introduced to me as John Jackman, and I just know that he has a wonderful home library, possibly with steps, and owns at least one velvet smoking jacket. The smile he gives me reaches his warm blue eyes, which crinkle at the corners, and I take to him at once. John pulls a chair over from the next booth, drapes his Barbour over the back of it, and settles himself at the end of the table.

No one seems in any hurry to start on their writing projects and I'm more than happy to learn a bit more about them all. Tom mentions his wife often and fondly, which is very endearing. I also learn that John is a widower, and has devoted his time since his wife's death to researching the history of the town and writing books from his findings. Pippa talks engagingly about her dogs and I tell her about Dexter. We both bring up photos on our phones to show one another. That leads to a few jokey remarks about how often Jenny posts photos of her cats on Facebook. They're such a friendly bunch, and I relax into their company.

I suppose we chat for about twenty minutes, and then Jenny starts to get fidgety. I get the impression she wants to get on with the interview: once she has planned to do something, she needs to do it. So, we make our excuses, ask Tom and Pippa to let us out and head to another table.

Jenny sets up the audio recorder on her phone and has pad and pen to make supplemental notes as needed.

'I've got a list of questions,' she says, 'so I s'pose I'll just get started.'

'Fire away.'

Jenny starts by asking some general background questions about me, my life, career and so on, before moving on to the writing process itself, and how I plan my books.

'Er…' I begin. Great, Amy. Very eloquent. 'I don't, really,' I continue, looking and feeling decidedly sheepish.

Jenny looks surprised. 'But how have you written two novels then?'

'Um... I suppose I do have a vague overall idea when I start writing. I don't really plan though, I just sort of start and then ideas come as I'm writing. It's quite an organic process. I might end up going off in a completely different direction than I thought I might. I never know how things will end.'

'Ah! You're a "pantser"!' Jenny pronounces.

I haven't heard this expression before, but guess it means someone who flies by the seat of their pants. 'It's probably not the best way to write a novel,' I say. 'It gets quite difficult to control the material after a while. I eventually reach a point where I can't manage it in my head, and then I make index cards for each chapter. I sometimes have blips in the timeline. I remember this happening once and I thought I'd have to do a big rewrite, but then I had a lightbulb moment and used the blip to write a twist into the story.'

Jenny asks me if I'm a procrastinator next, and if I get writer's block.

I groan. 'I'm a terrible procrastinator. I can always find reasons not to write. And when I do finally sit down at my computer, my split ends suddenly become endlessly fascinating. As for writer's block, I think every writer must suffer from it at some point. I find that if I just start writing – it doesn't matter what – then it will come. And I can always delete it if it's rubbish. The times I'm really stuck? That's where walking the dog comes in. Never fails.'

We then talk about the publishing process and how I went about finding an agent. Jenny looks surprised but delighted when I tell her I met my agent on a dating site. I hasten to add that I did no more than have a cup of tea with him. I'm pretty sure I'm blushing by now.

'You shouldn't be embarrassed,' Jenny says. 'I'd've been well up for it.'

She continues to surprise me.

We round off the interview by talking a bit about the books themselves, and Jenny says I should be really proud. 'Honestly, Amy, your books are a lot better written than some of the mainstream chick lit I've read.'

I can feel my cheeks turning pink again. Not with embarrassment this time, but with relief and gratitude. Someone thinks I, Amy Archer, am a good writer. Yippee!

Jenny thanks me for talking to her and we move back to join the others.

'Amy met her agent on a dating site,' Jenny announces to them, and I find myself re-telling the tale. I'm actually starting to enjoy talking about my life as a writer.

CHAPTER 8

Kidnap!

January slipped seamlessly into February, with the weather staying mild. The members of the writing group kept in touch via Facebook, seeking inspiration, accountability and virtual company. Little did we know how much we would come to rely on our little community in the coming months.

Jenny and the others were all busy penning short stories for a competition. I'd had a brief stab at writing one, but found it impossible, even after reading numerous 'how to' articles. I read a book of short stories in search of inspiration, but just found them unsatisfying. I did wonder if part of my reluctance stemmed from the knowledge that any stories selected would have to be read out at an event later in the year. So, I returned to book three, which still had no name, and tried to help it decide what it was. It really wasn't being very cooperative. I just hoped that if I kept at it a brainwave would strike when I least expected it. And walked Dexter. A lot.

Our third meeting of 'Write Time, Write Place' came around quickly and I was in good spirits when I arrived at our usual table. Jenny had obviously just beaten me to it and I found her organising her things and chatting to a young man who was finishing eating breakfast. I smiled and said hello. I knew we were expecting a new member today, from the online chat. His name was Ian Lambert and he'd just moved down from London and was looking for a writing group to replace the one he'd left behind. We didn't know what he looked like from Facebook as his profile picture was of a baby, but had surmised him to be younger than the rest of us. So, the young man in front of me appeared to fit the bill. Or rather the Ian.

'This is Robert,' Jenny said, breaking her no introduction rule.

I paused. 'Oh.'

'I know. You thought he was Ian, didn't you? I did too, and I said "Hello, Ian, nice to meet you and welcome to the group". Like a knob. Because he's not Ian at all. He's Robert. And he's a leftie like me.' I took her to mean he was left-handed rather than a socialist.

'Well, hello, Robert-slash-not-Ian. It's very nice to meet you. I'm Amy-not-Ian-either.' I take the seat next to him as I'm speaking.

'Hello, Amy, great to meet you.' Robert smiles. He has a very nice smile; blue eyes underneath a slightly messy mop of dark-blonde hair. I can tell he's tall, even though he's seated, and is wearing faded blue jeans and a t-shirt that says "Engineers are all torque".

'I kidnapped him,' Jenny says, straight-faced, making me laugh.

'What? How?'

'Well, because he was sitting at our table, and I just assumed he was Ian, and started talking to him as if he was, he couldn't really just get up and leave. And it's not really *our* table, of course. He has every right to sit here and eat his breakfast. Because he's Robert. Not Ian.' Jenny pauses for breath. 'So, anyway, then he tells me that he actually sat here on purpose to have his breakfast, so that he could meet us!'

'Really?' I look at Robert in surprise and confusion, hoping for an explanation. He really does have a *very* nice smile. Stop it, Amy, you're old enough to be his mother.

'Really!' Robert affirms. 'I usually sit at a table on the other side of the stairs to have breakfast on a Monday and I've seen you all meet up. I will admit to being envious and I really wanted to be a part of whatever it was you were doing. I'd guessed it was a writing group, and you're always so animated. I hope you don't mind me gate-crashing?'

'No, of course not, the more the merrier,' I assure him. 'You'll lower the average age of the group a bit, mind you.'

'How old do you think I am?'

I study him for a few moments. 'Mid-twenties?'

Jenny nods in agreement.

Robert laughs. 'I get that a lot. I'm actually thirty-four.'

'Positively ancient then. I was worried we might have to change the name of the group from "The Saga Seekers" for a minute,' I joke.

'Clever. Playing on the word saga. I like it.'

Jenny and I look at each other and grin.

'Am I missing something?' Robert asks.

'We're old, but we're not ready for a Saga cruise just yet,' I tell him. 'The group's actually called 'Write Time, Write Place', which seems pretty apt where you're concerned. You do realise though that you will hereafter be known as RobertIan?'

'I think I can cope with that. Thank you for letting me join you.'

'Don't thank us yet. You might want to reconsider after a couple of hours with us. And if you're here to write, you might be disappointed to find we spend most of our time chatting.'

'That's okay. I'd just like to be in the company of like-minded people.'

'Fair enough. So, do you write?' I ask him.

'Not really. Well, sort of, I suppose. *(Yep, he's a writer, I think to myself.)* I've written 100,000 words of a travel diary.'

'Bloody hell,' Jenny and I say in unison.

'100,000 words is impressive,' I tell him.

'I'll say,' Jenny agrees before returning to whatever she's looking at on her phone. 'The real Ian can't make it today after all. His son's ill and he's on babysitting duty.'

'Ooh!' A thought has suddenly struck my writer's brain. 'Robert could have killed the real Ian and stolen his identity! We didn't know what Ian looked like, so you assumed Robert was him. Robert could've just gone along with it.'

'Yeah!' Jenny addresses Robert. 'You could've hacked his social media and stolen his phone.'

Robert is saved from any more madness by the arrival of Pippa and Tom. A round of hellos is exchanged, and an extra chair brought to the table.

'You must be Ian?' Pippa says from her place next to Jenny.

Robert, Jenny and I all laugh.

'This is Robert. He killed Ian and stole his identity,' I enlighten the new arrivals.

'And I kidnapped him,' Jenny adds, just to confuse Pippa and Tom further.

We spend the next few minutes explaining.

We'd already agreed to spend some time brainstorming a short story that Jenny was writing for the competition. It involves time travel which I find confusing at the best of times, and I didn't think my recent rereading of *The Time Machine* was going to help. There followed a rather hilarious ninety-minute session where we discussed in great depth whether it's possible to have a time-travelling serial suicide bomber. I kid you not. He was to be called Keith. In spite of the lunacy of the plot, enough good ideas came out of the discussion to help Jenny progress her story.

If Robert wondered what on earth he'd got himself mixed up in, he didn't show it, and we all parted on good terms just after midday.

Later that night, we caught up online. The chat went something like this:

Jenny: I really enjoyed today's session. Thanks for brainstorming my story.

Robert: I'm feeling a touch of Stockholm Syndrome!

Me: Hope we didn't scare you off?! Great to meet you RobertIan.

Robert: You made my day!

Ian: Welcome Robert. I didn't know I had an understudy!

Pippa: Being kidnapped, killing and mass murder. I think you may have joined a weird cult! Welcome, Robert.

Jenny: Don't forget the suicide bomber called Keith.

Robert: I wasn't sure if I was Robert, Ian or Keith today.

Jenny: I hope you're not Keith!

CHAPTER 9

Murder!

Our fourth meeting took place on February twenty-fourth, and I had no nerves at all as I parked the car in my usual spot just down the hill from the pub. I'd heard my phone beep in my bag as I was getting the car park ticket, so I sat back in the car to quickly check. It was a message to the group from Robert informing us that the side of the pub upstairs where we normally sat was taped off, and that he'd bagsied a table directly opposite. He included a photo showing striped tape, a bit like the stuff police use to cordon areas off, stretched across from the top of the stairs.

I found Jenny a few minutes later at the hot drinks dispenser.

'Did you see Robert's message about our section being closed off upstairs?' I ask her.

'Yeah. What's that all about then?'

We'd had some gale force winds and torrential rain in recent weeks, so I voiced an opinion that maybe there was a leak in the roof or something else weather-related. I followed Jenny up the stairs and we turned right at the top, taking in the taped off area as we went. There's no obvious sign of ceiling damage or a leak as far as we can see. We find Robert at the expected table and shimmy onto the bench opposite him. He smiles broadly, seeming absolutely delighted to see us.

'It looks like a crime scene,' I say, looking over at the closed area again, and noting that this end, by the organ pipes, is also taped off. 'Any idea what's happened?'

'Nothing as exciting as a crime, I'm afraid, it's just closed for maintenance,' Robert informs us.

'That's disappointing,' Jenny says.

'Listen to you two ghouls,' I say, laughing. 'You sound as though you'd prefer someone got stabbed or something.'

At that moment, Pippa, Tom and John all arrive.

'What's going on over there then?' Tom asks, nodding towards the tape.

'There's been a murder!' Jenny and I pronounce this at exactly the same moment. We look at each other and laugh.

Tom, Pippa and John look alarmed until we enlighten them. 'It's just a lady removing chewing gum, stains and graffiti – that sort of thing,' I reassure them.

John makes a sort of harrumph noise. 'Well, if you ask me, the animals responsible for all that should be strung up!' he says forcefully.

Nobody disagrees with him.

'We just thought, bearing in mind our conversation last time about Robert killing Ian and stealing his identity, it seemed fitting to imagine there'd been a murder,' I say. 'One of us so needs to put this all in a story.'

And that's kind of how it all started. One minute we were joking about a murder in the pub, and the next we were discussing the best ways to kill a person and dispose of the body. I guess nothing's off limits when a group of writers gets together. Apart from one side of the pub.

'So, Tom, how would you do it?' Pippa asks the oldest member of our group.

'I'd bore them to death,' he pronounces.

I stifle a giggle. Tom does have a tendency to go on a bit. 'So, how long do you think that would take?' I fully expect his answer to be something along the lines of 'About fifteen minutes'.

'Depends on the size of the bore. A 6mm hand bore will take longer than a diamond-tipped industrial boring machine.'

We all laugh at Tom's brilliance. Although I do think fifteen minutes using the other method would do the trick. Or at least send his victim to sleep, thereby making the next part of his plan easier.

'What about you, John? Anyone you'd quite like to bump off?' I ask.

'Ah! Amy, that would be telling. Suffice to say the list is short,' he says, tapping his nose and smiling enigmatically.

'Crikey! There's a list? I hope none of us are on it?' Pippa says.

'No, my dear lady, you are all safe from my machinations.'

I love the way John speaks. I think maybe he was born in the wrong era. I can quite imagine him being a Victorian doctor in London, carrying round the tools of his 'machinations' in his leather Gladstone bag, and bumping off undesirables as he went about his work.

'If you were going to murder someone from your list, though, how do you think you might go about it?' I'm not giving up that easily.

'Well, I must confess I haven't thought too much about the "how". I know what my "why" would be. I have motive, certainly. But "means"..? I think perhaps I would seek inspiration from literature: Edgar Allan Poe's short stories, or perhaps Conan Doyle. I should very much like my murder to be worthy of a detective story.'

I don't know whether to be slightly alarmed by John's admission that he has a motive for murder, or just accept that we've all said we'd like to kill someone in a heated moment. I can think of a few clients at the vet's I'd happily have throttled. I'm sure Cameron would've helped me get them in the freezer.

'I always think the hardest part of killing someone must be getting rid of the body. Although, obviously, actually "killing" someone would be pretty hard.'

'Would it, though?' Robert, who has been pretty quiet up until now, asks. 'Would it, really?'

'Er… I think I'd find it pretty tough. I cried when I accidentally sucked a spider up the hoover,' Jenny says.

'Me too. The killing, and the spider thing,' I clarify. 'I rescue them from the bath too.'

'Oh, I think given the right motivation, anyone could kill another human being,' Robert insists.

'Well, hopefully, we'll never find out,' Pippa says, shuddering. 'Personally, I can't imagine ever hating anyone enough to want to take their life.'

'Do you think murder's more of a man thing?' I ask, starting to wonder if the male members of the group are psychopaths.

'Oh, absolutely,' John nods. 'I think you'll find in excess of ninety percent of murders are committed by men.'

'Blimey, that is high,' Jenny says.

'Going back to the disposing of the body thing – men have an advantage there too, being physically stronger than women,' I say. 'I wouldn't have a Scooby Doo about how to get rid of the body. I've lifted a few dead dogs in my time, so I'm pretty sure I couldn't move a dead human.'

'Well, I think there would be an element of adrenaline

immediately after the killing. You might be surprised at what you can do. Or you would have to either get creative, or have an accomplice,' John says.

For some reason, Jenny and I look at each other and smile. Alrighty then, I know who my accomplice would be.

No one says anything for a few minutes, obviously lost in their own murderous thoughts. Or wondering whether they can be bothered to traipse downstairs for another drink.

I break the silence. 'Here's an idea. What if we all went away and wrote our perfect murder? Does anyone fancy that? Something a bit different?' I look around the table to gauge interest.

'I'm game,' Jenny says.

'Yes, me too,' from Tom. 'I quite fancy the idea actually.'

Soon, everyone has agreed to go off and hatch their perfect murder, complete with how they would dispose of the body. We part company soon after, promising to keep in touch online.

CHAPTER 10

Aiding and avetting

I'm more than happy to abandon my third novel, which is still no nearer revealing its identity to me, and turn my attention to the business of murder. I've read many a murder mystery in my time. How hard can it be?

Jeez, how did Agatha Christie do it? I ask myself a couple of days later, when I still have no idea how I should go about killing someone. I have no shortage of ideas. Ideas are easy. But the actual details and logistics are another matter altogether. Take poison for example (you know what I mean) – I can name half a dozen poisons: arsenic, cyanide, hemlock, nightshade, strychnine. Okay, so I can name five without looking them up. But how would you actually go about obtaining them? And how would you leave no paper or electronic trail?

Then, assuming you manage to get your hands on the poison, you've got to find a way of administering it. And you just know that a post mortem will reveal the poison and somehow lead the police back to the dodgy search you did in an internet café, from CCTV on the street. Or, knowing my luck, the internet café owner would remember me because I looked so sodding guilty as I sat there hunched over the screen, furtively typing 'murder for beginners' into the search engine.

I wonder idly why poison is the first method to come to my mind? I think I remember hearing that it's a woman's weapon. Wasn't it in *Game of Thrones* someone says: 'Poison's a woman's weapon. Men kill with steel'? I certainly can't imagine stabbing or beating someone to death. I suppose if it was a crime of passion, then maybe, but you can't plan that. Perhaps shooting would be easier. Something that can be done from a distance, less personal, not so hands on. But where the heck would a normal person like me get a gun from? Although the more time I spend thinking about killing someone, the less normal I feel. I decide to check in with Jenny to see how she's getting on, and send her a quick message:

Killed anyone yet?

Very nearly. (These two words are followed by a smiley face. Disturbing.)

Really? Oh God, I'm rubbish at murder.

I'm quite enjoying it. Got a victim, a motive and a means. Working on opportunity and getting rid of the body.

Wow! I'm dead jealous.

I think you'd be more of a crime of passion killer. With you not being very good at planning. (Laughing emoji. Rude.)

So, I need to Google 'murder for pantsers'?

Murder with pants? Don't think that's been done too often.

You're not helping.

Sorry. You'll come up with something.

I won't! It's killing me.

Don't think you're meant to be the victim.

If I am, it'll be death by chocolate the way I'm going.

You could bash someone over the head with a Terry's Chocolate Orange – they're pretty hard.

It's not Terry's, it's mine. Right, well done you anyway. Back to the drawing board for me. Catch up soon.

Drawing pins, ironing board… get creative, Amy. Speak soon.

Right, Amy, start at the beginning, I say to myself, settling comfortably on the sofa with a bar of Dairy Milk. Who would you like to murder? My secondary school PE teacher? That man who cut me up on the roundabout the other day? Mr. Cadbury for making me fat? Then I remember some of the pet owners I had to deal with at the vet's. There were a few times Cameron and I agreed we should've euthanised the owners instead of the pets. Maybe I should kill one of them? There was one particularly nasty man who mistreated his dog in the waiting room. I remember thinking at the time that I'd like to kick him. The man, not the dog. I had to settle for informing the RSPCA.

I cast my mind back to the man in question, remembering that he was actually a homeless man who came to see us at the free clinic. Well, being homeless is no excuse for kicking your dog, matey. I could kill him and then the dog could be rehomed with people who wouldn't mistreat it. Two birds with one stone. I'm quite getting into the idea now. Maybe this plotting lark isn't so bad after all.

Okay, so I have a victim. I need a fitting method now. I think the time has come to call in reinforcements, and I reach for my mobile and text the best person for the job: Cameron Clarke, vet extraordinaire and all-round drama queen.

Hello, my lovely! How are you? I need help killing someone!

That should grab his attention. I check the time. He ought to be between clinics now, so I might be lucky and get a quick reply. I absent-mindedly finish off the bar of chocolate. Damn you, Mr. Cadbury. It's not long before my phone beeps.

Ameeee! I miss you. Who are we going to kill? After the morning I've had, I'm up for a bit of murder. (I love the fact that he doesn't even question what I've said.)

Remember that horrid homeless man who kicked his dog? We're killing him. I need to pick your brain for ideas on how to do it.

No problemo. I'm your man. Just about to go into surgery – catch up tonight? How about the pub at 8?

Perfect. Thank you. You're my hero. (Damn, now I'm thinking about chocolate again.)

That night I arrive at the pub at around seven fifty to give me time to exchange hellos and hugs with whoever's working behind the bar. I'd worked at the pub part-time a couple of summers ago, and it was always nice to go back in and see everyone. I'm delighted to see my favourite barmaid, Ellie, working alongside the landlord, Richie. If Cameron is as camp as a row of tents, Richie is as camp as a row of pink ones. I can't wait to introduce them.

I take a seat at the bar, order a couple of G&Ts and wait for Cameron. His goldfish bowl of a glass is bedecked with strawberries, an umbrella and a sparkly swizzle stick. It's not long before the door swings open and he makes his entrance, flouncing extravagantly across to greet me. Cameron can't somehow just walk into a room. We hug and share air kisses. I wouldn't do this with anyone else, but Cameron somehow demands it. He shuffles onto the stool next to me and heaves a sigh of relief.

'What a day! Ooh, gin! Fabulous, dahling, thank you.' He picks up the drink and somehow manages to take a glug from somewhere in between all the trimmings.

I pick up my somewhat plainer glass, 'Cheers, my dear!' I say and take a sip. I nearly made the toast, 'Up your bottom'. Thankfully my brain engaged in time to stop me. 'Tough day?'

'Aren't they always? Did my first eye enucleation though,' he says proudly.

I'm momentarily relieved that we don't have lychees in our gin. I'd been surprised at how common eye removal was when I worked at the vet's. The thought of it still turned my stomach though. 'Go okay?'

'Textbook,' Cameron nods.

'Yay! Well done you.'

'Thank you. Sooo… tell me… what's been happening with you?'

'In a minute. First I want to introduce you to Richie.' I call the landlord over from the other end of the bar where he's stacking glasses in the washer.

'You rang?' he drawls as he saunters over. Richie is kind of cool camp.

'Yes, I just want to introduce you to my favourite vet in the world. Richie, Cameron. Cameron, Richie. So now when he comes in you won't try and redirect him to the nearest Wetherspoons,' I say with a wink. Richie has a reputation for being a frightful snob where pub clientele is concerned. If he doesn't like the look of you, you know where you can go.

The two shake hands and take a moment to size each other up. I'm holding my breath to see if Cameron passes muster. Then Cameron says something about some obscure fashion designer and, that's it, he's in. (At the time, I had no idea who he was talking about, but he enlightened me afterwards. And I promptly forgot. I think it must be some sort of gay code. Anyway, it did the trick.)

'Lovely to meet you, Cameron,' Richie says. 'See you again soon, I hope. I must get back to work – no rest for the wicked.'

'Yes, you too,' Cameron agrees as Richie heads back over to the glass washer. The in a loud whisper, he turns to me, 'Ooh!

I bet he can be really wicked! Thanks for the intro, Ames.'

'You're welcome,' I laugh.

'Now, where were we? Oh yes. YOU WANT TO KILL WHO?' He says this loud enough for everyone in the room to hear, and accompanies the words with a shocked expression and his hands up around his face.

I can feel all eyes on us. 'You dick!' I'm laughing, and probably blushing too.

Cameron looks around the bar. 'It's okay, ladies and gents, don't panic – she's a writer.' He smiles benignly at his audience.

'You are such a twat,' I tell him.

'I know. But you love me.'

'Yes, I do love you. And I need your help.'

'Right. Yes. Fire away.'

I fill him in on the writing group and our idea to try and pen the perfect murder. His first concern is to make sure he'll feature in the story. After I've agreed to that, we get down to the grisly business of murder in the veterinary degree.

'If I was gonna kill someone, I'd definitely use insulin,' Cameron says. 'Can't be tox screened after death.'

'Yeah, I thought about that. I saw it on a TV drama recently though – hasn't it been done to death?'

'Pun intended,' Cameron chuckles. 'I s'pose it has been used a fair bit. There was that "Angel of Death" nurse too, wasn't there? Didn't she use insulin? And I think it would take ages to off someone in the formulations we get.'

'Okay, so what else would work?'

Cameron thinks for a second. 'There's Marbocyl. One tiny prick of the finger can make a person go into anaphylactic shock in minutes.'

I resist the obvious joke. 'Right, that might work. Anything else?'

'Ooh! Etomidate. It's like elephant tranquiliser – even spilling it on your finger can knock you out.'

'So, it wouldn't take much to overdose someone with? I quite like the idea of a tranquiliser. Lovely. Thank you.'

'My pleasure. So, if we're offing the homeless dude, how are we getting rid of the body?'

'I really want to use the pet crematorium. Haven't got that far in the planning yet.'

'Hmm. Tricky. I'm sure you'll come up with something.'

The subject switches to work and Cameron fills me in on all the latest gossip. I'm secretly pleased that my replacement packed the job in after less than three months, and that her replacement isn't much good.

'Oh!' he says, 'And Mrs Reed still comes in looking for you. Doesn't matter how often we tell her you've left. Bless her!'

'Poor Mrs Reed. I do feel bad about letting her down. How's Kiki? Still smiling?'

'Yes, still smiling, but I think she misses you too. We all miss you!'

I reach over and squeeze Cameron's hand. 'I miss you all, too. But I do not miss killing things!'

'And yet, here we are, plotting a murder!'

We both laugh and raise a toast to a successful mission.

CHAPTER 11

Death by chocolate

That night I have the strangest dreams. I'm trying to get Kiki to eat a lychee while Mrs Reed rides around on a pink elephant. Cameron is sitting in a black swivel chair stroking a fluffy white, rather angry-looking, one-eyed cat, like some sort of Bond villain.

I text Cameron as soon as I wake up.

Lovely to see you last night. Thanks for your help. And btw, had the strangest dream last night – you were stroking a pussy. Bet that's never happened in real life.

His reply pings back almost at once.

I shudder at the thought! My pleasure, lovely. Catch up soon. Mwah!

I'm chuckling as I head downstairs to make a coffee, which I take back up to bed, settling myself against the pillows with a notebook and pen. For once in my life I need to plan something.

I have a victim, a motive and means.

Ninety minutes later.

I have a victim, a motive and means.

I am not a planner. I give up, get up and go out shopping.

I mooch into WHSmith to browse the bookshelves. As I walk past the racks of newspapers, I see that all the front pages feature articles about this new virus which is threatening the world. What started as faint mutterings about bats in a Chinese food market has become louder and more insistent. Maybe it's time I started listening? Nah, I think, carrying on to the back of the shop and heading straight for the crime thrillers section in search of inspiration. I pick up and read the back pages of a few murder mysteries. To be honest, though, I can't really afford to buy books at the moment – I think I'm hoping for inspiration via some sort of osmosis – so after a few minutes I head towards the exit. That's where the chocolate stand sticks its foot out and trips me up. Well, it's on offer and I have a budget for chocolate. I pick up two Chocolate Oranges. Purely for research purposes, obviously.

*

By the time the next writing group rolls around on March ninth, the rumblings about the virus are growing louder. Everyone knows its name now: Corona. Or Covid-19. We're hearing that it could be serious. A pandemic. And not to visit Northern Italy. As I can't afford to hop on a plane right now, I remain pretty unflustered and head off to meet the others at the pub.

It's the usual suspects: me, Jenny, Pippa, Tom, John and Robert. Ian never did make it. After a brief chat about the Coronavirus, and the rising death toll in China and Italy, we move on to discuss our own plans to kill people.

'So, how's everyone getting on with their murderous plots?' I ask.

'I've finished mine,' Jenny says matter-of-factly.

Everyone looks impressed. I'm dead jealous. Jenny seems to find writing effortless.

'Blimey! Well done. I'm getting absolutely nowhere with

mine. This whole planning malarkey…' My facial expression completes my sentence.

The others join in with their congratulations.

'I quite enjoyed writing it actually,' Jenny says.

'Are we going to be able to read it now, or should we wait until everyone's finished?' Pippa asks.

Jenny shrugs. 'I don't mind.'

I look around the table for a consensus, which is that we wait until the killing spree is complete.

'How's your story coming along, anyway, Pippa?' I ask. Of all of us, I think that Pippa will find this the least comfortable exercise. She's a carer, not a killer.

'Not too bad, thanks Amy, I think I'm about halfway there. Haven't got a body yet, but plans are afoot.'

'That's brilliant,' we all agree. I'm feeling more of a failure by the minute, and vow I will go home and kill someone right after the group finishes. 'Are we allowed any clues?'

'Um… no, I think I'd rather wait until it's finished and I'm really happy with it.'

'Fair enough,' I say. 'Although, you know, as writers we're never *really* happy with our work!'

Everyone laughs and agrees that we are our own worst critics.

'I don't mind sharing the first idea I had with you all though,' Pippa says. 'It's pretty far-fetched, but I rather liked it. I thought that maybe my killer could poison someone by way of their contact lens solution. God, sounds mad saying it aloud.'

'Well, I don't think it sounds mad at all. I think it sounds rather brilliant and highly original,' Tom says, and we all agree it's ingenious.

Pippa continues. 'And I wanted my victim to be someone

who was known to have watched child pornography – you know, so the punishment was through his eyes; fitted his crime. That type of idea.' She looks a little embarrassed, but we're all really impressed with her originality.

'So, you had your victim, motive and means… that's pretty much where I've got to. It's the execution that's the hard bit, isn't it?'

Tom and John admit that they haven't really given their stories too much thought yet, as other 'life' stuff has taken priority.

'I have no such excuse,' I admit glumly.

'I did have one idea while I was hoovering the other day,' John says.

We all look at him expectantly.

'I was thinking about those robotic vacuum cleaners – you know, those round things that buzz around the floor automatically. And I started to wonder if maybe you could programme one to explode. I only did a vague bit of research into it. Not sure if it's even feasible, but it did appeal to me.'

'Ooh! I love that idea, John,' I say. 'Why didn't you pursue it?'

'Well, how could you ensure the right person, i.e. your victim, was in the right place at the right time? For starters.'

We're all quiet for a few minutes as we ponder the possibilities. It's Robert who finally speaks up.

'I reckon it could be done. Would need a fair bit of technical know-how though. If you could modify the machine to include cameras and have control of it yourself, you could get around your time and place problem. In fact, I believe there are some Robotic cleaners that are compatible with Alexa – you could potentially use her to control the bot.'

'Oh my God! Alexa as your accomplice. That would be so

cool,' Jenny says.

Robert nods. 'And then you've just got the problem of the explosive device. Wouldn't be that hard for the right kind of expert. And, of course, when the thing blew up it would destroy the evidence. Pretty neat and tidy.'

'As much as I love the idea, I'm not sure I could write such a story convincingly. I think it's back to the drawing board for me,' John says. 'How about you, Tom, any initial ideas you want to share?'

'Only one really, and that hit me on the way here in the car. I was listening to the news on the radio and they were talking about this Coronavirus. I got to wondering about deliberately infecting someone vulnerable with it. Sounds awful saying it out loud.' Tom pauses.

'Go on,' John encourages.

'Well, I remembered those cases of men deliberately infecting others with HIV… and it made me think. But the idea has so many flaws in it.'

'Hmm… if you had to contract the illness yourself in order to pass it on, you'd have no way of knowing how seriously ill you might become yourself,' Pippa muses.

'It would solve the problem of disposing of the body though, wouldn't it?' Jenny adds.

'Good point, death by natural causes,' Pippa nods.

'Getting rid of the body is definitely a biggie,' I say gloomily.

'Kill a very small person then, Amy,' Jenny adds helpfully.

'You're not clever and you're not funny,' I say sulkily. 'Well, actually you are, both, but…' As is my wont, I stick my tongue out to finish my sentence. If only facial expressions could finish my stories as satisfactorily.

We pass the remainder of the two-hour session talking happily about killing people and, just after midday, we all depart with assurances to keep in touch in the online group. I return home with renewed determination to bump someone off. Now, where did I put those Chocolate Oranges and just how hard are they..?

CHAPTER 12

Panic!

As the days pass, the news from around the world grows scarier. Businesses start to close, with many people now working from home. I'd like to say I'm one of them, but my story remains undeveloped, like a supermarket egg. I think my boss is just too lenient.

Events are suddenly being cancelled, and we've all learnt the art of social distancing. We're being told that the Coronavirus is a pandemic, and that the measures being put in place are to ensure the NHS doesn't become overwhelmed by too many people getting sick at once. We all understand that we must do our bit to flatten the curve. It's a whole new language that we're being asked to learn fast, at a time when the nation's anxiety curve is an upwards vertical line.

I still feel pretty safe in my little bubble of home, and writers are usually quite good at being reclusive anyway. We've had to cancel the writing group for the foreseeable future which makes me sad, but we all seem to be coping with the threat of the pandemic reasonably well, although I know Jenny is quite anxious.

The new language keeps coming (just not in my story) and the country goes into lockdown. We are self-isolating. Some of us more than others. We're only allowed to make essential journeys for food, medical needs and work if we can't work from home. We can also leave the house to exercise locally for an hour a day. Gatherings of more than two people are forbidden and we must stay two metres apart. Schools close, along with pubs and restaurants, and all other non-essential shops and businesses; and people start panic buying toilet rolls, soap and hand sanitiser. And paracetamol. And then pasta and rice. It's all very bizarre. And starting to get real and scary. If only my story was.

More and more cases of the virus are being reported from around the world, including here in the UK, where London seems to be ahead of the curve from the rest of the country. Daily briefings from the government are shown on television and we're told that we *must* self-isolate to protect the NHS and save lives. Social media, of course, goes mental, with the crisis bringing out the very best and the absolute worst in humanity. From punch-ups in supermarkets over loo rolls, to free online opera. It's a crazy time. Poets, writers, singers, musicians, start to share on Facebook. Timelines are a mass of memes and funnies, videos of families singing and dancing together, and a whole load of creative genius. If only. I seem to be paralysed and unable to write.

I'm also, apparently, unable to buy loo rolls. And not because there aren't any on the shelves. When I finally brave the shop, my timing is spot on for once and they are in the process of unloading a trolley full onto the shelf. I pause next to the them, but it's no good, I can't bring myself to pick up a pack of sodding loo rolls and put them in my trolley because I feel too guilty. Even though I actually need them. But I don't want people to see them in my trolley and think that I'm jumping on the panic-buying bandwagon. Madness. And probably terribly British. I note that the shelves are empty of paracetamol, hand sanitiser, and hand wash. Although there are still bars of soap which baffles me. I buy some of the bars and also some boxes of tissues. Adapt or die, I think to myself as I unload my no-bandwagon onto the conveyor belt at the checkout.

When I get back to the car with my shopping, I use some hand sanitiser from my nearly empty bottle and breathe a sigh of relief. Going out has become a scary exercise. And I've always found exercise a bit scary anyway. As I drive the short distance home, I wonder if I could improvise some hand sanitiser. Worst case scenario, I could probably drink it.

Once I've unpacked the shopping and washed my hands, again, I make myself a coffee and sit down to scroll through Facebook for a while. Sharing Coronavirus funnies has become a big part of everyone's day. Amongst the scare-mongering and the humour, are many posts about how people are using the time to learn a new skill or a new language. They've redecorated their houses from top to bottom, manicured their gardens and learnt Mandarin. Apparently if we haven't done anything like this then we are utter failures. Well, they can fuck right off, I think to myself. I hate the idea that people are being made to feel like losers by these smug gits. I'm so cross I have to eat some chocolate orange.

It's actually three weeks before I shake off the creative paralysis and start to flex my mental muscles again. And as the muscle memory returns, it feels good. Really, really good. I blast out my murder story and then throw myself headlong into a new novel. It might be no coincidence that my creative juices started flowing at the same time as the weather changed. April brought some beautiful sunshine with it and I got into the habit of writing until midday and then reading in the garden in the afternoon. Some of the best ideas for the book came when I was sunbathing, and I came to the conclusion that my brain must be solar powered.

The evenings were harder, when the sun went down, but again we were adapting and creating a virtual social life; replacing actual events with online versions. Video conferencing apps came into their own – no longer just used for business, but for family get-togethers, quizzes and more. We'd managed to persuade Jenny to continue the writing group on Zoom and all downloaded the app in readiness.

The first online 'Write Time, Write Place' meeting takes place on March 23, the first day of lockdown, and is a novel experience for most of us. Tom can't seem to get his webcam to work and we see more of Jenny's cat's bottom than Jenny's face, but it's lovely to actually see everyone and interact as if we're together. Robert's wearing a The Killers T-shirt which makes us all laugh. Jenny says we should be honoured as she's actually washed her hair and got dressed for the first time in a week. Her normally hot pink hair is fading to more of a strawberry bon bon shade.

'So, how's everyone getting on with their stories?' I ask, once Tom's resolved his technical issue with the camera. We knew that Jenny's was completed, of course.

'Mine's finished,' Pippa says, smiling.

'That's great, well done you,' I say. 'Are you happy with it?'

'Yes, actually, I think I am.'

We all congratulate her and say how much we look forward to reading it.

Tom and John both admit to not having made much progress still. As do I. (This first video meeting took place before I had my solar-powered breakthrough.) Robert says he's got some ideas. Big ideas, at that.

'I'm intrigued,' I tell him. 'Any clues?'

'Let's just say I want to write about the sort of killer who's worthy of a nickname.'

'Ooh! Like Jack the Ripper or the Boston Strangler?' Pippa says.

'Or the Acid Bath Murderer,' Tom chips in.

'Let me liquidate your assets,' John says, with a fake villain laugh that makes the rest of us join in.

'Yep. Exactly like them,' Robert nods. Something about the way he says it sends a shiver down my spine. I shake off the feeling.

'Robert the *Grues*ome,' Tom pipes up again, pronouncing the name in a broad Scots accent, heavy emphasis on the 'grues'. We all laugh.

'The Bob Slayer,' I slide in with my suggestion, relieved that the mood is lighter once more. 'I was thinking, as things have been turned upside down in the world at the moment, if maybe we could share a story each week? We could take it in turns to email our story and then discuss it at the next Zoom meeting. What do you think? We have two completed stories now, and that would take the pressure off the rest of us. Especially Robert, who sounds as though he's planning to commit multiple murders.' Yes, I have an ulterior motive. I look around the faces on my laptop screen.

After a bit of toing and froing, we all agree to this idea, and Jenny volunteers to go first. This seems only right as she finished first, and she promises to email her story to us all after the meeting.

The discussion then moves away from writing, which is not so unusual for our group. Tom's wife makes an unscheduled appearance in her pyjamas as she walks behind him. I don't think she realised he'd fixed the webcam problem. Both of Jenny's cats put in an appearance too.

It's been nice talking about something other than the bloody Coronavirus for a while, even if it was still about killing people, but naturally Covid-19 is at the forefront of everyone's minds.

'How's everyone coping, anyway, in this strange new world?' I ask.

'Not too bad, really. I'm doing deliveries in the town – you know, prescriptions and things. Gets me out of the house. And, of course, there are the dogs to walk once a day,' Pippa says.

'I've put my name down as a volunteer for the NHS. Not sure what they'll have me doing – probably just talking to people on the phone who might be feeling lonely and isolated. They won't want an old bugger like me doing deliveries, I shouldn't think,' Tom shrugs.

'Well done, you two. That sounds perfect for you, Tom,' I say, chuckling at the thought of him boring people to death, whilst simultaneously feeling a bit guilty for not volunteering. 'How about you, John?'

'I have been happily reading Émile Zola's *Les Rougon-Macquart*. All twenty novels. Been promising myself I'd read them for years. This seemed like the perfect opportunity. It's been rather wonderful. And, perhaps, more than a little inspiring for a fledgling writer of murder most foul. When not reading, I have been tending my new raised vegetable beds.'

I'm feeling like a complete failure of a human being by now. I've been lounging in the sun, ready trashy novels and eating biscuits. I look to Jenny, hoping she'll make me feel better.

'Well, my life hasn't really changed much, let's be honest. I stay at home with the cats and write. I think the only thing I'll be coming out of this situation with is agoraphobia.'

'Or not,' I add.

'Eh?' Jenny looks confused.

'*Not coming out*... agoraphobia?' I explain. Jenny continues to look confused. 'Never mind,' I say with a wave of my hand. If I have to explain a joke, then it wasn't a good one.

Suddenly, the penny drops. 'Oh! I get it! That's actually quite funny,' she says.

I smile and bow my head. 'Here all week, folks.'

We wrap the meeting up, with assurances from Jenny that she'll email her story to us, all waving goodbye as we click on Leave Meeting. I head straight to my bookcase and hunt for a copy of Zola's *Le Docteur Pascal* to read in the garden. On the way I stop off in the kitchen to see if there's a vegetable or anything healthy I can snack on. There isn't. Apart from the orange. It's still not Terry's.

CHAPTER 13

Jenny's story

Later that night, I check my emails and, sure enough, there's one from Jenny with her story attached. I'm excited to read it, so I make a cuppa and settle myself down comfortably on the sofa.

PIGGY BANK

It's two years since I left *him* but he's still trying to ruin my life. Bastard. I hate his guts. No, I do, I really do. Leaving him is the best thing I ever did. Apart from getting my cats. My cats top everything. I don't have any children. Not a fan. But I love my cats. I couldn't have cats when I was with him; he hated cats. More than that, though, he suffered with asthma and was actually very allergic to them, so I suppose he had a pretty good reason not to like cats. That's not the point though. He's still a twat for not liking them. I don't like olives, but I don't have some sort of hate campaign against them.

Now I'm single again I have three rescue cats. They rescued me. Splodge, Podge and Dodge, all from the same litter, but as different as chalk and cheese. And something else beginning with 'ch' – chocolate. As different as chalk, cheese and chocolate. The one thing they have in common is that they love me unconditionally. They don't try and control me – apart from at feeding time – or criticise everything I say and do.

He made me feel like I was cat shit on his shoe. I shouldn't have stayed as long as I did, but he eroded the chalk cliff of my self-esteem so badly that I didn't have the strength to leave. He made me believe that I was nothing, and would be even less without him. He made me feel like a negative. He criticised my choice of clothes, the way I did my hair, my make-up; he belittled me in front of friends and sneered at my opinions. Eventually I just stopped seeing my friends, and I let him choose what I wore and how I looked. It was just easier than pushing back. He wore me down to a chalky pile of rubble. He wore me away to nothing.

I'm not nothing any more. I'm something. Someone. I matter. I wear what I like and I've dyed my hair pink. Tomorrow I might dye it blue. The cats don't care what colour my hair is.

I don't really know how I found the strength to leave him. I knew I had to get out or go under. So, I started to plan my escape. I couldn't just walk out without a plan – that's not who I am. I am a planner. So I started to make lists which I kept stashed at work. Before long I'd decided to move to the south coast and I'd applied to relocate with work, and started looking for somewhere to rent. It was surprising how quickly things fell into place, and then I just packed up my personal belongings when he was out at work one day, got in my car and left.

Life is good now. I started painting, seascapes mainly, after I moved. I'd always wanted to be an artist, but of course he just mocked me if I mentioned it and told me I had no talent, laughing at the idea that I could ever make a living from it. Well, he was wrong, and I am now making a living from my art. I keep a local gallery stocked with my works and also sell online through my website and social media. I'm not making a fortune, but I'm surviving and I'm happy. I have my art and I have my cats. And I'll never again let someone control or belittle me.

But then he found my website and my artist pages on social media and began a relentless, hate-filled, trolling campaign. I asked the police if they could help. They said unless there was a threat to my safety they couldn't really do anything. So I'm going to do something. He doesn't get to ruin my new life.

And that's why he has to die. That's why I have to kill him.

I haven't told you his name. Did you notice? That's because he doesn't get to have a name. He made me feel like a nobody. I'm just returning the favour. He's nobody and soon he'll be nothing.

*

Hello, stranger. How's life? I type the text through gritted teeth. I never, ever thought I'd contact him again.

I wondered how long it would be before you realised the error of your ways. Arrogant bastard. I could picture the smug, self-satisfied look on his face.

Yeah, you were right, as always. Can't make it on my own. I'm clenching my hands and my jaw as I wait for his reply.

Surprised you survived this long. Inside I'm screaming.

I was wondering... maybe I could come and see you? Next weekend? If you're not busy.

Must be your lucky day, I'm free all weekend. You can stay over. I feel sick to the stomach at the thought of seeing him again, let alone sharing a bed with him.

Thanks. I'd like that. Can I come on Friday night? I think I might actually vomit. I take a deep breath and remember why

I'm doing this. Short term pain for long term gain.

My, we are keen. Yeah, Friday night's good. I can hear the sneer in his words.

Great. I'll see you then. About 8 if that's okay with you? Playing the little woman, getting his permission.

Don't be late. You know I don't like to be kept waiting.

I won't. And thanks. See you Friday.

One more thing – you haven't been stupid enough to get a cat, have you?

No, I didn't get a cat. Well, I wasn't lying. I got three.

I drop my phone onto the sofa and run to the loo to throw up. God, if I'm like this after an exchange of texts, how on earth am I going to cope with seeing him? Being with him? I wipe my mouth, wash my hands and shake the thoughts away. One step at a time.

I tried to keep busy for the next few days. I had a few errands to run and stuff to organise. I hated leaving my fur babies, but I knew they'd be okay. It would only be one night; I could leave plenty of food down on Friday evening and they'd be fine until I got back. I dyed my hair brown – a temporary alteration, I hasten to add – and chose my outfit carefully, knowing how he liked me to dress. I knew that no matter how I looked, he would find something to criticise, but I had to negate how bad it would be. I had to protect myself as much as possible.

Friday evening arrived way too quickly and my nerves were jangling like a big old bunch of jailer's keys. I'd actually dug out some Diazepam tablets from the bad old days and been taking them now and then. I was also in danger of overdosing on Rescue Remedy, dropping the bitter-tasting drops on my tongue every half an hour or so. I hated him all over again for reducing me to this mass of exposed nerve endings. My heart was in my mouth as I packed up the car, said goodbye and be good to the cats, after giving them all lots of cuddles and kisses, and set off for London.

I'd left in plenty of time to allow for Friday night traffic. I didn't want to risk being late. I needed him relaxed and in a good mood. He'd contacted me mid-week and told me to pick up food and beer for us. I'd meekly agreed, of course, but it was the last time he'd give me an order. I'd gone one better than picking up food, and cooked a batch of his favourite beef curry. He'd never know about the cat food I'd put in it. I'd overfed the cats and scraped their leftovers into the pot of simmering, spicy meat. It gave me a sick sort of satisfaction to think about him eating it. It was his own fault. He'd made me into this person. Thankfully I'm a vegetarian.

As I drove, my mind drifted back to the years BC. Before Cats. It's not that I wanted to think about those times; I couldn't seem to help it. I suppose it was understandable, considering that I was heading back into the lion's den. When I first met *him*, I think I was a pretty normal twenty-nine-year-old woman. Like anyone, I wasn't without my hang-ups, but I was a bubbly, sociable, healthy young woman. I had a degree in Linguistics and a job I loved as a speech therapist. I specialised in working with children who had speech and language disorders. As a child I suffered with a lisp and endured a fair bit of teasing at primary school. I couldn't hear the speech defect myself, apart from on a tape recording, which made it all the more confusing. It knocked my confidence a fair bit. Finally, when I was ten or eleven, I asked my mum if I could see someone about it. Before that age, I don't think I knew that such things as speech therapists even existed.

It bugs me a bit, looking back, that my mum didn't do anything to help sooner. I suppose as a kid I didn't make a fuss and she didn't realise it was a problem. It was though. To this day, even though I know I don't have a lisp anymore, I still hate any sort of public speaking. That self-consciousness never really left. So, having the opportunity to help children like me to speak clearly, to articulate, communicate, and see their self-confidence increase, brought me absolute joy.

Maybe when I met him, he saw someone with a vulnerability, something just under the surface that he knew he could exploit. I don't know. I remember the night I met him, as clear as day. I was at the pub with a couple of girlfriends, and he was there with his mates. They came over and we all ended up sharing a table. He was chatty and charming, and really good looking, with hair that flopped into deep brown eyes you could lose yourself in. There weren't any warning bells going off in my head. And I don't think that was just because of the vodka. Long story short, we exchanged numbers and started dating. And my opinion of him didn't change from the one I formed on that first night. He was thoughtful and romantic, considerate and caring. That's why it's so hard to understand why he changed once we moved in together. I still can't get my head around it now.

I gave up my flat and moved into his house about six months after we started dating. I knew it was quick, but it felt right, so why wait? For a while, everything seemed perfect. We bought things for the house together and started making plans for our future. I had honestly never been happier.

And then, I began to notice little changes in his behaviour towards me. At first they were just little digs, here and there; he began to criticise my appearance, telling me if he didn't like something I was wearing. This top didn't suit me, that skirt made me look fat. Those old feelings of self-consciousness, never buried deeply enough, started to rise to the surface once more. I became anxious about my clothes not meeting his approval on a daily basis. After a while, I let him choose my clothes for me. It was just easier than enduring the sneering look on his face and the cruel words.

When he had control over what I wore, he turned his attention to my hair and make-up and did the same thing. I no longer recognised the woman looking back at me in the mirror. There was some essence of me in the sad blue eyes, but it wasn't me. My self-confidence spiralled downwards as the months went on. I hoped that once he was happy with how I looked, he would stop being cruel. I realise now that I was stupid and naïve, and I should've got out the moment he began to change. If only it was that easy. At first, I thought it was just a blip: this wasn't the man I'd fallen in love with. And I made excuses for him. And then it was impossible to leave, because he'd made me believe that I was nothing without him. It's ridiculous, I know, that an intelligent woman could be brought to her knees like that, but I was. He chip, chip, chipped away at my self-esteem until he'd whittled me down to a slither, a splinter. Something barely there. Barely visible.

His criticisms of me continued, and began to extend to the way I did things. I sliced the cheese wrong; I ironed his shirts incorrectly; the way I hung the towels in the bathroom was not to his liking. Nothing I did was right, or good enough. I dreaded his fault-finding and berating. And it wasn't limited to when we were on our own. He did it in front of my friends too; mocking me and trying to make me feel small, look small. Eventually, I stopped seeing them. I felt ashamed and embarrassed and unworthy. It was easier to not see them than feel like that. Apart from work, I stopped going out on my own.

My anxiety slid into insomnia, depression and eating disorders. I plucked up the courage to see my GP one day and went home with prescriptions for Diazepam and Mirtazapine. I didn't tell the doctor the real reasons behind my mental health problems, blaming the stress of work and non-existent family issues. I was too ashamed. I just wanted something to take the edge off the pain and maybe help me sleep. I dreaded going to bed. Most nights I lay on the very edge of the bed, tense and anxious, pretending to be asleep. Not that it made any difference. If he wanted to have sex with me, then that's what happened. He just took what he wanted. This man who'd once been tender and loving, was aggressive and domineering. He didn't beat me up. Not in the sense of punching and kicking. But he was rough and cruel when he took me, taking fistfuls of my hair, pulling my head back and putting his hand across my throat or mouth. And then he would roll over and sleep, as I tugged my nightdress back down to try and cover my shame, and wept silently, longing for oblivion.

More than once I thought about taking my own life, and putting an end to the misery. I wrote letters to my friends and family in my head, and thought about how I would do it. All my pills and a bottle of vodka. A hot bath and a razor. Slip quietly under and disappear. But some spark, some instinct to survive, persisted.

Looking back now, I think I know the moment that something snapped in me; when I knew I had to find the strength and courage to leave him. It was such a small incident in the scheme of things, but it ignited a touch paper that fizzed up and lit a dormant anger, long suppressed, somewhere deep inside me. I received a birthday card and small gift in the post from a childhood friend who'd tracked me down via my mum. We'd been at primary school together and he was the first boy I ever kissed. We were never even really proper boyfriend and girlfriend, but he held a special place in my memory. He had torn up the card and smashed the little snow globe which was a replica of one I'd had as a girl, leaving me to clear up the glass and glitter and mess. As I'd knelt there on the kitchen floor, a glass shard in my hand, I could feel the first flicker of a furious flame seething inside me.

*

It was dark by the time I reached his house, and a shudder went through me as I recalled my life inside it. I never thought I'd set foot here again. I was pleased to find no parking space directly outside and had a valid excuse to park a way down the road. I didn't want the neighbours remembering my car being parked out front. I unloaded just the essentials from my car and walked to the house, reminding myself to breathe and trying to control the rising panic in my chest. My heart was beating fit to burst. I wasn't too worried though – he'd just think I was nervous and excited to see him again. Arrogant son of a bitch.

I fixed a smile on my face and rang the bell. The feelings of nausea washing over me were almost overwhelming. I could see his outline through the half-glazed door as he approached down the hall. Breathe. Stay calm. You can do this. The door opened. I smiled at him.

'Hello,' I squeaked. It was all I could manage.

'Well, look what the cat dragged in,' he said, with more of a sneer than a smile.

Part of me wanted to turn around and run, but I just sort of shrugged and walked past him, heading straight for the kitchen at the back of the house to put my stuff down. It gave me a much needed few seconds to try and compose myself after seeing him for the first time in so long. All the old fear responses had come flooding back. But I'm not that person anymore, I tell myself. I'm in control now.

He's followed me into the kitchen and put his arms round me from behind, where I'm standing at the island unit. He leans into my neck. 'So, did you miss me?' he says, before biting my earlobe quite hard. He forces me to turn around and face him, tipping my head up to look at him. His eyes bore into me: bottomless pits of black tar. How had I ever thought those eyes were beautiful?

'Yes.' Again it's all I can manage. My words are trapped in my throat by feelings of fear and revulsion.

'You can show me how much later,' he growls.

I just nod, and try and wriggle out of his grasp, but he holds onto my arms, keeping me in place in front of him. 'Let me look at you properly.'

All I can do is stand there and endure his scrutiny, trying not to let how I'm feeling show in my face.

'Not too bad, I suppose,' he says. 'Could do with losing a few pounds. It's no wonder you're still on your own.'

Bastard, I think. I'm not on my own and my weight is fine. I'm a healthy size twelve, not the anorexic stick insect I used to be. 'Well, I'll only give myself a small helping of dinner then. We should eat before it's gets too late,' I say, pulling away and busying myself with the bags on the counter. 'I made your favourite. Beef Madras. Just the way you like it. And beer – I got you Cobra.'

'Good girl,' he says.

I just smile. Inside I'm screaming. I'm not your girl.

Finding my voice, I say, 'You go and sit down and I'll dish up.' Before he leaves the room I force myself to hug him, ensuring as much contact between our torsos as possible. I lift my hands to his face, stroking his hair away from his eyes and touching his lips before kissing him briefly. Then I pull away from him and turn my attention to the food. 'Go on, go and make yourself comfortable. I'll bring the food into you.'

'Mmm... I look forward to continuing that later,' he says. Before he leaves the room, he takes a fistful of my hair, pulling my head back to expose my neck which he grazes with his teeth before leaving the room.

I realise I'm trembling and that tears are pricking my eyes. 'Bastard, bastard, bastard.' I feel in that moment I could take a knife to his chest. But this isn't going to be a crime of passion, because I'm a planner. And I'm in control.

We eat dinner in front of the television. I've given him a generous portion of cat food curry and am trying to force small mouthfuls of my own veggie one down. In reality I eat very little. I take some small satisfaction from the knowledge that he's eating my cats' leftovers. I've made the curry a bit hotter than I used to.

‘This is giving me a bit of a sweat,’ he says, wiping his sleeve across his forehead and eyes. I can see that his eyes are starting to stream and are looking a little red.

‘Oh! Sorry, maybe I made it too hot. Here,’ I say, passing his beer over. ‘I’ll get you another, this one’s nearly empty.’ I pop to the kitchen and bring the remaining beers through, together with the bottle opener. While I’m in the kitchen I also grab a packet of tissues from my bag, and pass him a couple. He wipes his eyes and blows his nose. He doesn’t need to know that I took the tissues out at home, brushed the cats with them, especially around their faces and mouths, and then refolded them into the packet. He gulps down the second beer in one go.

By the time we finish dinner, he’s not looking or feeling too great, but is putting his runny eyes and nose down to the curry. He keeps rubbing his eyes which are obviously starting to itch. I know that he must be starting to feel bad, because he’d normally be bitching at me by now.

I need to keep control of the situation. I pass him a beer and another couple of tissues, pick up the plates and head to the kitchen. Grabbing my overnight bag, I hurry upstairs to the bedroom. Another involuntary shudder hits me, but I force myself to do what I need to do.

I jog downstairs to the lounge, making a quick stop to the kitchen en route. He doesn’t look too good. I try to look concerned.

‘I think we should get you up to bed. You look like you need to lie down. Come on,’ I say, reaching out an arm to him. He doesn’t object, but instead plods up to the bedroom. He seems a little confused and his face is quite red.

'Don't worry about getting undressed now – just lie down and rest for a bit.' I'm relieved when he heads for the same side of the bed he slept on when I was living here. His head hits the pillow and he closes his eyes.

'I don't feel so good.'

No. And you're about to feel a whole lot worse, I think to myself. 'Shh,' I say, lying down on the bed next to him and stroking his head. Underneath his head, trapped between the pillow and pillowcase is the collection of cat hair I took from Splodge, Dodge and Podge's brushes over the course of the past few days. They'd all have wanted to contribute, I was sure.

I can hear him starting to wheeze as his airways begin to constrict. He's starting to look panicky.

'My inhaler,' he manages to wheeze out the words.

'Where is it?' I ask. I'm playing for time. I know he always kept one in his bedside drawer.

He points over to the cabinet. He barely has the breath to speak.

I get up and go around to the bedside cabinet and open the drawer. I know the inhaler won't be there though. Because I removed it and put it in my handbag downstairs. I pretend to rummage around for it. 'I can't find it. It's not here!'

He rolls over with difficulty. Don't worry, I think, there's cat hair that side too. 'EpiPen,' he croaks, clawing at his throat.

'What? What are you saying? I can't understand you.'

'Epi...Pen...'

The EpiPen is also downstairs in my handbag. Again I pretend to look for it. 'It's not here, it's not here!' I exclaim. If he should survive this by some freak chance, I need to look like I cared. Like I tried to help.

But looking at him now I can tell he isn't going to survive, not without the life-saving shot of adrenaline from his EpiPen. I leave the room and go and stand on the landing. It's getting hard to watch now. He has terror in his eyes. I can hear the wheezing getting worse as he desperately tries to get air to his lungs.

I'm standing at the top of the stairs, leaning against the wall, just waiting and wondering how long it will take, when he suddenly comes staggering towards me. How he's on his feet I don't know. He always was a stubborn son of a bitch. He practically falls the couple of steps to me. I move aside before he can clutch at me with his flailing arms, and the next thing I know he's fallen down the stairs.

I hear myself gasp and feel my hand on my mouth. He's in a crumpled heap at the bottom of the stairs. I can't hear any sounds coming from him. I sit down on the top step and promptly burst into tears. I'm not crying for him. I'm crying because it's over and he can never hurt me again.

I don't know how long I sit like that. I realise after a while that I'm not crying anymore though. And that I feel quite calm. I still have work to do. The first thing I need to do is make sure he really is dead. As I walk tentatively down the stairs, I can't help thinking at least I don't have to drag the body all the way from the bedroom. He's actually done something to help me for once. How ironic.

I step gingerly over him when I get to the bottom. I stand a little way from him and listen. Nothing. I take a deep breath and reach down to check for a pulse. I can't feel anything in his wrist, so I check his neck. Nothing. I hold my own breath for a moment or two. Silence. He's dead. I have killed him. I am a murderer. And I feel strangely calm.

*

I had thought about calling 999 when I was planning the murder. Wait until it would be too late to save him and then make the call. I wasn't convinced I could have acted well enough though, and I could then foresee problems down the line, like explaining what I was doing there and why he hadn't used his inhaler or EpiPen. I couldn't risk it.

The next stage of the plan was the bit I was dreading the most. Before I tackled it, I went into the kitchen and got some thin rubber gloves, a jar of Vicks and an anti-sickness pill from my handbag. I put the gloves on and swallowed the pill down with a mouthful of Jack Daniels from a bottle I found in the same cupboard it had always been kept in.

I knew I had an hour or so before the anti-sickness pill would be in my system, so I made a start on clearing up. I washed and dried all the dishes and put them away. I also washed the beer bottles before putting them in the recycling. I packed up the food containers I'd brought with me and took them to the car, exchanging them for another bag I'd brought with me. It was late now, close to midnight, and there was no one about in the quiet street. Back indoors, I put on one of those disposable white decorator's overalls over my clothes.

Next I retraced my steps around the house, carrying with me a bottle of bleach cleaner and a cloth. I was careful only to clean the places I'd touched. I didn't want to remove all traces of him, just me. Mostly, I'd touched kitchen surfaces and cleaning them shouldn't arouse suspicion anyway. I did the same in the lounge and bedroom, and also removed most of the cat hair from the pillowcase, flushing it down the toilet. I didn't think the few I missed would cause suspicion. I put his inhaler and EpiPen back in the bedside drawer. I'd been careful not to get my fingerprints on them. If I'd had to clean them, I thought it would be suspicious that his fingerprints weren't on them. Like I said, I'm a planner.

When I was confident I'd removed all possible traces of me from around the house, and given the tablet time to work, I turned my attention to him. I removed a large tarpaulin from the bag I'd brought in from the car and laid it on the kitchen floor. I spread layers of large, super absorbent puppy training pads over it. Next I dragged the body along the hall and into the kitchen. He weighed a ton and it took several minutes and a few stops before I finally had the body on the plastic sheeting. I was breathing hard from the exertion, and stopped to get my breath back.

Just for a moment I wonder if it's too late to call an ambulance and move his body back to the bottom of the stairs, but I know that's impossible. I'm just delaying the awfulness that comes next. I put a dab of Vicks menthol rub under my nose, and take out a pair of dressmaking scissors and a pruning saw from my bag of tricks. I'd bought the saw and the tarpaulin at one of those outdoor Sunday markets, along with some heavy-duty black sacks. I'd paid cash, of course. The first thing I had to do was cut his clothes off. He wasn't wearing shoes. I peeled off his socks, and then cut off his jeans, shirt and underwear and bundled them all into a black sack.

I knelt down next to the body. Where the hell did I start? I decided on an arm. Placing my left hand on his lower left arm, I started to saw away at his shoulder. I started to gag as soon as the blade went into the flesh. I was glad I'd barely touched my dinner and taken the anti-sickness pill. Even so this was going to be harder than I thought. Blood spatter went everywhere. I was glad of my overalls and that I'd thought of the puppy pads.

It took a lot of strength, both mental and physical, but eventually I managed to remove an arm. I took a break before tackling the next one. I placed the severed arms in one of the black sacks and then moved on to his legs. I had to stop often. Eventually, both legs were in a sack. I sat back against one of the kitchen cupboards after all four limbs were off. The puppy pads were saturated and I had to place a load more all around the area I was working in. The next bit was going to be even worse. I'd read that pigs couldn't digest human hair or teeth. I'd brought hair clippers and a hammer for this reason, and I set about shaving his hair off and removing his teeth. I'm not going to lie, there were times when I thought I couldn't finish the job. But then I thought about my new life on the coast and my cats and my art, and I dug deep. I think there was still some adrenaline in my system too, which helped. All I had to do now was saw his head off. I pushed down on his forehead with my left hand and began to saw across his throat. I had to tilt my head away and close my eyes as I dragged the pruning saw back and forth. And I had to take breaks. Dismembering a body is really bloody hard.

Finally, I had four sacks containing the six body parts and they were all sealed up tight using cable ties from the market. I carefully folded the tarpaulin and put that in another sack, together with the saw, hammer, hair clippers, scissors and gloves. I peeled off the bloodied overall and shoved that in too. Pulling another pair of gloves from my bag, I took down the bottle of Jack Daniels and had another swig. Not too much – the last thing I needed was to be stopped by the police and breathalysed on the drive home.

'Could you open the boot please, madam?' Can you imagine?!

I went to the front door and checked that all was quiet in the road. It was still dark, around 2.15 a.m. I made three trips to the car with the sacks, stashing them out of sight in the boot. I cleaned the site of the butchery and checked around the house once more, making sure I hadn't missed anything. And then I left. I pulled the front door shut with my coat sleeve pulled down over my hand, walked the short distance to my car and drove off.

I was absolutely exhausted by this point, and all I wanted to do was crawl into my bed and sleep. One more thing to do first though. I fought the bone-weary tiredness as I drove the seventy or so miles to the coast. I arrived at my destination a while before dawn and parked in a lay-by right next to the pig farm. I'd agonised over the best time to do this to stand the best chance of getting away with it. I figured the pigs would be up before any farm workers came by, and I just hoped they were hungry.

I unloaded the first sack from the boot. I picked the heaviest one first – the torso – and lugged it into the field, using the torch on my phone to see where I was walking. I approached one of the corrugated shelters and dropped the bag. Taking a small knife that I'd retrieved from the glove box in the car out of my pocket, I slit the bag open and let the big lump of flesh fall into the mud. I could hear snuffling noises from the dozing pigs. I ran back to the car as quickly as I could on the uneven ground and repeated the process with the other three sacks, dropping the contents of each in front of a different shelter. By the time I had finished, I could make out shapes of adult pigs woken by the noise and no doubt the smell of an early breakfast, investigating the parcels of meat delivered to their doors. I hurried back to the car, bundled the now empty sacks into a bag in the boot, jumped in the driver's seat and drove off as quickly as possible.

I don't think I began to breathe again until I was some distance down the road. I know my knuckles were white from gripping the steering wheel so tightly. Nearly there, I told myself. Not much longer. I drove about ten miles to an old deserted aerodrome. I knew that it attracted teens on mopeds and that it was the site of the occasional burnt out stolen car. There were no houses nearby. It was getting light now, but that was good as I figured daylight would actually be better for the next job.

I drove past the aerodrome to check that the area was clear, and then doubled back and pulled over not far from a burnt out car. I bundled all the used sacks, tarpaulin, his clothes and my gloves and overalls into a heap in what remained of the passenger footwell of the blackened shell. I stripped off my jeans, jumper and shoes too, adding them to the pile and quickly redressing in clothes from my overnight bag. I doused everything liberally with lighter fluid, lit a match and threw it into the pile. Flames whooshed up to the roof of the car, flattening out as they touched it, fiery fingers reaching out sideways towards me. I watched for long enough to be sure everything had been destroyed and then got back in the car and left. Another step closer to being finished.

Any adrenaline I'd felt earlier had well and truly evaporated now, and I was shattered - mentally, physically and emotionally. I drove home, being careful not to speed, and about thirty minutes later I was parking outside my little terraced house. I emptied the rest of the stuff from the boot and carried it indoors.

As I closed my own front door behind me, I was on the verge of collapse. I stood in the hallway for a moment. When I looked up I saw the cats on the stairs: Splodge on the top step, Podge somewhere around the middle, and Dodge sitting at the bottom. I couldn't help laughing at the welcoming committee of my unwitting accomplices. I spoke to them all by name and they tailed me into the kitchen. I put down some food in each of their bowls, giving each of them a stroke as they padded over. 'Good job, my lovelies. Couldn't have done it without you.'

I removed the scissors, knife, hammer, hair clippers and saw from the bag they were in, grimacing as I saw his blood on the saw. I scrubbed them thoroughly with bleach before putting them away in suitable places. I thought I might still get rid of them at some point – throw them into the sea perhaps.

All that remained was a small clear plastic bag – like the ones you put sandwiches in. In it are his teeth and hair. I have some vague notion of taking up sculpture, or pottery... I can visualise my first piece being a fat, contented-looking pig. And concealed within the clay pig will be the mementoes of a murder...

THE END

CHAPTER 14

The new normal

The next morning dawns bright and sunny once more. Maybe lockdown isn't so bad, I think to myself as I throw open my bedroom curtains to reveal a cloudless blue sky. The only sound is of birdsong.

I have no idea what day it is. The calendar has pretty much become redundant. It's like an extended version of that dead time between Christmas and New Year, but with sunshine. And solitude. The only point in the week that I know the time for sure is eight o'clock on a Thursday night, when we all go out on our front doorsteps and either clap or bang on a saucepan to say thank you to the NHS. And the only reason I manage to get that right is because of all the reminders on Facebook. I have slipped into a pattern of writing (also known as writing avoidance or counting split ends) in the morning, and then reading in the garden from about midday. Some days, midday arrives earlier than others. The lure of the sunshine is often too great to resist. Besides, as we Brits know, we have to make hay when the big yellow thing in the sky shines, because God knows when it could disappear again.

I make my first coffee of the day and spend a few minutes checking my emails and social media. The endless Corona-inspired funnies never seem to dry up. A post of Jenny's cats pops up on my Facebook timeline and I decide to message her to say how much I enjoyed her story.

Morning, killer. LOVED your story!

Jenny's always quick to reply and her message pings back almost immediately. *Really? Aw! Thank you. That's made my day.*

Yep, really, it's terrific. You're a great writer. You should definitely write more fiction.

Hm...maybe. I don't find it at all easy though.

Well you sure as hell can't tell from the end result. It flows beautifully.

Thank you. Maybe I'll give it a go. I am actually writing a lock-down diary – a sort of stream of consciousness. About a thousand words a day. Probably the most boring thing ever.

I bet it's not! That's the thing about your writing – it's never boring, even when you're writing about boring things! You could easily have a whole book by the time we get out.

The only thing I'm likely to get out of this situation is a drink problem.

It's only a problem if you start putting vodka on your cornflakes in the morning.

Well I am getting low on milk...

You know what the answer is? Forget the cornflakes.

Ha! What are you working on at the moment?

Er... my tan.

Seriously, what are you hoping to come out of lockdown with?

I am being serious. A tan. Oh, and maybe a novel. I've also taken up hula hooping. So, maybe a hula hooping habit.

There's a slight delay before Jenny's next message arrives. When it does, it's accompanied by a picture of a packet of ready salted Hula Hoops crisps. *Better than a drug habit. I was never any good at hula hooping.*

Ha! I used to be a bit of an expert in my younger days. I bought one of those weighted ones a few years back, but didn't get round to using it. To be honest, it hurt like hell when I tried – feels like it's bruising your belly. Actually, make that bellies – they're the others things I'm bringing out of lockdown with me. I persevered with the hoop this time though, and the pain stopped after a few days.

It's a weird time, isn't it? Some days I'm just paralysed by anxiety and totally lethargic, and others I'm like the sodding Duracell bunny. No rhyme or reason.

I know. Me too. I think it's kind of normal though. In the circumstances.

The new normal. The uncertainty's hard, isn't it? Not knowing when it will all end, and we can get back to the old normal.

Yep. I don't think we'll get back to normal for a long time. And I think even when we do, it'll be a different kind of normal.

Scary times. I hate leaving the house for anything. I tried ordering an online shop, but the delivery slots are weeks away.

Me too! I sneak out under cover of darkness when the queues have gone for the day. I popped into B&M the other day for urgent chocolate supplies and nearly had a nervous breakdown when I touched my face at the checkout. I think I must touch my face about a million times a day normally.

Lots of new habits to get into. What's with the panic buying though? Didn't people wash their hands before the Coronavirus? Dirty buggers.

I know! And the loo rolls? I didn't think getting the shits was one of the symptoms. I felt too guilty to buy loo rolls the other day.

Ha ha! Muppet.

I know. I have lots of boxes of tissues though. And bars of soap, because the stupid people only buy hand wash. Go figure.

As long as I've got enough cat food, that's all that matters.

Yep, you can always make a curry!

We wrap up our chat soon after, with promises to keep in touch. I tell Jenny I'm looking forward to discussing her murder story with the others, and to reading her lockdown diary.

The rest of the day looms large and shapeless. If today was an item of clothing, it would be a maternity dress, I think with a sigh. Clothes have become an interesting part of lockdown. It's all about being comfortable. Women have abandoned their bras and tight jeans, safe in the knowledge that nobody will be knocking on their front door. Certainly the only time I wear 'proper' clothes is if I have to go out in the real world for essentials. I think there may actually come a time, if this situation goes on for too much longer, when I just say sod it, and go to the shops bra-less. That day hasn't come yet though.

Today's outfit comprises pink and white polka dot bikini under a short, floaty summer dress of every colour under the sun, with cardigan and slippers. Nothing matches. It's most fetching. It's also the most efficient outfit for the day ahead. With the mornings still being a bit chilly, the cardigan and slippers are vital, but can be discarded as the day warms up, culminating in the bikini once I finish work and go and sunbathe. Practical. No unnecessary costume changes.

After a breakfast of instant porridge, I settle down at my desk to write. I'm actually pretty engrossed for once, when the doorbell goes. In these times of lockdown, this is a rare occurrence, and I should have stopped to think, but my mind was on my book and it was a rather absent-minded Amy who went and opened the door, only to be met by a socially-distant delivery driver snapping a photo of me on his phone. I think my mouth dropped open in a most unattractive fashion as he took it. I started to speak, but he turned tail and jogged off back to his van.

Still a little stunned, I look down at the doorstep to the parcel there, examining the delivery address label: it's not even for me. Well, that's annoying. Anyway, now I'm wondering, should I leave it there for several hours in case it has the virus on? There's probably some protocol to follow, so I close the door and head back indoors to look up what I should do.

So, apparently Covid-19 lives for twenty-four hours on cardboard, and I'm supposed to let the parcel sit for that period of time before I touch it. I can't help wondering what would happen if it was raining. Apart from the obvious. At least it's not plastic-wrapped – the virus survives for seventy-two hours on plastic. I write myself a note to deliver the parcel the following morning.

The following morning arrives and I see my note on the kitchen table. I then wrestle with whether or not I should put 'proper' clothes on to deliver the parcel to the correct recipient. I decide that I should, and grumpily put on a bra and struggle into my jeans (which have clearly shrunk). Then I wonder if I should photograph the neighbour when they open the door, to prove I had delivered it? It seems only fair as there is a god-awful picture of me out there somewhere, probably on a wall with a load of other hilarious lockdown delivery driver pics. It's all such a minefield, I think with a sigh. My jeans are digging into my bellies rather painfully and I'm not a happy bunny, Duracell or otherwise. Oh well, just get it over with, Amy. I then have a moment of panic. Is this little jaunt essential? Does it count as my one 'leaving the house for exercise' opportunity? (I know

I don't actually leave the house to exercise. At all. But that is irrelevant. It's the principle.)

I grab my mobile and front door key and open the door.

The parcel is gone.

For fuck's sake.

CHAPTER 15

Ice cream

The rest of the week is a whole wardrobe full of maternity dresses. Each day seems to last about fifty-three hours. I have binge watched so many Netflix shows and binge eaten everything in the house. I start to worry that I will lose the ability to speak. And I long to cuddle someone. When lockdown ends, I will probably just hug the first person I see. With my luck, it'll probably be the person whose parcel I failed to deliver, and they'll recognise me from the photo the delivery company shared with them to prove who took it. I may not be able to leave the house ever again. The rate I'm going I'll be too fat to fit through the door anyway. And they'll have to take out the big windows at the front of the house and crane me out. I think I might actually be losing my mind.

On the plus side, I'm writing steadily, and have mastered hula hooping in the opposite direction.

I'm glad when Monday rolls around again, bringing with it our next virtual writing group.

'Morning, all,' I say once everyone's joined the meeting. Only Robert is missing. A chorus of good mornings follows. 'I've tried to recreate the Wetherspoons' ambience – I'm drinking a pint of lager and have cordoned off half the dining room.'

'I'm drinking my usual hot chocolate and will be giving disapproving looks to people who are drinking at 10 a.m.,' Jenny says, holding up her cat mug for us all to see.

‘Hmm… this beer tastes a lot like coffee…’ I say with a giggle, holding my own mug aloft. My mug has a picture of a fox on and says “Oh! For Fox Sake!” ‘How are you all doing, anyway?’

Everyone starts to talk at once and we all laugh. ‘I guess we should take it in turns to speak,’ Jenny says. ‘Why don’t you go first, Pippa?’

‘Okay, thanks, Jenny. I’m doing pretty well actually. Keeping surprisingly busy with local deliveries, walking the dogs once a day, and the usual domestic tasks. Been baking quite a bit too. I haven’t done any writing since I finished my story.’

My mind goes straight to cakes. ‘Ooh, what have you been baking?’

‘Banana bread, Earl Grey tea cake, honey and oat cookies. All sorts.’

‘Yum. Next times there’s a pandemic, I’m coming to self-isolate at your house,’ I tell Pippa. ‘Dogs and cakes. A perfect combination.’

‘And the pleasure of my company, too, naturally, Amy?’

‘Goes without saying, Pippa. Now, tell me about those cakes again,’ I say with a wink.

Tom goes next. ‘Well, I’m keeping myself out of mischief too. Lots of jobs around the house and garden that I’d been putting off. Going for a walk every day – the bluebells are out in the woods near me. Haven’t made much progress on my story yet, though, I’m afraid. It’s hard to focus on much apart from the pandemic. I see Prince Charles and the PM have both got the virus.’

‘It does rather take over, doesn’t it? Makes it real, somehow, when people like that get it. Anyway, plenty of time to get your story done, Tom. I'm sure you'll come up with something,' Pippa says. 'How about you, John? What have you been up to?'

'I am pleased to report that my murder story is almost complete. I don't have a body yet, but it won't be long. It has actually been a rather satisfying little project.'

'I know, right?' I say enthusiastically. 'Who knew killing someone could be so much fun?'

'Have you written your story too then, Amy?' John asks.

'Yep. Done and dusted. In true pantser style.'

'Can't wait to read it,' Jenny says. 'I've been doing my usual stay at home things – writing, sewing, taking photos of the cats.'

'Speaking of your writing, we need to talk about your brilliant story,' I chip in. Again, we all start to talk at once, wanting to congratulate Jenny on how much we enjoyed her story. Everyone stops talking and looks at the other faces on their screens. By some sort of unspoken agreement, we let Tom, as our most senior member, open the discussion.

'I thought it was terrific; really original and well written. I loved the fact that the cats were her accomplices. My favourite bit, though, was when he fell down the stairs. I laughed, probably very inappropriately, at that.'

'Yes! I loved that too. When she just steps out of the way and he goes tumbling down the stairs, saving her the job of dragging the body down. That was great,' I agree.

'It was so beautifully planned and detailed. Organised.'

'Yep, it kind of reflected the sort of writer you are, Jenny: a planner, a plotter. Wonderful attention to detail, nothing overlooked, or left to chance.'

'Apart from the pigs,' Jenny says. 'I wanted to feed him to

pigs, because he was one, but I had no idea how long it would really take them to eat a whole person, or if they would finish eating him before someone discovered the leftovers.'

'It was a fitting way to dispose of the body, certainly. It worked with your themes of animals and food. I've rather cheated on getting rid of the body,' Pippa admits.

'Care to share?' I ask.

'Maybe we can do my story next week and then I can send it to you all later today?' We all agree to Pippa's story being next.

'Has anyone else struggled to get rid of the body, or thought up any ingenious methods?'

'I was working in the garden the other day and did think about those big shredders that tree surgeons use. You know the things - you feed in branches and they spew out wood chips,' John says.

'Oh yes, I know what you mean. That would work I should think, as long as you could do something with all the stuff that comes out.'

'I think you'd have to freeze the body before you could put it through one of those machines,' Tom says, being the most practical-minded member of the group.

Pippa's looking a little green at the thought of shredding a body. 'I wonder if your killer would have got away with her murder, Jenny, if it had happened in real life?' she muses.

Jenny shrugs. 'I don't know. It was fun to write though. I honestly don't know if any of it would actually have worked, but that's the joy of writing, isn't it? We can make anything possible.'

'I was thinking about the amount of blood there would be when I was researching different ways to get rid of a body,' I say.

There's a consensus of nods across the screen. Clearly we've all been encountering the same sort of obstacles in planning our murders.

'I must admit, I thought about removing the blood from the body before chopping it up,' Jenny confesses. 'You can get a pump thing – stick it in the neck and draw all the blood out. But then I decided that was just another thing to get rid of, and to go with the messy option.'

'Hmm… I guess that's another instance where it would be best to freeze the body first?' Pippa suggests. 'I think all murderers need to invest in a chest freezer before they do anything else. That should definitely be at the top of their shopping list.'

'I can only foresee one problem for my killer,' I say. 'Her freezer would be full of Haagen-Dazs.' My mind drifts off to the possibility of making ice cream for pigs, from human remains. Told you, I've been in self-isolation for too long.

'Listen to us, what a gory lot we are,' Pippa says.

'I know! I keep expecting the police to turn up at my door because of all the dodgy things I've been googling,' Jenny says. I think she's only half-joking.

'Honestly, officer, I'm a writer! It's all perfectly innocent!' I laugh. 'Just don't look in the freezer in the garage...'

'Getting back to your story, Jenny, one thing I thought was particularly clever was giving him the curry to disguise the first symptoms of his cat allergy. Ingenious,' John says.

'Yes, that was genius. And putting cat food in it – that made me laugh.' Tom is chuckling again at the memory.

'It really is a terrific story, Jenny, you should be so proud,' Pippa smiles.

'Thank you, everyone, I'm just glad you didn't hate it.'

'You should have more confidence in your ability – you really are a superb writer.'

Jenny smiles modestly, 'So, Pippa's story next then?'

'Oh cripes! I'll be a wreck knowing you're all reading my story. I hope you enjoy it.'

'I'm sure we will. I really look forward to our meetings – I think they're the only thing keeping me sane,' I say.

'Er...?' Jenny raises an eyebrow.

'Okay, sane-ish. It's all relative,' I say with a grin.

'I guess that's it for today then,' Jenny says to wrap things up. 'Don't forget to email us your story, Pippa. Stay safe and well, all of you. Stay sane-ish, Amy.'

We all echo Jenny's words and wave goodbye. And that's it for another week. I feel a little sad as the faces pop off the screen one by one. At least I have Pippa's story to look forward to.

CHAPTER 16

Pippa's story

MURDER IN LAUREL CLOSE

'I'm going to kill him! I'm going to bloody kill him!' As I scream these words, much to the terror of my ancient black Labrador, who's following me around the house as usual, I'm running around closing windows. Nero looks rather dejected as I jog up the stairs to shut more windows. As much as he wants to be with me, his old legs really can't face the trek upwards.

'That bloody man,' I mutter as I come back downstairs and head into the lounge where my husband, Patrick, is studiously ignoring his ranting wife and trying to hide behind the Sunday paper.

'That bloody man!' I repeat, looking to Patrick for some solidarity.

'What's that, dear?'

I stand in front of him with my hands on my hips. I know full well he's not really listening. 'He's having another bonfire. The git next door. Thoughtless bastard.'

'Yes, bastard.'

It's better than nothing. 'Beautiful day like this – I'd thrown all the windows open and got washing on the line and blankets and things airing in the sunshine. Eleven o'bloody-clock on a Sunday morning. And there he is, standing next to the ruddy towering inferno holding a beer, as if he doesn't have a care in the world!' I follow this with a sort of growl. Nero, who's caught up with me again, looks at me in surprise. 'Sorry, boy,' I say, giving his head a rub.

'What's that, dear?'

'Jesus! I might as well talk to the bloody dog! At least he pays attention and tries to understand.'

'Mm.'

I turn on my heels and waste a dramatic exit on the dog, who plods after me into the kitchen. I flick the switch on the kettle and get the coffee things. My plans for spring cleaning have gone right out the window. Except, of course, ALL THE RUDDY WINDOWS ARE SHUT! I make two mugs of coffee and plonk one down in front of Patrick.

'Coffee.'

'Hmm... thanks.'

I take my coffee into the conservatory and settle myself into my favourite wicker chair. Nero collapses at my feet and is soon snoring quietly. At least I can appreciate the fact that the sun is shining, sitting here. And fume inwardly about the plumes of smoke billowing over the fence from next door.

Unfortunately, these bonfires are a fairly regular occurrence throughout the summer months. The village Facebook group, and the WhatsApp one for our little cul-de-sac, regularly have posts from people complaining about my neighbour's bonfires. It's not just me he pisses off. No amount of asking him nicely to wait until people have finished in the garden for the day, or at least forewarning us so we can get our washing in and close our windows, had worked. Several of us had complained to the council, more than once. But nothing made any difference. He probably chucked any warning letters he got on the bonfire.

He was an arrogant, inconsiderate bastard.

I'm not an angry person normally. These are not, however, normal times. We are actually in week four of lockdown due to the Coronavirus, or Covid-19, or whatever you want to call it. I call it a bloody nuisance, a bit like him next door. Arthur Bundt, that's his name. Apparently you're supposed to pronounce his surname to rhyme with punt. That's not what I rhyme it with.

I had hoped that with everyone at home in isolation, he might be a bit more considerate. I had even printed off the advice from the council about not having bonfires at the moment, and snuck out and stuck it through his letterbox one night. The next time I stuck something through his letterbox, it would be a little gift from Nero. This was what the council notice said:

Residents across the borough are being asked to think of others and to not light bonfires during the current Coronavirus pandemic lockdown.

The effects of bonfires at this time are likely to be much more serious and have a bigger impact. The Coronavirus is known to cause serious respiratory problems, which could be made much worse if the sufferer is exposed to smoke from bonfires.

It is important to be especially considerate at this time, when people are confined to their home and unable to escape unpleasant fumes.

Bonfires can also become out of control or cause accidents, creating extra pressure on the already busy emergency services.

We understand that the changes to collection services and

the closure of the refuse and recycling centres may create a storage issue for some residents. Please think of others, compost your garden waste where possible, and stack or bag up rubbish for disposal when the current emergency is over, rather than burn it.

The Council will take enforcement action against any persistent offenders where bonfires cause an impact on neighbours.

In other words, don't be a dick. All very self-explanatory and reasonable, I thought. Well, either Arthur can't read, or he doesn't care. I very much suspect it's the latter, as he couldn't do his job as a delivery driver otherwise. I bet he's one of those awful, lazy ones who chucks parcels over fences in all weathers and doesn't give a monkey's what happens to the contents.

I don't know how he turned out to be such a vile human being. His parents were such lovely people when they had lived in the house. They'd died tragically in a fire on holiday. Awful. And then Arthur had inherited the house. Punt. We had hoped he would sell it and buy somewhere else. No such luck. He really didn't fit in with the other residents of Laurel Close. The words 'lower the tone' sprang to mind.

Clearly, though, the council notice hadn't made a jot of difference. Arthur obviously didn't care if some poor soul was battling respiratory disease or this bloody virus. Well, quite frankly, today has been the last straw. Arthur has to go.

*

'Patrick, how do I keep internet searches secret?'

For once, I seem to have got his full attention. He peers at me over his glasses and across the breakfast table, frowning. 'Why on earth do you want to know that?' he asks.

'I just do. Can you help or not?'

'Well, I suppose there's incognito browsing for Google. I know that keeps stuff out of your search history, but I don't know much more than that really. What on earth do you need to keep secret anyway?'

I tap the side of my nose. 'Mind your own beeswax.' Let him wonder what I'm up to. Might make him take a bit more notice of me.

'Don't go booking anything for my birthday, Rosie – we might still be locked up.'

'Locked down,' I correct automatically.

'No, I was right,' is what I think he mutters.

I stick my tongue out at him.

'Very mature.'

'Oh, just eat your porridge!'

We finish breakfast in silence. Afterwards, as I'm clearing away the dishes, Patrick announces he's taking Nero round the block.

'Okey dokey, don't forget poo bags.' I want to add that anything he scoops can be deposited through the punt's letterbox, but I resist.

With Patrick out of the way, I switch on the laptop and open Google. Eventually I find the drop down menu with 'New Incognito Window' and select it. Not for the first time, I wish I was more computer savvy. It's not my fault I was born into the wrong generation. My two grown up sons tease me mercilessly, and take the mickey out of me every time I say, 'When I was a girl....' They have both been known to add 'And dinosaurs roamed the earth'.

It doesn't take long to find what I want. I'd already had a bit of a notion, and this had confirmed it. I carefully close the open tab and turn off the laptop. I sit at the kitchen table for a bit longer, a plan starting to form in my head. I check my watch; Patrick will be at least another ten minutes at the rate Nero walks. I get up and check out the lounge window to make sure Arthur's van isn't on the drive, and then head into the back garden.

Laurel Close is made up of a semi-circle of detached properties, each with a large, mature back garden. The front and rear boundaries of most of the gardens are planted with Laurel hedging, hence the name. It's a place where nice people live; friendly, chatty people who get on, without living in each other's pockets. We look out for one another without being a collection of curtain twitchers. Most of the residents are middle-aged couples whose children have flown the nest, like me and Patrick. The only blot on the Laurel landscape is you-know-bloody-who. Cuckoo.

I walk the length of our garden, wrapping my cardigan around me as there's a chill in the air today. At the far end of our garden, and adjoining Arthur's plot, is our shed. It's concealed from view by a rather rampant bamboo. I make a mental note to dig some of it up. I know I won't find what I'm looking for in our shed, however. I need to look in Arthur's. I drag a garden chair out of the shed to stand on, and proceed to clamber inelegantly over the fence. I'm puffing now and my heart is racing. I'm definitely not cut out for this sort of nonsense. Any dreams I might have had of being a cat burglar have now gone up in smoke.

Looking around guiltily, I walk the few feet to Arthur's shed, praying that I find it unlocked. Yes! I open the door and go in, feeling a cobweb wrap itself around my face. I shudder, wipe it away and look around. It's just as I hoped. Arthur's dad had been a very keen gardener, and his shed was a veritable treasure trove of old tools, equipment and chemicals. It looked like several generations had contributed to the shed's contents over the years, and nothing had ever been thrown away. Arthur, of course, hadn't bothered to sort through it, and it remained a sort of garden shed museum. I check various items, finding exactly what I want. I don't remove anything though. Closing the shed behind me, I trot back to the fence. Sodding hell. How on earth am I going to climb back over without the chair?

I don't want to talk about it. But I ripped my nice cardigan. And injured both my pride and my bottom.

The rest of another day of isolation looms long. Typically, the sun isn't shining today, so I can't make up for yesterday's abandoned jobs. Bloody Arthur Bundt. I decide that I might as well curl up in the conservatory and read for a while. I pad through to the bookshelves in the hall and browse the unread section, smiling as my eyes alight on Tom Wolfe's *The Bonfire of the Vanities*. That'll do nicely, I think as my smile turns into a wicked grin.

*

Arthur only ever has his bonfires at the weekend, and usually a fortnight apart, so I have a frustrating wait before I can carry out my plan. Most evenings, if it's dry, he does a little bit of work in the garden, cutting things back and so on. He invariably chucks assorted household waste on too, cardboard and such. I wonder what's wrong with recycling it like normal people? Probably a pyromaniac, I mutter to myself as I watch him from the back bedroom window one evening. The weather has been amazing for the past few days, and the forecast is for more dry and sunny days to come. Rain would most definitely spoil my plan. Well, delay it at least. I'm afraid Arthur Bundt's card is marked, come rain or shine.

Another week of isolation passes surprisingly quickly. With the nice weather and a large garden to tend to, I keep busy. Patrick spends most of his time reading or in his home office. He's working his way through a stack of *Dentistry News* and *The Probe* magazines. It's no coincidence he has no trouble sleeping. Really we just meet up for meals, when we sit silently across the table from one another. I suppose after thirty years of marriage we don't have much to say.

One night over dinner, I attempt to engage him in conversation. Always the optimist. I'm trying to think of something to say. I can't ask him about work, or how his day was, because his dental practice is currently closed.

'So, what are you reading at the moment?' is all I can manage.

'Hm?'

For God's sake. 'I asked what you're reading at the moment? Thought I'd give conversation a go. We've been obeying this self-isolation thing to the extreme – I feel like I haven't seen you for days.'

'Don't be daft. We share a bed, for goodness sake.'

Ah! The marital bed. Don't get me started. I couldn't remember the last time anything started in our bed. Apart from Patrick's Kindle. Previous attempts to rekindle our sex life had been a washout.

I decide to scrap the idea of conversation with my husband and instead turn my thoughts to Arthur Bundt. It's so nice to have something to look forward to in these trying times.

*

By the following Friday, Arthur has an enormous bonfire erected at the end of his garden. Knob. Make it a good one, Arthur, I think to myself, because it's going to be your last. There's no way of knowing if he'll have the bonfire on Saturday or Sunday. The weather forecast is bright sunshine for the whole weekend, so I have to act today.

I've already checked that Arthur's van isn't on the drive, and made a long shopping list for Patrick. He's grumbling about having to go to the supermarket, but secretly I think he's glad to get out of the house for a while. I've put a few rather obscure things on the list that he'll have to hunt for. I know he won't ask a member of staff for help. He should be grateful, it's a bit like a treasure hunt. I'll have well over an hour to myself as he'll have to queue in the car park before he can even get into the shop. I pack him off with list, bags and hand sanitiser.

'See you later. Don't touch your face. Use the hand sanitiser! I'm going to potter in the garden,' I tell him as he leaves the house. Not strictly true, but not far off. I am going to potter in a garden; just not *ours*.

I close the door after him and head to the utility room, where I don my gardening shoes. I double check my pocket to make sure the dental face mask I pinched from Patrick's office is there.

'Right. Ready. Stay,' I say to Nero, as I open the door to the back garden. 'Won't be long.' He looks sadly up at me, and then plods back to the kitchen where he flops resignedly down in his bed, giving a big sad, doggy sigh. I can't risk him freaking out and alerting the neighbours to the fact that I've disappeared from our garden.

I trot up to the end of our garden, to a big pile of cuttings from the Laurel hedges that I'd pruned rather heavily yesterday. I gather up enormous armfuls of them and hoist them over the fence into Arthur's garden. I keep some back which I pile next to our compost heap. That done, I go into the shed and grab my gardening gloves and the larger of our two gardening forks, along with two old garden chairs. I lower the fork and one of the chairs over into Arthur's garden, and then use the other chair to stand on and climb over. I don't make the same mistake twice. No, sometimes I have been known to make the same mistake many, many times. Just ask my husband. But this time, I have learned the error of my ways. My bruised bottom taught me that lesson for many days. The fact that Patrick hadn't noticed the purpling bruise on my arse said even more about our marriage than last night's failed dinner conversation, I think with a sigh to match Nero's.

Once in Arthur's garden, I go into his time warp of a shed and don my gloves and face mask before taking down three bottles of pesticide from the dusty shelf. Next, I turn my attention to the enormous bonfire heap. This is the part that I'm not really looking forward to. Before I do anything else, I take my mobile phone out of the back pocket of my jeans and take photos of the bonfire heap from all angles. Then, I grab the garden fork and start to disassemble the pile, carefully placing the stuff from the top to one side. Next I use the fork to carry the material from the centre of the bonfire to the fence, where I sort of fling it over into my garden. It's heavy tiring work, and I wonder more than once if I've made a big mistake. But I've started now and, like childhood dinners, I was always taught to finish what I started. I leave the base of the bonfire heap untouched. It's a mixture of garden waste and household packaging, including boxes and plastic bottles.

'What sort of moron burns plastic?' I say under my breath. No wonder the smoke from his bonfires was so toxic and black.

The next thing I do is carry over the green Laurel branches which I hurl into the middle of the heap. One of the things I had checked on the internet during my incognito search was that Laurel gives off cyanide when burned. I wasn't sure how toxic the resulting smoke would be, hence my use of the pesticides which also contained the deadly poison. Pinching my face mask tighter over my nose, I fetch the bottles and spray the contents liberally over the Laurel cuttings. For good measure, I throw the empty bottles into the middle of the pile too. Finally, I fork on all the stuff from the top.

I stand back and check that the heap doesn't look too different to the original, comparing the photos I took with the reconstructed one. I move a couple of obvious bits, including a large washing powder box and a load of plastic packaging, to match the pictures. Finally, I take a last look around, picking up a few stray bits that had fallen off the fork and chucking them into my garden. Once I'm satisfied, I lower the fork over the fence and start to clamber back to the safety of my own garden. I've literally just got my leg over when my mobile rings in my pocket, almost making me topple off the fence. It's the most excitement my nether regions have experienced in some considerable time. I quickly complete the climb, and pull my phone out. The display reads 'The Dentist'.

'Yes, Patrick. What is it?' I answer rather shortly. I'm feeling more than a little flustered.

'You okay? You sound a bit breathless.'

'Fine. Just gardening, you know, hard at it. What do you want?'

'Two things: what the hell is agave syrup and where would I find chia seeds?'

'Have you asked a member of staff?'

'Of course not. That's why I phoned you. Stop rolling your eyes.'

He knows me too well. 'Oh, don't worry too much about them – I can make do without them,' I tell him. Now that I've almost completed my mission, it's safe for him to finish up the shop now. Besides, I didn't have a clue what I would've done with either item had he brought them home.

'Oh, for God's sake, Rosie,' Patrick says huffily. 'Right, I'll see you soon.' He hangs up before I have a chance to remind him to use the hand sanitizer.

It's an immense relief to be back in my own garden. I put the chair back in the shed, tidy the stuff I'd thrown over the fence onto the compost heap under a few laurel branches, and put the fork and my gloves away. I'm going to flush the facemask down the loo when I go back in the house.

I walk back up to the house, dusting off my trousers as I go. I open the back door and am greeted by Nero, wagging his tail delightedly. Like all dogs, he has a sixth sense for the return of his favourite human.

'Good boy,' I say, crouching down to make a fuss of him. 'It's lovely to see you too. Want a biscuit?' It's a rhetorical question. I often ask myself the same thing.

I get Nero a gravy bone from his treat jar and set about making myself a well-earned coffee. Well, I'll need something to go with the biscuit. Mug in one hand and biscuit in the other, I sit down at the kitchen table with a sigh of relief.

'Buggering bollocks!' I exclaim a moment later, jumping up out of the chair and startling Nero. I run out into the garden, not even stopping to put on shoes, and leg it up the lawn. I've only left the ruddy chair in Arthur's garden! I reach over and pull it back, putting it away in our shed. My poor heart is going like the clappers. I wonder briefly what a heart attack feels like. I lean against the shed door for a few seconds until my heart rate drops to something less likely to need an ambulance. The last thing I want in the middle of a pandemic is to be admitted to hospital. That reminds me, I still have the mask in my pocket. Must get rid of that too. Don't want Patrick to see it and ask questions I don't want to answer.

Back in the house, I flush the mask down the loo and return to my coffee. The biscuit has disappeared. I look over at Nero who can't make eye contact. I'm not cross with him. I'd've done the same. Coffee finished, I head upstairs and change my clothes, putting everything I was wearing in the wash. I don't want to take any chances with having pesticide or anything on me.

When Patrick arrives home a short time later, I'm sitting in the conservatory reading the Tom Wolfe book and looking as though butter wouldn't melt.

'The butter melted a bit in the car,' Patrick calls from the kitchen, where he's unpacking the shopping. 'I bought a cooked chicken for lunch and stupidly put it in the same bag.'

*

That night I send a message to the WhatsApp group for the Laurel Close residents. Everyone is in it except, of course, Arthur-rhymes-with-punt.

'Evening everyone, just to give you the heads-up – you-know-who has built the most enormous bonfire and is bound to light it over the weekend. So, I'm afraid it's washing in and windows shut. I'll try and let you all know when he lights it. Stay safe. Rosie x'. The last thing I want is to risk any of my lovely neighbours breathing in toxic smoke.

*

Saturday dawns clear and bright, not a cloud in the sky. It's a lovely day for a bonfire.

I potter about upstairs, ostensibly sorting out my overflow wardrobe in the back bedroom. In reality, I just want to know if and when Arthur decides to light the bonfire. Nero has made the ascent to keep me company. Eleven o'clock comes.

'Are we having coffee this morning, or not?' Patrick shouts up the stairs.

'Can't you make it?' I yell back. The eternal optimist in me again.

'You know I can't work the machine.'

'Then maybe you should learn,' I mutter under my breath as I leave the bedroom, telling Nero I won't be long, and head downstairs. I make us both coffee and take mine back upstairs and into the back bedroom, just in time to see Arthur light the enormous bonfire.

'Oh my God!' My heart rate quickens as I stand at the window watching, whilst also texting the neighbours to warn them about the smoke. 'Bonfire is a go.'

The heap goes up quickly thanks to the dry spell of weather and the amount of highly flammable stuff on it. Dirty black smoke, probably from the plastic, swirls into the air. Arthur stands there with the usual beer in hand. He walks around the bonfire, as if trying to evade the smoke. Somehow the wind keeps changing direction and the smoke seems to follow him.

I think I'm probably holding my breath as I watch and wonder what will happen. At one point, Arthur goes back up to the house and I think my plan has been thwarted, but a few seconds later he reappears pulling the recycling bin after him. He then proceeds to chuck the contents of the bin into the flames, empty plastic milk bottles, cardboard, anything that will burn.

I let the fire burn for some time, watching the smoke pursue Arthur, imagining it being sucked into his lungs. I imagine his heart rate quickening and him starting to feel faint. He swigs on his beer and continues to add fuel to the fire.

After quite some time, I go to the top of the stairs and call down to Patrick. 'He's having another bonfire next door. Do you think we should call the fire brigade?'

He appears at the bottom of the stairs. 'What? Um... I don't know, really. Isn't that a bit of an overreaction?' he says, after weighing the question up in his mind.

Take your time, I think. 'Well, it is against the guidelines at the moment, so...'

'I think, unless the fire gets out of control, we shouldn't interfere, Rosie. Just leave it, eh?'

'Okay,' I shrug, going back into the bedroom. Nero looks up at me as I go in. He's looking decidedly sheepish. For a dog. It's then I notice the wet patch on the carpet. Poor old boy is getting a tad incontinent. I can't be cross with him. 'It's okay, boy,' I reassure him. 'Although you are supposed to fiddle, not tiddle, while Rome burns.'

I take up my place at the window once more. Arthur Bundt is looking a tad unsteady on his feet.

I gasp and my hands fly to my face. Running to the top of the stairs, I scream:

'Patrick! Better call the fire brigade after all. And an ambulance. Arthur Bundt just fell into his bonfire.'

THE END

CHAPTER 17

Mint Matchmakers

I love Pippa's story and send her a quick message to tell her as much, knowing she'll be on tenterhooks while we're reading it. I won't lie, though, I'm feeling a bit anti-climactic after the high of seeing the others on my computer screen. The solitude has slapped me round the face again and the uncertainty of when it might all end has me in its grip. There's only one thing to do when I feel like this: FaceTime Cameron. I make a coffee and head to the lounge, sitting in my swivel chair with my feet on the window sill.

'Ameeee!'

'Hello, you! How's your day going?'

'Not too bad ta. Just had to induce vomiting in a bulldog that ate the contents of its owner's handbag – including chocolate and paracetamol, wrappers 'n' all.'

'Could you come round and do that for me every time I eat chocolate?'

'Jeez! I'd have to move in with you, be there 24/7, Ames.'

'True. I s'pose that's not practical. What you up to now?'

'Lunchtime! Hurrah!'

'Yuck. How can you think about food after watching a dog barf up the contents of its stomach? What's on the menu?'

'Cheese and lettuce toasted sandwich.'

'I've heard of lettuce…'

'I don't recommend it.'

'I'm not sure I fancy it in a toasted sandwich.'

'Well, when I say toasted sandwich, I just mean I put some cheese and lettuce between two slices of toast. Bread was a bit stale. It was actually quite nice.'

'I can't remember the last time I ate anything green.'

'Bogies?'

'Ew. Do green M&Ms count?'

'Absolutely. So does Peppermint Aero.'

'Excellent. I'll get that next time I fancy a salad. Seriously, though, I'm fully expecting to have scurvy, and… I dunno… rickets when this is all over.'

'What are you? A pirate? You're not gonna get scurvy. And, with the amount of sunbathing you're doing, you're definitely not going to be lacking in vitamin D, so rickets are out too.'

'I'm not sunbathing for fun, I'll have you know. Didn't the leader of the free world say UV light kills the virus? The lovely golden tan I'm getting is simply a side effect from taking my medicine.'

'Oh, sweet Jesus. He'd have people shoving a UV light up their bums. Please tell me you haven't swapped your G&T for Dettol on the rocks?'

'Don't be ridiculous. Bleach Schnapps.'

Cameron snorts with laughter. 'I miss you, crazy person.'

'I miss you too, snot face. Can't wait until this is all over and we can go to the pub again. We still have a lot of gins to try.'

'Indeed we do, lady, indeed we do.'

'Did I tell you I've taken up hula hooping?'

'What flavour?'

'Oh my God. Why does *everyone* say that when I tell them I've taken up hula hooping? Have I got a reputation as a junk food-eating exercise-phobe?'

'Er… yep.'

'Fair enough. Mind you, the amount I'm eating at the moment, I'm going to need a bigger hoop.'

'They make Big Hoops and giant Flavarings too now. The spicy ones are amazing.'

'Sod off.'

'You know you don't mean that,' Cameron pouts at me. 'So, what have you been up to apart from consuming large quantities of hoop-shaped snacks?'

'Cracking on with the new book. And doing lots of research.'

'Let me guess… for "doing research", read "lying in the garden with a book".'

'Yep,' I grin. 'How are things at work in the crazy time of Corona?'

'Very odd. But actually okay. The receptionists are all furloughed on eighty percent pay, so they're pretty happy, and probably also "doing research". We're running emergency clinics, but also doing a lot of online and phone consultations.'

'How are you managing social distancing at the clinics?'

'Wherever possible, the owners stay outside, or in the car and we bring the animal in to treat.'

'Must be quite nice – not having to deal with some of the more challenging and neurotic owners.'

'Hell, yeah! Although I do miss the nice, chatty ones.'

'And the attractive male owners?'

'Well, of course! Although I have been in touch with Richie and we're going to meet up when lockdown ends.'

'Really? Yay! That's great.'

'It is rather. Super grateful for the intro, you little

matchmaker.'

'My pleasure. I think the two of you are a match made in Armani heaven.'

'Hope so. What's happening in your love life anyway?'

'Cobwebs mainly. You know I joined that dating site before Christmas?'

'Indeedy.'

'Well, the only even vaguely eligible sounding men are bloody miles away.'

'I don't think you should rule them out. After all, what's actually keeping you here? You could spread your wings and go anywhere. You have no real ties; you can write anywhere. Just keep an open mind.'

'I s'pose. It's all immaterial at the moment, anyway – until lockdown is over, which I can't see being any time soon.'

'Maybe, but you can still cultivate some online friendships in the meantime, and then explore them further down the line, once we're allowed to actually touch people again.'

'Oh, don't! I'm craving physical human contact. I pity the person nearest me when we get out – I'm probably going to break their ribs.'

Cameron laughs. 'I feel you! At least I get lots of animal cuddles at work. And cuddles with the nurses. Although they'd be more enjoyable if I was straight.'

'Aw! Give everyone my love. I do miss you guys.'

'We miss you too. Just hang in there – this won't last forever.'

'Thanks, Cameron. You've cheered me up.'

'Aw! It's been lovely chatting with you, Amy. I must away though. I have an urgent appointment with a nasty abscess.'

'Yum. Don't fancy my scrambled egg and ketchup on toast

anymore.'

'Ha! Fare thee well, my lovely. Mwah!'

'Arrr! Bye, Cameron.'

As ever, a chat with Cameron has lifted my spirits, and I decide to take a more positive approach to the internet dating thing. I grab my laptop and log on, scrolling through the likes and messages I've received, and glancing at the thumbnail photos which accompany them. My spirits take a bit of a dip when they prove to be the usual suspects. Police suspects. Either that, or they're holding a giant fish or have taken their selfie in a toilet. Or, worse still, they have their kids in the picture. I'm determined to persevere this time though. After all, it might be fun just to have someone to chat with during lockdown, even if it doesn't go anywhere.

I start scrolling through the profiles, stopping now and then if someone's picture takes my fancy, and reading their profile. For once, I don't let their location be a determining factor. I come across a face I'd noticed on my previous visits to the site. It's a ridiculously handsome face, belonging to a professional-looking be-suited torso. His profile is quite brief, and his location says Berkshire. Nothing to put me off, apart from the loud, insistent warning bells that his photo is too good to be true. He honestly looks like a male model.

I send a brief introductory hello message – I can see he's online. He replies quickly and we exchange a few cursory messages. I quickly start to feel that his messaging doesn't match his picture, with too many spelling errors to be put down to typos. By the time he suggests we meet halfway when we can travel again, I finally listen to the warning bells. He hasn't used his own photos: the man in the pictures is not the man I'm chatting with. I swear under my breath and log out in disgust. Sorry, Cameron. I think the only relationship I'm going to pursue today is with chocolate. No false advertising there.

CHAPTER 18

Tom: it's major

The next virtual meeting of 'Write Time, Write Place' finally rolls around and I log in eagerly at ten, watching the others pop up on my screen. Robert's there this time, but there's no sign of Tom.

'Morning, all. Shall we give Tom a couple more minutes? He might be having techie trouble,' I say, looking around the faces on my screen. I realise that Jenny is looking awfully serious.

'Tom won't be joining us, I'm afraid. I did think about cancelling today's meeting actually. His wife got in touch with me this morning. Tom's in hospital. He's got Coronavirus.'

Everyone looks shocked and upset.

'Shit. How's he doing?' I ask.

'Not great, apparently. They're talking about the possibility of him needing to go on a ventilator.'

I feel close to tears. We all know how serious this is. 'This fucking virus.'

Pippa is crying. 'Poor, poor Tom. And his poor wife. She won't be able to be with him. I can't bloody bear it.'

'I'm so very sorry to hear this. It makes it all horribly real,' John says. 'To know someone who's in hospital with the damn thing.'

'That is awful news, for sure,' Robert says.

'How does everyone feel about today's meeting? Would you rather postpone it?' Jenny asks.

We all sit and think for a bit. 'Personally, I think Tom would want us to carry on. He'd hate to be the reason we cancelled. But I'll go along with what everyone else wants.' I wait for the others to speak.

'I agree with Amy. Tom wouldn't want his having the virus to stop us. We should carry on. Stiff upper lip and all that,' Pippa say, wiping her eyes with a tissue.

'Stiff upper lip over a quivering bottom one,' Jenny adds with a sad smile.

The consensus is very much that we carry on.

'Can't help thinking what a horrible irony it is that Tom has caught the virus – remember what he said before about the idea of deliberately infecting someone with it?' Robert says.

I shudder at Robert's words. Something about the way he spoke didn't match the words. There was a little sinister edge somehow, as if he rather enjoyed the irony. 'It's just plain horrible,' I say.

'Jenny, will you please keep us updated with any news?' Pippa says.

'Yes, of course. All we can do is wait and hope. And pray, if that's your thing.'

'I bet Tom loved your story, Pippa. I think it would have made him chuckle,' I say.

'If he had the chance to read it,' Pippa says sadly.

'I'm sure he would've done – probably read it as soon as he received it. I know I did. Loved it too!'

Pippa blushes. 'Thank you, Amy. That means a lot coming from our published author.'

It's my turn to blush, and pooh-pooh the bit about me being a published author.

'It is a brilliant story, Pippa. I loved the Rosie/Patrick relationship. They seemed so real, so authentic. I know murder's not funny, but you did get a tremendous amount of humour in the story,' Jenny tells her.

'Couldn't agree more, very well done indeed, Pippa,' John adds. 'I adored Nero, the dear old black lab. A couple of bits I particularly enjoyed were Rosie's dramatic exit being wasted on a dog, and at the end when Nero tiddles while Rome burns next door. Very funny.'

'It was a cracking little story, Pippa,' Robert agrees. 'Very original, I thought, and quite ingenious. Rosie was a beautifully drawn character, and I laughed out loud at some of her antics.'

'Yes! And Patrick, the long-suffering husband. I chuckled at the thought of him trawling round the supermarket looking for… what was it… chia seeds and something else?' John is laughing at the memory.

'Agave syrup,' Pippa says.

'That's right. I did laugh at the episode, because I'd have been just the same – wouldn't have asked someone in the shop. We, as men, are simply unable to ask for directions,' John concludes.

'I did really enjoy writing Rosie and Patrick's marriage into the story. Very much an old married couple who get on each other's nerves, but would probably be lost without one another.'

'When I was reading it, I was picturing Dawn French as Rosie. Do you know what I mean? I could just imagine her comic timing and physical comedy working brilliantly; stuck halfway over the fence with her phone ringing,' I giggle at the image in my head.

'Yeah, I can see that too. I'd happily watch a sitcom about Rosie and Patrick,' Jenny says.

'Oh my God, that would be amazing! Yes! Pippa, you have to write some more Rosie and Patrick stories.' I say, enthused by the idea.

'Crikey! Really?' Pippa looks stunned. 'Well, I suppose I could give it a go, if you really think…'

'Yessss!' we all chorus.

Pippa looks chuffed to bits and we're all happy to have made someone's day. Tom is obviously still very much at the forefront of our minds.

'You know what Tom would've loved best in your story?' Jenny says. 'That bit where Patrick says "locked up" instead of "locked down". He'd've belly laughed at that. I bet he saw a few resemblances with his own marriage – he and Cheryl have been together for forty-six years.'

'Wow. That's a lifetime. That's longer than you've been alive, Robert,' I point out.

'That is quite something. I can't imagine being with the same person for that length of time. I've only really managed a year in a relationship,' Robert admits.

'Relationships are hard,' I agree. 'God, I really hope Tom pulls through.'

'Yes. Imagine losing your partner of forty-six years. How would you keep going?' Pippa is shaking her head.

'I know. I can't even begin to imagine. I don't think I'd want to keep going,' I'm close to tears again at the thought of what Tom and his wife are going through, and the fact that she can't be by his side in the hospital.

'One of my friend's mum's died a few days ago. She'd been moved to a hospice, and only one family member was allowed to visit. They couldn't even take it in turns. So, she didn't get to spend time with her mum during her last days, or say goodbye properly. It's all so rubbish,' Jenny tells us.

'It is. It's shit. And then you can't even have a proper funeral, can you?' I shake my head.

'Nope. They can only have ten people max at the funeral, and if they're from different households they still have to practise social distancing. So they can't even hug their family members. And… after the funeral, the body has to go back to the undertaker, or to some temporary mortuary, to be stored until the graveyard reopens.'

'That's awful. You can't have proper closure at all. Or give the person the send-off they deserve. So, so sad,' Pippa says.

'I can't get my head around so much of what's happening in the world right now. It's all so surreal,' I press my fingers into my temples.

'On a lighter note, you know everyone's putting up posters in their windows thanking the NHS? Have you seen the photo doing the rounds on Facebook of the Funeral Directors with a 'Thank You NHS' sign in its window?' Robert says.

Everyone's quiet. I know the photo he's talking about, but now doesn't seem the appropriate time to mention it. I had laughed at the black humour when I'd seen it, and I had shared it with my friends. Once more, I'm slightly put off by the way Robert sees the world. He doesn't seem to think like the rest of us.

'Hmm… maybe wrong time, wrong place for that one, Bob Slayer,' I tell him, trying to break the awkward silence that has descended on the group.

'Perhaps now would be a good time to wind up,' Jenny says, looking like she's getting wound up.

The faces on my screen all look rather subdued again. Well done, Robert, I think to myself.

'Congratulations again on your story, Pippa. Would really love to see more of Rosie and Patrick,' I say, trying to end the meeting on a positive.

Pippa smiles. 'Thanks, Amy. And, Jenny, please do let us know when you have news of Tom.'

Jenny nods. 'I will. Take care, everyone, and stay safe.'

I suddenly remember that we haven't decided whose story to do next and jump in with a quick reminder. John says he's more than happy to take his turn and promises to email us all a copy straight after the meeting. We all call out goodbyes and stay safes and leave the meeting.

I feel low again now. The news about Tom is devastating and, although I'm not religious, I do say a few words to whatever higher being is listening. As John said, it makes it all horribly real. I'd felt quite safe in my little bubble until now; the threat of the virus had seemed somehow distant and unreal, as though it wouldn't touch me here in my little corner of Kent. I just had to wait it out – read, write, lie in the sun; not too difficult. But now the Coronavirus felt like a possibility, something that could happen.

I've never met Tom's wife, Cheryl, but I feel the need to reach out to her. I find her on Facebook and type out a message:

Hi, Cheryl, I'm one of Tom's friends from the writing group. I just heard the news that he's in hospital and I wanted to let you know I'm thinking of you both at this difficult time. Please send Tom my love and support, and tell him he doesn't get out of writing his short story that easily! Keeping everything crossed for good news. Take care. Amy.

The other person on my mind is Robert. I've started to get an uneasy feeling about him. I can't quite put my finger on what it is. I stop to think about how much we actually know about him. I might do a bit of digging. I'm also looking forward to reading John's murder story.

CHAPTER 19

Robert who?

Who is Robert? Really? I'm on a bit of a mission to find out a bit more about our newest member. Thinking back to the first week we met him, even that was a bit odd. The way he just sat at our table, and we sort of kidnapped him as Jenny said. But we didn't pressgang him at all, did we? He facilitated the whole thing.

He seemed nice, and pretty normal, that first week. I remember how I'd been struck by his smile and his blue eyes. I had been single for a long time though. Since then, I've been noticing more and more that he has a bit of a warped sense of what's appropriate, and what's downright distasteful. And I don't mean the Wetherspoons breakfast he normally tucks into on a Monday. He doesn't seem to have the right filters somehow. Roberts verbalises the stuff other people might be thinking, but would never say because it was downright offensive.

I make a mental list of what we know about him for sure.

1. He's an engineer. (He wore that 'Engineers are all torque' T-shirt on week one, and he talks about technical stuff and writing drawing standards documents.)
2. He likes The Killers. (Another T-shirt, Amy – not sure that's very enlightening. I think you have a Black Sabbath T-shirt somewhere, and you don't even like them.)

3. He loves to travel, and has written a very long travel diary, although we have never seen any proof of that. (Hm… lots of people love to travel.)
4. He has never had a relationship that's lasted more than a year. (Proves nothing, Amy – plenty of people are scared of commitment or simply haven't met the right person.)
5. Er… he has nice blue eyes.

Great list. Very useful. Very enlightening. Robert's definitely a psychopath, Amy. Okay, so I'm being ridiculous, but he has said some really inappropriate things. And what was all that about wanting his murderer to be notorious? To be worthy of a nickname? I suppose that doesn't mean anything either. When was the last time you read a novel featuring a serial killer, and thought, ooh, this writer's clearly a murderous nutjob? So, Robert sometimes says tactless things. Have you met my mother? I come to the conclusion that I've been in isolation for too long and am overthinking everything. Robert's just a bit different. My phone pings with message.

What the actual fuck?! (It's from Jenny.) *Is Robert some sort of psychopath, or what?*

Funny you should say that… I've just been asking myself the same thing!

What answer did you get?

I rather talked myself out of it. Told myself I was imagining it and blamed it on lockdown-itis.

But some of the stuff he said?! I couldn't quite believe my ears.

I know. He's said some inappropriate shite.

Do you think I should ban him from the group?

Um... I think that might be an overreaction, don't you?

Maybe. I don't know. I guess I could leave it for now. Give him another chance.

Yeah, I think so, for now. As odd as some of his behaviour is, it would be horrible to be shut out of anything right now. I know for me, the group is really helping me keep it together.

You're probably right. Besides, if he is a headcase, I don't want to be the one to push him over the edge!

Let's just take it a week at a time and see. Have any of the others said anything?

No, although they must have noticed.

Leave it for now then. Have you seen John's story yet? I haven't checked my emails. Can't wait to read it – I bet it's far more literary than mine!

Haven't seen it yet. Will check in a mo. Just wanted to vent about Robert.

Fair enough. Catch up soon. Have a good rest of day!

You too. Bye for now.

I try to put thoughts about Robert and worries about Tom to the back of my mind and focus on my writing. It soon becomes clear that today is going to be a write-off as far as the work in no-progress-whatsoever is concerned. I've sat with my fingers poised over the keyboard, staring out of the window, for about ten minutes. And the only thought now going round my head is why the opposite of write-off isn't write-on.

I close the word document with a sigh and head to the lounge. Via the kitchen. And the fridge. Gin or chocolate? I look at my watch. It's one-fifteen. Both then. Sounds like a pretty balanced lockdown lunch to me. Breakfast had been two chocolate biscuits with my coffee. A biscuit in each hand definitely qualified as balanced.

Plonking myself dispiritedly on the sofa I switch on the TV and load Netflix. Everyone's been raving about *The Tiger King*, and I've been meaning to watch it to see what all the fuss is about. I manage about twenty minutes of the first episode, but it's simply not my cup of tea. I can kind of see why it appeals to a lot of people, but I can't get into it. I scroll around looking for something to watch, but I'm finding it hard to settle to anything today. I know it's all part of the coronacoaster ride we're on, but I never did like rollercoasters. I just want the world to get back to normal.

I click the TV off and grab my laptop. I've just remembered John's story. Perhaps that will occupy my mind for a while.

CHAPTER 20

John's Story

LET NO MAN PUT ASUNDER

The inky black night was no match for the darkness of my thoughts since I'd heard that my wife's killer had been released from prison. The judge had reduced the maximum sentence from fourteen years down to ten, because he pleaded guilty. I was the one who got a life sentence.

Michael Pascal. That was his name. It was burned onto my brain forever. Michael Pascal. The man who got behind the wheel of his car when he was four times over the limit, and ploughed down an innocent woman walking home from her book club. My beautiful, my beloved, Sarah. She was just thirty-nine years old when he ended her life. She would always be thirty-nine years old now. He denied her any more years. And he might as well have killed me too, for my life ended that day. When the police finally gave me back her belongings, I found a battered and bloodied copy of the book they'd been discussing that night: *The Lucky One* by Nicholas Sparks. I hated Michael Pascal all the more for that horrible irony.

It wasn't his first offence either. He'd been arrested for drunk driving before, but got away with a fine and losing his licence for eighteen months. Because that time he hadn't killed anyone. They tell me he was trying to light a cigarette when he lost control of the car and swerved up on to the pavement, crushing Sarah against a wall. A lousy bloody cigarette. Smoking kills. And sometimes it kills the wrong person. How could it be right that he was still living, breathing, walking around, when Sarah was nothing but ash?

My life ended on that day in 2008, and yet here I am, somehow, fifty-one years old, with my hair grey and lines around my eyes. In my head, time stopped on that fateful day ten years ago. I'm still shocked when I look in the mirror and see a middle-aged man staring back at me. It's how Dorian Gray must have felt when he gazed upon his aging portrait. I have *existed* for all these years, not lived; my existence made bearable by the knowledge that Sarah's killer was locked up. But now? Now that his liberty has been restored? I cannot live with that. I cannot exist with that. Either I go, or he does, but we cannot both continue. One life must end. I choose his.

*

I keep a photograph of Sarah on my bedside table. There is so much life and movement in that still. We're on a beach in France – Biscarrosse, in the south west of the country, with its unspoilt white sand and foaming Atlantic breakers. Sarah has run ahead to the sea, and I call to her, camera ready. As she turns, I capture a snapshot of perfect happiness. The sun's rays pick out the golden highlights in her auburn hair as it dances around her smiling face, green eyes sparkling. That beautiful face. The summer's pencil has drawn dots across her nose. She hates her freckles. I adore them. Her face is free of make-up: she had no need of it. Sarah was a natural beauty, inside and outside. Until he, Michael Pascal, smashed into her, crushing her pelvis, her hips, her internal organs, leaving her bloodied and broken, inside and outside, on the pavement.

There are many more photographs of Sarah dotted throughout the house. I want her in every room with me. I could never bear to take them down, to be without her company. Even after all these years, it would still feel disloyal to even consider removing them; as if I was somehow being unfaithful to her. Sometimes I mourn the fact that we never had a child together. Other times I am grateful, as I don't think I could bear to see a physical reminder of what I'd lost.

Of course, there have been other women – I'm only human and I still crave that physical contact with another. With a woman. But I never managed to find anyone who I could connect with on more than a physical level. Sarah was, is, my soulmate, however corny or pathetic that may sound. She is irreplaceable, so I think I've stopped trying; I no longer have any expectations of meeting a woman with whom to grow old. On the couple of occasions I thought I may have met someone special, it was more a need for companionship that drove me on. I was lonely. And anyway, they both told me I would have to take down Sarah's photographs, so that was that. I understood they felt they couldn't compete with my late wife, with her ghost, but I knew she would never stop haunting me. And I didn't want her to.

I still speak to her every day; tell her my worries, ask her opinion, her advice. I still miss holding her at night, caressing the curve of her hip, and losing myself in the depths of those fathomless, sea-green eyes. What we shared was more than a marriage; it was a fusing of souls, a melding of minds and bodies. Was it Plato, or Aristophanes, who wrote of humans as being cut in half, doomed to wander the earth searching for their other half for eternity? Sarah was literally my other half. I know that because I haven't felt whole since the day she died. The day he killed her. Michael Pascal.

*

The police told me he was being released. Claire, the family liaison officer who'd supported me after Sarah was killed, telephoned me. I remember being glad she didn't come to tell me in person as I could not have disguised the rage which engulfed me. Every fibre of my being tensed and clenched. Had the officer been there, I'm sure she would have heard my heart thumping in my chest. She would surely have seen the fury on my face.

'Thank you for letting me know.' I heard the words coming out of my mouth. Some autopilot in my brain knew what to say. Of course I knew this day would come, but I had been in denial I suppose. And now it was here? Now it was here, I felt as though Sarah had been murdered all over again, and I could not bear the injustice of it. I would not bear the injustice of it. And so, I started to plan.

The police wouldn't tell me where Michael Pascal was living. I understood their reasons. So, the first thing I had to do was find him. I wondered if ten years in prison had changed him. Did people ever really change though? I had to assume he was still living in the same area, so I decided to start with the pubs. I did a bit of research into the most likely pubs for a man like Pascal to drink in and made a list.

I started with the first one on the list on a Monday night. I ordered a ginger ale at the bar and sat quietly in the corner of the Red Lion in Lewson Street from 8 p.m. until closing time. I never drink alcohol. Not anymore. But I bet he does. I repeated this on Tuesday. And Wednesday, and every day until Sunday. I crossed the Red Lion off the list. On the second Monday, I sat in the Lord Nelson and waited. And watched. There was no sign of him for the whole of that week. I drew a line through the Lord Nelson. On the third week, it was the turn of The Eagle. Nothing. It was week four, Tuesday evening at about eight thirty, and I was sitting quietly in The Ship Inn. I had just lifted my glass to my lips when the door opened and he walked in. I'd know him anywhere, even after ten years.

My hand tightened around the glass. I lowered it to the table for fear I would crush it and give myself away. I could feel the tension in my jaw, the black fury in my eyes, as I watched him approach the bar. He ordered a pint of bitter and took a seat on a stool, as if he belonged there, and had never been away. He shared a joke with the barman. I felt sick to my stomach. How dare he laugh? How dare he be free to enjoy his life again? How could that be right? How could that be just?

I forced myself to sit there, nursing my glass and my murderous thoughts, watching, waiting. I couldn't go to the bar to order another drink in case he should recognise me. I didn't think he would after all this time, but I couldn't take that chance. He would probably complain I was harassing him and the police would have to warn me off. No one must know I'd found him.

He got up from his stool after about forty-five minutes, and headed for the exit. I thought for a moment he was leaving and readied myself to do the same. But then I registered his unfinished pint on the bar and his jacket still draped across the adjacent seat, and realised he must be going outside for a cigarette. I relaxed back into my chair.

He didn't actually leave until after last orders were called. I'd lost count of the number of pints he had drunk. He was unsteady on his feet, almost tipping the stool over as he got up and staggered off to the Gents. I gritted my teeth as I watched him go. He hadn't changed, and it was only a matter of time before he destroyed more lives. It was all I could do not to follow him into the toilets. I imagined myself smashing his head against a sink, over and over again, his blood and brains redecorating the room like an abattoir floor.

I waited until he'd left the pub, the door swinging shut behind him, before I got up and followed. I wondered if he would go to a car, but he continued on foot. It was only about seven or eight minutes' walk before I saw him stop outside a little two-up two-down mid-terrace, and fumble to get the front door key out of his pocket and successfully into the lock. I noted that he took the key from his right jacket pocket. Once he had gone in and closed the door I walked past the house, making a mental note of the number on the filthy, peeling, red-painted door. Thirty-nine. Well, I wouldn't forget that in a hurry: the same age as Sarah when he killed her. I walked back to my car and went home. Sitting down at the kitchen table, I pulled my pad and pen to me and drew a circle around The Ship Inn. I'd found him. I knew where he lived.

I knew I wouldn't be able to sleep after seeing him. I sat in an armchair in the pitch black lounge and let the Stygian maelstrom in my head swirl. I didn't have a plan and I just hoped that when the storm in my head calmed, some idea of how to proceed would remain, like tidewrack.

I must have drifted off at some point, and I woke cold

and stiff in the chair just after 7 a.m. I made a coffee which I downed, before standing in a hot shower to ease the aches in my body. As the hot water streamed over my head, I knew what I wanted to do. And the first thing was to make sure Michael Pascal lived alone.

I cleared my diary for the rest of the week. One of the benefits of being a self-employed Chartered Accountant meant I was accountable to no one. I made a flask of coffee and some sandwiches and set off in the car at about 9.30 a.m. I drove to the street I'd followed Pascal to the night before and found a parking space on the opposite side of the road, a few doors down, with a good view of his front door. And I prepared to wait. I had the radio on, but I couldn't tell you what was played. My focus was solely on that front door, silently willing no one to come out of it other than Pascal himself. For my plan to work, he had to be living alone. I knew that had been the case when he had gone to prison, but I didn't want to make an assumption which could cost an innocent life. Although, could anyone mixed up with a man like him really be innocent? Weren't they guilty by association? Surely no decent human being could be involved with a man like that? Even so, I only had reason to kill him.

It was a quiet street, not many comings or goings at all. There was no sign of life at number thirty-nine until just after midday, when the front door opened and Pascal came out alone. He got in a battered, dirty-blue VW Passat and drove off. A different car. The ancient BMW he'd been driving when he hit Sarah had been written off. I didn't bother to follow him this time. It was the house I was interested in. I just sat and watched, but no one else appeared. Pascal came back a couple of hours later and carried some supermarket shopping bags into the house. The bags looked especially heavy. If I was a betting man, I would've put money on them containing mostly alcohol. I decided to come back later that night and watch some more.

Back at home, I caught up with some work-related emails and also did some Google searches on Pascal's name and address to try and find out if anyone else lived with him. As far as I could tell no one did. I went back to his house and continued my stake-out several times over the next few days, and was reasonably confident with my conclusion by the end of the week.

'I've found him, Sarah. Michael Pascal. I'm going to make him pay. I'm going to get justice for you.' I spoke these words as I stood in the kitchen making my morning cup of tea. Her photograph was on the fridge, under a magnet we'd brought back from a holiday to The Seychelles, and I paused to look at it before opening the door to get the milk out. My eye caught the magnet next to it – we bought that one from The Paris Catacombs. It was a small block of marble inscribed with the words: 'Arrête! C'est Ici l'Empire de la Mort'. Sarah had been fascinated by the 'Empire of the Dead' with the bones of more than six million people concealed deep under the Paris streets. If everything went according to plan, the body count would be going up by one.

For once, I chose not to listen to Sarah's advice. She told me to let it go, to leave it. Killing Pascal wouldn't bring her back. To move on with my life. I stirred my tea and shook my head at her. 'I'm sorry. I have to do this.'

The following Tuesday evening saw me back at The Ship

Inn. I sat there until gone ten, when it became clear Pascal was not coming in. Frustrated, I went home, promising myself I'd try again tomorrow. I didn't want to go to the pub on a night when they were more likely to be busy. By 7.30 p.m. on Wednesday evening, I was in my usual spot in The Ship with my glass of ginger ale, waiting and hoping. At just after eight, in he came, heading for his usual stool, ordering a pint, removing his jacket and placing it on the next stool. We are predictable creatures of habit. I waited until he went outside for his first cigarette and went straight to the bar to order another drink. I perched on the stool next to Pascal's jacket and, while the barman turned and reached down into the fridge, I dipped my hand into the right hand pocket, closing my fingers around Pascal's keys and surreptitiously transferring them to my own. I was careful how I touched the keys, holding them by the edges, not wanting to leave even a partial print.

The barman placed my drink on the bar and I handed over the correct change. Time was now of the essence. I went back to my table and downed the drink in a few gulps. As soon as Pascal came back in and settled himself at the bar, I left the pub. I jogged to my car and headed for the twenty-four-hour supermarket, parking as close as I could to the entrance and walking briskly into the store. I made my way straight to the booth where they did shoe repairs and key cutting, thankful that they stayed open until 10 p.m., and asked for a copy of the front door key I'd removed from Pascal's jacket. The only other key on the ring was a car key.

All I had to do now was return to the pub and slip the keys back into Pascal's jacket, which was easily accomplished, this time when he went to use the bathroom. I didn't hang around after that, relieved to head home and close my front door. I had come to the conclusion that I was not cut out for this kind of subterfuge and my stress levels were high. For the first time in years, I could have done with a brandy myself. But I had sworn after Sarah died that I would never touch alcohol again. And I always kept my promises to Sarah. I had never promised I wouldn't kill Michael Pascal. And now I had his front door key, I was one step closer to achieving my goal.

That night, I lay in bed, unable to sleep again as I thought about the next stage of my plan. Eventually, I think I dozed off just before dawn. I woke muzzy-headed and lethargic soon after ten, grateful once more that I did not have to go out to work. Coffee and a shower revived me sufficiently to do the accounts I needed to do, and speak to the clients I'd been putting off for the past couple of weeks. I knew that my full concentration would not return until after I had accomplished my objective, but I could keep the business ticking over until then. My clients had all been with me for years, and I was grateful for their loyalty.

After work, I made myself a coffee and sat at the kitchen table with my laptop. I felt closest to Sarah in the kitchen somehow. I suppose because she made it such a warm and welcoming room. There was somehow more of her spirit in here than anywhere else, and I needed to draw on the strength she gave me to get through this. I spent an hour or more reading articles and studies on the subject I was interested in. The more I read, the less confident I felt that my plan would work. Eventually, feeling frustrated, I closed the laptop, grabbed my keys and coat and went for a drive.

Focussing on the act of driving centred me once more, and I let my mind drift to happier times. Sarah and I used to go for drives together often when we first started dating, back when going for a drive was more of a thing. We'd met at university. She was in her first year of an English Literature degree and I was in my final year of Accounting. I'd seen her across the room at the Student Union bar one night, laughing with her friends. She was, and still is, the most beautiful woman I have ever seen, made all the more so by the fact that she was totally unaware of it. It was love at first sight. For me, anyway. Sarah took a little more convincing. I think I grew on her. Like mould, I remember saying at the time. Sarah could have had her pick of men, but she chose me, and I never stopped being grateful.

I drove down to the beach as dusk settled over the town, and parked the car, rolling down the window and inhaling deeply, the cool sea air reinvigorating my tired mind. I could hear the waves washing over the pebbly beach, and I closed my eyes and tried to switch off my thoughts, letting my senses take over. After a while – I don't know how long – I closed the window and got out of the car, walking down onto the stony beach and sitting down at the top of a slope, looking out to sea. The moon was almost full, shining torch-like on the sea, its light bouncing off the ripples of the tide.

I picked up a smooth pebble and turned it over and over in my hand, its cool smoothness adding to my sensory abundance. I had a sudden urge to take off my shoes and socks and tread painfully down to the shallows to paddle. That's what Sarah would have done. She had such a lust for life; she embraced every opportunity for experience; she was fearless and adventurous. I should have been the one to die, not her. I brought no colour to the world, but Sarah had brought a kaleidoscope of colour and light, beauty and motion everywhere she went. She left a gaping abyss when she died. I would have left a shallow divot. What would Michael Pascal's death leave? I wondered. Would anyone miss him? Would he leave a hole in anyone's life? An aching pain in their chest that never ever went away? I found it impossible to believe that he would be missed. The world would be a better place without him in it.

*

The next part of the plan necessitated gaining entry to Pascal's house while he was out. That was easily achieved by ensuring he was safely ensconced at the pub, before donning a dark jacket, hat and gloves and letting myself in with the key I'd had cut. The street was quiet and not particularly well-lit. I had no idea about CCTV in the area, but I had not seen any obvious cameras during my surveillance. I kept my gaze down at the ground just in case. I'd parked my car some way down the road.

The interior of the house smelt musty and unpleasant. I wrinkled my nose in disgust. I had a quick scout around the downstairs. A check of the kitchen cupboards and fridge revealed cans of beer and a couple of bottles of cheap-looking vodka. There were dirty dishes, and foul overflowing ashtrays on the table and work surfaces, together with rank takeaway containers and empty cans. The lounge wasn't much better, with a filthy coffee table covered in the same sort of detritus. I suppose it was pretty much what I expected from a man such as Pascal.

The thing I was most interested in was the seating in the lounge. It was obvious by the way the room was arranged that Pascal favoured a particular chair. There was a small side table next to it with another disgusting ashtray and an empty glass. The chair had moulded itself to the shape of a regular occupant and the back bore a greasy imprint from an unwashed head. The rest of the room was quite sparsely furnished: a sagging settee covered in stained yellowy-coloured velour, a metal television stand with TV and DVD player on, and an old seventies-style sideboard. The floor covering was a dated kind of linoleum, cracked in places, and with a dirty beige rug over the middle.

I had seen everything I needed to, and couldn't wait to get out of the squalid hovel that Michael Pascal called home. Taking one last look around, I headed for the front door and, after checking the street was clear, I left and hurried back to my car. All I wanted now was to get home, chuck my clothes in the washing machine and take a shower. I felt dirty after being in that house. But I was a step closer to reaching the endgame.

*

I picked the night that I would do it. It wasn't a random date. It was Sarah's birthday. The fourteenth of September. She would have been fifty years old. A half-century. Another milestone denied her, stolen by Michael Pascal. It fell on a Sunday. It wasn't a problem for me, and I didn't see Pascal as being the religious type. The Ship Inn was his regular place of worship on a Sunday, and I planned to be in the congregation also. No prayers were going to save him from my wrath; there could be no redemption for the man who killed my wife. The devil take you, Michael Pascal. I damn you to hellfire for all eternity.

D-day, deed-day, death-day, was still some weeks off and, I won't lie, my nerves were getting pretty ragged. I didn't have any trouble persuading my GP to prescribe me a short course of strong sleeping medication: I looked like death myself. There was another reason for waiting to do the deed. I wanted Pascal to have time to pickle himself in alcohol once more, and saturate himself with fatty takeaways. He had been overweight when he went into prison, with the unhealthy pallor of someone who obviously did not care what he put into his body. He hadn't changed.

Finally, my anxious wait came to an end, and Sunday September fourteenth arrived. I woke early – I hadn't actually been taking the sleeping meds – and lay in bed holding Sarah's photograph. 'Happy birthday, my love.' I hugged the picture to my chest and could feel tears pricking the corners of my eyes. And it made me angry. I clenched my jaw as I thought of what today should have been, and my rage returned twofold. Michael Pascal would die tonight. He didn't get to have any more birthdays.

I couldn't settle to anything all that day. I drank too much coffee and paced up and down the kitchen. I really felt as though I might be losing it. I just had to get through tonight, and then my existence could return to something I could live with. At last evening came, bringing with it huge, nauseating waves of anxiety. Could I go through with it? Would it even work? There were factors outside of my control, and no guarantees my plan would work. I strengthened my resolve with thoughts of Michael Pascal, laughing in the pub, living, breathing – all the things he had denied Sarah. And all the years with her he had stolen from me. I had to redress the balance once and for all.

At around 8 p.m. I checked my pockets to make sure I had everything and departed for the pub. I'd left my mobile phone switched on in the kitchen. Should I become a suspect, I didn't want my phone giving away where I was. I'd thought a lot about being caught, and the conclusion I'd come to was that it would still be worth it. Could life in prison be much worse than life on the outside without Sarah?

I parked some way away from The Ship, in the opposite direction to Pascal's house, and made my way to the pub. As I pushed open the door I was silently praying that he would be there, on his usual pew. Previous Sundays suggested he got there after lunch and drank until closing time. I just stuck my head in the door, long enough to confirm his presence and then ducked out and walked briskly to his house, putting on my gloves as I went. Checking all around, I let myself in and went into the lounge. The filth and stench were even worse than before. The curtains were closed – I don't think he ever opened them. I raised the feet of the armchair enough to pull the rug out from underneath it, and repositioned it on the other side of the room under the sofa. I moved the armchair a little so it was more isolated in the room. I went to the kitchen and brought back one of the bottles of vodka and left it on the coffee table for later. There was already a glass on the little side table I'd moved with the armchair. I locked up and walked the short distance back to the pub.

I went up to the other end of the bar and quietly ordered my ginger ale from the barmaid there, before taking a seat at a different table than my usual one. I needed to trick the regular barman's memory a little. I still had a clear view of Pascal. All I had to do now was wait.

I could hear Pascal's loud, slurring voice as he talked to the barman. I had to hide my clenched fists under the table and look at my drink so no one could see the rage on my face. I couldn't wait to silence him for good. Not much longer, I thought, looking at my watch. Timings were going to be key, and I couldn't control them the way I would've liked.

The gods were on my side, though, and just after nine thirty Pascal staggered off outside to smoke. I was ready with the correct change for another drink in one hand, and a small bottle of liquid Zopiclone in the other. I'd told the doctor I had trouble swallowing tablets. He'd swallowed it. I went to the bar, by Pascal's stool this time, and ordered a drink. It was simple enough to quickly tip the contents of the bottle into Pascal's glass when the barman turned away. I was pretty sure Pascal was too drunk to notice the taste. Closing time was less than an hour away, and the drug should take about an hour to work. I'd put a fairly hefty dose in his glass. The leaflet that came with the Zopiclone advised against taking it with alcohol as the combination could result in a deep sleep from which you might find it difficult to wake. I was counting on it.

Pascal came back into the pub and staggered off to the toilets before returning to his seat. I could feel the expression of disgust on my face as I watched him. Foul creature. It was now 9.45 p.m. He downed the remainder of his pint and I saw the barman pass him a shot glass, which I assume contained vodka. Then another. I prayed that I'd got the timing right and he wouldn't suddenly pass out at the bar. Last orders came and went and, at dead on ten thirty, Pascal half fell from his stool and walked unsteadily out of the pub, his head beginning to look as if his neck could no longer support it.

I let the door swing shut behind him before following him out, again putting on my gloves as I went. It took some time for the drunken, swaying Pascal to reach his house. He bounced off walls and fell against a car at one point, but he staggered on, somehow, and arrived home. As I watched from a few feet away, I wasn't convinced he was going to be able to find his keys, let alone get the door open. He leant against the door, swearing and mumbling and fumbling in his pockets. It looked as though he could collapse at any second. Making a decision, I jogged over and held him up.

'Woah there! You okay? Let me help you,' I said, trying to sound like a friendly Samaritan, when really all I felt was utter revulsion. 'Got your keys?' I felt in his pocket and took out his keys, inserting the door key in the lock and opening up. 'Here, let me get you inside,' I said. Pascal wasn't in a fit state to object and let me lead him into the lounge, where I got him to sit in the armchair. His eyelids were drooping and, once he sat down they stayed closed.

My heart was pounding in my chest by this time. I stood and watched. And waited. It was only a few minutes before it was obvious he was out cold. His breathing was slow and a little laboured. I kicked his foot. Nothing, no reaction except a slight break in the snoring that had started. I said his name and clicked my fingers next to his ear. I clapped my hands. No response.

I got started. I checked the time on my watch. It was ten fifty-six. As much as I was loath to touch him, I pulled up his sleeve to reveal his watch, and altered the time. It was all guesswork, but I set it to eleven fifty. By then I would *be safely* back at home and sending some emails from my PC. 'Well, you see officer, I'm a bit of an insomniac, and I work all sorts of odd hours... Just ask my doctor...'

I got the bottle of vodka from the table and poured some on Pascal's upper body and some on the inside cushions of the chair, careful not to spill any on the floor. I put the glass from the side table in his left hand – I'd observed him often enough to know that he held his drink in that hand and his cigarette in his right. I let his left hand rest on his thigh, with the glass tipped. Then I took the packet of cigarettes and lighter from his jacket. I removed one of the cancer sticks from the pack and lit it. Sorry to deprive you of a victim, big C, but this one can't wait. It was fiddly trying to get it between Pascal's fingers, but when I had done it, I let that hand rest on his other thigh.

Then I stood back. I realised I'd been holding my breath as I inhaled a lungful of air. Pascal had not stirred at all. I think he was pretty much unconscious from the sleeping draught and booze combination.

The lit cigarette had started to burn through the fabric of his trousers, a small orange flame flickering hypnotically. Still he didn't show any sign of waking. I stared transfixed. I could now see his naked thigh through the hole, and the flame started to burn blue. I knew what was happening from the reading I'd done. His skin was splitting and the fat beginning to melt. The liquid fat fed the flames which began to lick up towards his belly. His alcohol and fat-soaked clothes were now acting like the wick of a candle. The wick effect. I knew

I had to get out of there. The smell, and the knowledge of what was happening, was making me gag. I couldn't control what happened next, but I needed to get home and try and establish some sort of alibi.

I crept out of the house onto the deserted street and walked as quickly as I could to my car. My head and heart were pounding. All I could think about was Pascal burning up like Guy Fawkes on a fifth of November bonfire. I hoped that the fire would be contained to the chair; I'd made sure there was nothing flammable in close proximity. I checked my watch when I got home: eleven thirty-five. I'd left my home PC switched on and logged in to my emails with a couple of draft messages ready to send. I completed the process and hit send on them a few minutes apart. I then did a little bit of work on a spreadsheet which would clearly show the time I last amended it. I had no idea if the fire would stop Pascal's watch, but it had been worth a try.

*

I'm not going to lie, I was a wreck afterwards, waiting and wondering if the police would turn up on my doorstep. Obviously I would be the prime suspect if this turned into a murder enquiry. I watched the local news religiously. All they'd said so far was that a man had died in a house fire late sometime on Sunday night. No name had yet been released, and nothing said about whether the police suspected foul play. I'd driven past the house on the Monday, and there was no sign of a fire from the outside, which had been a huge relief. My worst nightmare had been that the fire would spread to the neighbouring properties.

It was a few days later, on the Thursday morning, that there was a knock at my front door. My heart leapt into my throat. I took a deep breath and walked up the hallway, opening the door to see the police family liaison officer standing there.

'Claire, this is a surprise, come on in. Don't tell me he's killed someone else,' I said, gesturing into the house.

We went into the lounge and Claire indicated that I should sit. She remained standing. 'No, he hasn't killed anyone else. It's...er... as a matter of fact, he's dead. Michael Pascal is dead.'

I tried to look shocked. 'Oh. Did he crash his car?'

She shook her head. 'No, Mr. Pascal died in a fire at his home on Sunday night.'

I was silent for a few moments. 'Well, I can't say I'm sorry he's dead. Is that a terrible admission?'

'I'd say it was understandable, in the circumstances.'

'Do you know how the fire started?'

She paused. I knew she was probably not supposed to give me any details. I also knew she was about to. After Sarah had been killed, we'd built up quite a relationship. 'It looks as though he passed out drunk in his chair with a lit cigarette in his hand...' she pulled a face to illustrate the gruesome nature of his demise. 'I shouldn't tell you this, but all that was left of him were his lower legs, still with bits of his trousers on, and his socks and shoes. Nothing else in the room burned except him and his chair. We even know what time he died because his watched stopped at eleven fifty.'

'Christ! What a horrible way to go,' I said, in what I hoped was a convincing tone. 'Thank you for letting me know.'

Claire just smiled as she turned to leave. 'You take care.'

'Yes, I will. You too,' I told her as I followed her to the front door.

I closed the door and leant back against it, exhaling with relief. I'd done it. I'd got away with murder. I could get back to getting on with my existence now. My dull, grey little life, but with one less shadow looming over me, and one wrong righted.

Smoking will kill you. One way or another.

THE END

CHAPTER 21
Fingerprints

I'm really impressed by John's story and impatient for Monday to arrive so we can talk about it. I send John a quick 'Loved your story' message, although I'm sure he won't be as anxious as Jenny and Pippa, waiting for the verdict.

The amazing weather continues and my days drift in a strange, seamless oneness of writing and sunbathing. Both tan and book are developing nicely, but I'm starting to feel the isolation more and more. Lockdown shows no sign of being relaxed as we all do our bit to protect the NHS from being overwhelmed. I force myself to watch the government's daily briefing at least once a week, but very little changes day by day. And I find myself screaming at the television when the journalists come on and ask stupid bloody questions, that have either already been answered or are simply seeking blame. It's a learning curve for everyone, and I have now learnt to switch off before the questions. The Prime Minister is in intensive care, and the four-thousand-bed Nightingale Hospital has opened in London. The daily death rate rises alarmingly every day, and the death toll has exceeded five thousand. It's scary.

We've heard from Tom's wife that he remains seriously ill, but has so far held his own and not had to be put on a ventilator. We're all praying that he continues to fight this bloody virus. I think of Cheryl often, and how awful it must be for her. She must be beside herself with worry. She should be beside her husband. Their situation makes the next Thursday night clap all the more poignant, and it's gratifying to hear the claps and cheers from around the village. Hang in there, Tom, we're all rooting for you.

By the following Monday, April 13, the death toll has risen to over ten thousand, but we're being told we still haven't hit the peak of the pandemic. Thankfully, Boris is out of hospital though. The strangeness of the time is highlighted by a broadcast from the Queen, as well as her first ever Easter message.

It's a gloomy bunch of faces that greets me when I join the Zoom meeting.

'Hey, all,' I open with a sad smile. 'How's everyone doing?'

A few quiet 'Hey, Amy's' echo round my screen. No one seems in a hurry to speak though. Finally, Pippa breaks the silence.

'Did you all hear from Cheryl this week? It sounds as though Tom's battling bravely.'

'Yes, poor Cheryl, it must be awful just waiting for news all the time,' I say.

'Tom's a fighter. I do believe if he can stay off a ventilator, he'll see this ruddy virus off,' John says.

'God, I hope so. I just want him back with us, and being his lovely jolly self again,' Jenny adds with a sad smile.

'Amen to that,' I agree.

'You've got to admit, though, it is easier to get a word in edgeways without him here. He could talk for England.' This from Robert. And in the past tense. As if he's never coming back.

I can see shocked faces across my screen. I know I'm guilty of tarring Tom with the boring brush, but really? It's like Robert's filters are missing. I dive in before the others have a chance to speak, worried that shock will turn to anger.

'Well, I'd give anything for him to be here now, talking the proverbial hind legs off a donkey.'

'Me too,' Jenny nods.

'Me three,' from Pippa.

John looks too angry to speak.

Robert opens his mouth to speak again, but I pre-empt him. 'So… John's story… what did we all think? I thought it was brilliant. So much darker than Jenny's or Pippa's.'

'Yes! I loved how dark and brooding it was. You could really feel the cold, calm menace of revenge,' Jenny agrees.

'And the way it contrasted with the light and love when he talked about his wife,' Pippa added.

'A crime with passion at its heart, but tempered by time and distance. Chilling!' I say.

Robert stays quiet.

John looks gratified. 'Why, thank you kindly, ladies,' he says, bowing his head slightly. 'I wanted to depict a man whose broken heart had never fully mended, and to give the reader an insight into how a normally sane and rational man could be driven to kill.'

'And you succeeded,' Jenny said. 'We, as readers, could sympathise; almost condone his behaviour.'

'I appreciated the literary references too, and the nods to Zola and *Doctor Pascal*. I had to chuckle at how different it is to my mad murder,' I tell him. 'And it was all so beautifully planned and executed. A bit like Jenny's in that respect – reflects the type of writer you are. God knows what you'll make of mine when you read it,' I say, pulling a face. I'm already anxious about the others reading my story next.

'I'm sure yours is great, Amy,' Jenny says. 'I'm fully expecting some black humour.'

'I hope you won't be disappointed. Back to John's though…' I say, wanting the spotlight back where it should be. 'What did you think, Robert?' I ask, crossing my fingers and silently praying he doesn't say something unsuitable. I want to include him in the discussion, but recognise it's a gamble.

'I agree with you all. I thought it was very well-written and convincing,' he says.

Phew! I think to myself.

'If I could pick up on one tiny detail…' Robert continued.

Uh oh.

'… it would be the fingerprints on Pascal's key. The killer is careful not to get his fingerprints on it, and I understand why wiping it clean of all fingerprints would be suspicious… but he doesn't account for the prints which the key-cutter would obviously have put on it. Was this just an oversight?'

Okay, I think to myself, could've been worse, and actually a fair point to make. I look at John, and wait for him to respond.

'Ah! Yes! The fingerprints. Well, Robert, you're actually right about it being an oversight on my part. The realisation didn't hit me until after I'd emailed the story to you all. I decided it wasn't worth re-writing. After all, it was just an exercise in writing and I would naturally have changed it had this been for publication. But, well spotted!' John says magnanimously.

I think for a minute. 'So, say the police had decided Pascal's death was suspicious and had checked the key for prints… presumably, unless the key cutter had a criminal record, he wouldn't be on a police database. And, if he was, he could easily explain away his prints being on anyone's key due to his job.'

'Yes! And Pascal couldn't dispute a claim that he had a spare key cut, because he's been reduced to a smoking pair of ankles,' Jenny adds.

'Unless they checked the CCTV at the supermarket,' Robert throws in.

Oh, fuck off, Robert, I think to myself. I'd like to see you do better. 'Well, anyway, it's a minor blip in an otherwise brilliant story which I bought into completely. And I loved how booze and fags, the very things that killed his wife, were used as the murder weapons. Well done, John.'

'Yes, very well done indeed, John,' Pippa and Jenny chorus.

'Thank you again,' John says. 'Like Pippa's Arthur Bundt, Michael Pascal was "hoist with his own petard" in true Shakespearean style.'

'Your turn next, Amy,' Jenny reminds me.

'Lordy. I should probably give you a bit of background before you read it, or it won't make sense,' I tell them. I explain about meeting vet Cameron at the pub and picking his brain about suitable drugs to use and that the plan was to "murder" a horrid man who abused his dog at the surgery one time. 'I hope you enjoy it. I will be hiding under the duvet for the foreseeable future.'

Jenny laughs. 'You've got to get over that, Amy. You should be proud of your writing. It's no accident that you've had two books published.'

'I know, but it's easier said than done. It's still scary as hell having people read my stuff. I'm terrified of being judged and found wanting. I know that my books won't be everyone's cup of tea, but I still care way too much what people think. One bad review can wipe out fifty good ones.'

'Well, I can't wait to read your murder story. Make sure you email it straight after the meeting, won't you?' Pippa says.

'Yep, will do. Let me know what you think. Lie if need be,' I say, with a grimace.

We wind the meeting up then, with the usual 'Take care, stay safe' messages. I log into my email account and send the story before I can chicken out.

CHAPTER 22

Amy's story

OOPS!

'I've killed Laura!' I blurt the words out as soon as Cameron answers the phone.

'You what now? You've killed Laura? Laura who?'

'Laura! My best friend, Laura!'

'Oh, that Laura. Why would you kill your best friend? I thought you were going to kill the homeless man.'

I realise that Cameron thinks I'm talking about the fictional murder.

'No. Listen. I've *really* killed Laura. Well, actually, strictly speaking, I suppose she killed herself, but...' I shake my head, 'that's irrelevant now. She's dead, however you look at it.'

'Shit. Are you serious?'

'Deadly serious! Cameron, what the hell do I do?'

'Do nothing. I'm on my way!'

I press 'End Call' and sit at the bottom of the stairs to wait for him. My legs are trembling. In fact, I'm trembling all over. My best friend is lying dead on my lounge floor. This is not the murder I had planned. Nearly planned.

About ten minutes later Cameron arrives, slightly out of breath. 'I hope this isn't a wind up, Amy. I was getting ready for a date – my first date with Richie, actually.'

'Definitely not a wind up, Cameron. I wish it was.'

'Where's the body then?' He seems remarkably calm about the whole thing, which is odd considering what a complete drama queen he is normally. My drama queen in shining shirt tonight.

'In here,' I say, leading him through to the lounge.

'Shit,' he says, having bent down to check for a pulse. 'You've killed Laura.'

'I know! Although, she did kill herself really, as I said...'

'What the hell happened?'

'Er... you might want to sit down for this,' I tell him.

We sit next to each other on the sofa and I begin to talk. I keep seeing Laura out of the corner of my eye though, so I pull the throw off the back of the sofa and lay it over her, shuddering as I do so.

'That's so much better,' Cameron says sarcastically. 'Now we can't see the sodding dead elephant in the room.'

'Don't. I know. Just listen. And please don't be angry.'

'I'm already bloody furious, Amy. I ironed a shirt for tonight.'

'I'm really sorry. I'll make it up to you. And you can tell Richie it was all my fault.'

'Oh, don't worry, I plan to. And if this is how you treat your friends, I'll give the former a miss thanks.'

I take a deep breath and begin.

'So, remember that day your keys went missing?'

Cameron nods, quiet for once.

'Well, that was me. I took them from your bag when I popped into the branch to say hello.'

He starts to speak. I shush him or I'll never get through the story.

'Anyway, I had copies cut of the branch keys: the front door and safe. And then I posted your keys through the letterbox, hoping you'd just assume you'd lost them and some kind soul had found and returned them.'

'What the hell, Amy?!'

'I know, I know, I'm sorry! I just wanted to see if it was doable – I wanted the murder I was planning to write to seem plausible.'

'For God's sake, woman. I take it killing the lovely Laura was not part of the plan?'

'No! God, no. So, anyway, I let myself into the surgery late one night and took the bottle of Etomidate from the safe. I knew it probably wouldn't be missed – it wasn't used the whole time I worked there.'

Cameron looks too stunned to speak at this point, as if someone gave him a small dose of elephant tranq. He makes hand gestures that clearly mean 'What the hell? Are you insane?'

I force myself to carry on telling the story. 'So, anyway, I decanted the contents of the bottle of Etomidate into an empty 'Joy' essential oil bottle and hid it in amongst the dozens of bottles I keep in the downstairs loo. You know – you've seen my shelves, the really cute ones that look like rooms in a house...'

Cameron is just shaking his head at me in disbelief. 'Oh. My. Actual. God. You are such a dick.'

'I KNOW! Don't you think I feel bad enough already? Laura and I went to primary school together. She was my chief bridesmaid, for God's sake!'

Cameron just keeps shaking his head. 'So, how do you go from decanting – stupidly – the Etomidate – deadly elephant tranquiliser – into an essential oil bottle - labelled 'Joy' no less – to your best friend – the lovely Laura - lying dead on your rug? I can't wait to hear this.'

'Well, Laura came round for a catch up – we hadn't seen each other for ages...'

'She won't be seeing anyone ever again,' Cameron snorts.

'Not helpful.' I glare at him. 'We'd been chatting for about an hour over coffee, and she went off to use the loo. When she came back, she said she hoped I didn't mind, but she'd used her favourite oil...'

'Don't tell me...'

I nod. '"Joy". She loved the stuff. Used to apply it liberally on her wrists and neck. Sometimes on her chest. The next thing I know, she's lying in a heap on my Persian rug, and I can't find a pulse. That's when I called you.'

Cameron is quiet for a few moments. 'I'm a bit surprised, really.'

'What? That I killed my best friend? Me too, as it happens.'

'No, no, that the Etomidate killed her like that.'

'Okay, two things. One, you're not surprised that I killed my best friend? Wtf? And two, you said just spilling it on your finger...'

Cameron waves his hands dismissively. 'I know what I said, but I'd say anything to get in a story. It is treacherous stuff – I just thought you'd need to inject it for it to be effective at killing someone. Curious.'

'Well, I'm pretty sure she wasn't shooting up "Joy" in my downstairs loo, so...'

'Was she on any medication for anything?'

'Um... beta blockers, I think. Couldn't tell you which ones

or what for though.'

Cameron nods. 'That might do it. Anything else?'

'She had a headache earlier – took some Co-codamol with her coffee.'

He nods again. 'I see. Yep. That's unfortunate.'

'Are you telling me she was killed by a headache?'

'By trying to cure one, perhaps. That combination of drugs wouldn't have gone down well with the Etomidate. Still, look on the bright side – she won't be getting any more headaches.'

I groan and put my face in my hands. This can't be happening.

'So, what do we do now?' I ask, finally.

'That's a bloody good question, Amy. Not one I have the answer to just at the moment.'

'Can't we just call the police? It was an accident. Sort of.' I look hopefully at Cameron.

'Er... and how do we see that conversation going down? "So, Mrs... Archer..."'

'It's Ms, actually, Officer.'

'"My apologies, *Ms* Archer, can you tell me how Mrs... er... Ms..."'

'Miss. Cates, Laura Cates.'

'"Miss Laura Cakes, came to be lying dead on your Indian rug?"'

'Not "Cakes", "Cates". Laura Cates. With a "T". And it's Persian. The rug.'

'"My apologies once more, Ms Archer. If you would care to enlighten me further?"'

'Yes, well, you see... she... um... she had a very bad reaction to an essential oil.'

'"An essential oil, Madam? Did she drink it?"'

'What? No, of course not. Don't be silly!'

'"Forgive my silliness, Madam... etc. etc." Do you see, Amy? *You* put the Etomidate in the bottle, you're responsible.'

'Bum.'

'Quite. I need some time to think. The first thing we have to do though is stash the body.' Cameron gets up and removes the throw from Laura's body. I can't look. 'Could be worse.'

'Excuse me? I really don't see how this could be any worse!'

'Laura could have been a chunkleberry.'

'A what now?'

'A chunkleberry. A fat girl, y'know?'

'I do now. And no, she wasn't a chunkleberry.'

'Chunkleberry Cakes,' Cameron says, and now he can't stop laughing. It's so inappropriate. And I'm trying really hard not to join in. I think we're both becoming hysterical. The whole situation is so surreal and messed up.

Eventually, Cameron stops laughing and wipes tears from his eyes. 'Sorry. Right. Body. As I was saying, it's a good thing she's not a...'

'Don't!' I interject.

'It's a good thing she's petite.'

I frown at him.

'The smaller the body, the easier it is to deal with, dopey. Jeez, you've dealt with enough dead dogs to know that. We need to get her over to the branch and into the freezer. That'll buy us some time while we work out how to get rid of her.'

'But...'

'No buts, Amy. That's what we're doing. How fond of that rug are you?'

‘I used to love it. Now, not so much.’

‘Great, ‘coz we’re rolling babycakes up in it. Come on.’

We lay the body lengthways on the rug and roll. Honestly, I’m just waiting for Cameron to make more inappropriate bakery jokes.

‘Okay, need to make sure the coast’s clear and get her into the car. We can take mine. It’s a pit anyway, and I had no connection to Laura, so there’s no reason why it should ever get searched.’

‘Good thinking, Batman.’

Cameron looks at me sideways, as if to say ‘Really?’

‘Sorry. It’s just a thing people say.’

‘Not my people, honey.’

I’m pleased that he doesn’t end that sentence with “bun”.

We carry the body to the front door, and Cameron makes sure the road is empty. It’s pretty dark in my lane, thankfully, and quiet at this time of night. It’s about ten twenty now. He opens his boot and comes back to help me carry the rug-wrapped body to the car. I pop back to the house, grab my bag and house keys and join Cameron in the car. He’s right. It is a pit.

He turns the key and nothing happens. He turns it again. The engine doesn’t even attempt to turnover. The word apple pops unbidden into my head.

Cameron bangs his hands on the steering wheel. ‘Right, plan B. Your car. Let’s move the body.’

I’m reassured to hear that there’s a plan B. I’d been worried we didn’t even have a plan A. We jump out of the car, open the boot of mine, and relocate the body. Thankfully, my car starts right away and we set off to drive the twenty or so minutes to the vet's.

'I'm really sorry about your date,' I say to Cameron. 'You did a great job ironing your shirt. Richie would have been putty in your hands.'

Cameron sniggers. 'Something a bit harder than putty, I should hope.'

'Ew.'

We drive the rest of the way in silence, and are soon pulling up right outside the surgery. Cameron gets out and unlocks the front door, checks there's no one around and then beckons for me to get out and help carry Laura inside. We lug the rug through to the back room and Cameron goes back and locks the front door. We don't turn the light on in reception, and only switch on the back room one once the doors are closed. The fluorescent tubes flicker into life.

I'm standing around like a lobotomised zombie by now, while Cameron scurries around gathering supplies. Soon he has several of the large-size heavy-duty black sacks we use for big dogs, a bag of cable ties and a couple of the labels we attached to the bags for the crematorium people.

'Help me unroll her, Amy.'

I do as I'm told. I try not to look as Laura reappears.

'Okay, we're going to put the rug in one bag and Laura in another. Then we'll double-bag them and label them up as 'On Hold' with my initials. If anyone asks, she's a St. Bernard.'

We bundle the rug up and stuff it into a sack, sealing it with a cable tie, and then repeat the process. Next comes the body. If I thought stuffing a dead cat in a bag was hard, stuffing my dead best friend in one was nigh on impossible. I understood what Cameron had been on about now. It was just as well rigor mortis hadn't set in yet. We somehow folded her knees up to her chest, as if she was about to do a cannonball into the pool, and jiggled her into a sack, which got the same treatment as the rug one. Once frozen, they would just be amorphous blobs. Cameron labelled both sacks and we dragged them over to the chest freezer. Thankfully, it had been a slow week on the killing front, and there was plenty of room.

We quietly close up and leave the surgery, checking all around before getting in the car. I start the engine and we head back. We're about five minutes down the road when I suddenly remember something.

'Bugger! Her handbag! And coat! They're still at my house.'

'Okay, don't panic. I'll take them with me and dump them in the freezer tomorrow. I'll also make sure her mobile is switched off.'

We're both quiet for the next few miles, lost in our own thoughts.

'Cameron... Thank you,' I say, finally.

'What are friends for?' he says and he starts laughing like a maniac as he adds, 'Murdering, apparently.'

'I didn't murder her,' I say, pouting.

'Whatever,' he says, in that infuriating way young people do these days.

'She killed herself.'

'With joy.' He's still cackling. 'Take some comfort in that, Amy, she died with joy.'

'What are we going to do with the body? It can't stay in the freezer forever.'

'It'll be okay for a few days, while I think what to do. You've just got to carry on as normal, Ames, okay?'

'I'll try.' I was pretty sure normal was now a thing of the past. 'You can borrow my car for now. I won't be needing it for anything. Until you can get yours sorted, anyway.'

'Coolio.'

Cameron parks back at my house, pops in to grab Laura's abandoned coat and handbag, and then heads off. I blow him a kiss as he gets in the car and drives off. And then I find the gin.

*

I don't hear from Cameron for the next forty-eight hours. Finally, however, he phones me. 'I have a plan.'

'Is it a cunning one?' I ask.

'It's the best I can come up with,' he says. 'Fortune is favouring us, Lady Macbeth – the pet crematorium owners are away on holiday next week, and the practice has been left with a spare key in case of any problems on site. Sooo... I suggest we 'borrow' the key and cremate the St. Bernard ourselves.'

'Okay, first off, I am not Lady Macbeth. And second off, do you even know how to operate a cremator?'

'No, but how hard can it be? There's bound to be a YouTube tutorial we can watch. It's only like a big, extra hot oven, isn't it? Have you got any better ideas?'

I have to admit that I have no ideas, better or otherwise, and we arrange to do the deed the following Sunday night.

*

Sunday arrives and, after dark, Cameron and I retrieve the sacks from the freezer and drive to the pet crematorium.

Thankfully, it's in a pretty remote location. Cameron opens up the building and locates the light switch just inside the door. We quickly bundle the sacks inside and lock ourselves in.

The cremator itself reminds me of a giant kiln, a bit like the one we used for pottery at school. I wasn't expecting to have a nice vase at the end of this though. There's a panel with buttons and a digital display. Cameron studies the switches.

'Do you know what to do?' I ask in a loud whisper.

He shrugs. 'Load her up and set it to "extra crispy"?'

'She's not a pizza,' I hiss back.

'Yeah, but you've got to admit, it is a bit like a giant pizza oven.' He flicks a switch and something powers up, with lights coming on in the display. 'We have lift off!' he says jubilantly. 'Help me get the sacks in.'

I find a low flat-bed trolley and we load the sacks onto it and angle it up to the open door of the giant machine. We slide the sacks in and pull the trolley away so we can close the door. It actually looks a bit like a giant dark-green Aga.

Cameron is back at the buttons.

'What do you reckon? Twenty-five minutes at one eighty and then stick a skewer in?'

'It's not bloody *Bake Off*, Cameron. Will you just light it, or whatever you do!'

Whether through luck or judgement, Cameron starts the process. 'Do you want to say a few words? A prayer? Sing "Ode to Joy" maybe?'

'Not funny. How long will it take do you think?'

'From what I've read, probably a couple of hours.'

'Holy shit. You mean we've got to sit here for two hours?'

'Yep. And then we've got to rake out the ashes and pulverise what's left. That's what the machine over there is for,' he says, pointing to something that looks a bit like a washing machine. 'It'll grind up any remaining teeth and bone fragments. We'll have to fish out any bits of metal, like coins or keys too, and dispose of them separately.'

I shudder. 'You really have done your homework.'

'Teacher's pet, that's me. Now we just have to hope the smoke dissipates quickly and that nobody in the surrounding area spots it.'

I hadn't even thought about smoke. 'Isn't there, like, some giant extractor fan thing?'

'Hey, you're the one who said it's not *Bake Off*.'

'Right. Great.'

We sit there in silence for the next two hours. Cameron has found a swivel chair in an adjoining office, and I'm sitting on the floor leaning against the wall with my elbows on my legs and my head in my hands. I think we both nod off at various times.

Eventually the great green Aga beeps at us. I look over at Cameron. He gets up and goes over to investigate. It's too hot to rake the ashes out straight away, but eventually we manage to do so, and we sieve out the bits that haven't burned. Cameron takes the teeth and remaining bits of bone and throws them into the drum of the pulveriser.

'What do you reckon? Whites with a full spin?' he jokes.

I barely hear what's he's said. I'm staring at a pile of coins, keys and the metal case of Laura's compact mirror. The mirror had been part of a set I'd given her for her birthday a couple of years previously.

Cameron sets the drum spinning and comes over to put

his arm round me. 'Chin up, chicken,' he says. I turn into his arms and burst into tears, sobbing uncontrollably. Eventually the sobbing subsides and I sit back down on the floor to wait once more. Cameron bags up the metal items and sweeps the ashes into a bag.

'I'll scatter all this off the cliffs somewhere, Ames. Unless you want...'

I stop him. 'No, I don't want to. I can't.'

After what seems like an age, Cameron sweeps out the pulveriser and adds the bits to his bag of ashes. He checks around to make sure everything is how we found it, and we leave, locking the door behind us.

Cameron drops me home just before dawn. 'Hang tough, lady. Speak soon.'

I just smile tiredly at him, reaching over to hug him as best I can in the car. 'Thank you,' I say, looking into his eyes. Wearily, I climb from the car and drag myself indoors. I don't look back as Cameron drives away.

I close my front door and am hit by a wall of pain. This is a pain I know will never go away. I go into the downstairs toilet and then slowly mount the stairs, clutching a small glass bottle...

THE END

CHAPTER 23

Pizza

I'm relieved and gratified a short while later to receive positive reviews of my story from the others. It takes the edge off my anxiety and I now won't dread next Monday's discussion half as much. Besides, there's so much madness going on in the world right now, that one short story pales to an insignificant dot.

Social media feeds have been full of conspiracy theories about Covid-19 pretty much from the start, and the latest one is that 5G technology is to blame. As a result, there have been over twenty arson attacks on 5G masts. It beggars belief. And at least one of the cell towers provided connectivity to a hospital.

Thankfully, the scaremongering and conspiracy theories are counteracted by touching and heart-warming stories of selfless acts and kindness. No one will forget ninety-nine-year-old Captain Tom Moore's one hundred laps of his garden, and his subsequent promotion to honorary Colonel, a knighthood, and the thirty-three million pounds raised. Our own Tom remains seriously ill in hospital, and in our prayers every day.

By the time our next meeting of 'Write Time, Write Place' comes around on April 20, the death toll has exceeded twenty thousand and lockdown shows no sign of ending. At ten a.m. I join the Zoom meeting and smile as the others all click in. Jenny is wearing a bright, cat-covered, fabric mask.

'Morning, all,' I say. 'Nice mask, Jenny.'

'Thanks,' she says, her voice slightly muffled. 'I made it. I've decided to start making them for people. I'll post something on Facebook later with all the different fabrics I've got, and costs and stuff.'

'Brilliant,' I say. 'I'll definitely order a couple.'

'Me too,' Pippa says. 'I don't think it will be long before they become compulsory in places where you can't observe the two metre rule.'

'I think you're right,' Jenny agrees, removing her own mask. 'I reckon travelling on public transport will be first.'

'Well, I won't be wearing a mask,' Robert says. 'They're not going to stop a virus getting through, anyway. Waste of time.'

I resist telling him to fuck off as a picture of Hannibal Lecter flashes in my head. 'Well, it's my understanding that a face covering will greatly reduce the chance of infecting someone with the virus. It's the right thing to do, don't you think? To put others before yourself? You could be carrying the virus, but be asymptomatic. How would you feel if you gave the virus to someone who then got seriously ill, or even died?'

Robert shrugs. 'It's no worse than the flu. I'm not going to be dictated to about what I can do and where I can go, and if I should cover my face.'

'Try telling Tom and his wife that it's no worse than the flu,' Pippa says, her voice trembling with the anger we're all feeling at Robert's insensitivity.

Robert looks unrepentant. In my usual role as peacekeeper, I steer the conversation to safer ground, as much as I'd be happy to put off talking about my story. 'So… anyway… put me out of my misery… what did you think of my story?' I put my hands over my eyes and peep through my fingers.

Jenny grins and says, 'I laughed so much! It was classic Amy.'

'I must admit, it made me giggle too,' Pippa agrees. 'At times I didn't know whether to laugh or cry.'

John is quiet. I'm pretty sure that my story isn't really his cup of tea.

'I was laughing and dying all at once during some bits. Amy and Cameron are a great double act.' High praise from Robert.

'Thanks, guys. I'm glad you liked it. I enjoyed writing it in the end, and I'm really happy that the black humour worked.'

'It really did, and I loved how it reflected your pantser style too. Very clever. And it somehow blurred the lines between fiction and reality,' Jenny says. 'I still can't quite get my head around that.'

'I know exactly what you mean – I did my own head in with that. Do you see why I told you about my meeting with Cameron now?'

'Yep,' Jenny says. 'Certainly do. It was really clever. I liked it a lot.'

'I know it was a bit far-fetched,' I say.

'But that's the beauty of what we do, isn't it? As writers? We can go anywhere, say anything. Does it always have to be believable?' Pippa shrugs.

'I suppose you're right. I wasn't sure if you'd be able to suspend disbelief with my story?'

'I don't know about the others, but I did,' Jenny reassures me.

'Oh good!'

'Me too,' Pippa adds. 'And I did laugh at Amy and Cameron. I know killing someone's not supposed to be funny, but you somehow achieved an awful lot of comedy.'

'All the stuff about "joy" cracked me up. And "Chunkleberry Cakes"! I had never heard the term chunkleberry,' Jenny grins.

'I googled slang terms for chubby women and that was my favourite. You wouldn't believe how many I found.'

Pippa laughs. 'Cameron was hilarious and beautifully written. I'd love to meet the real one. He sounds like a scream.'

'He is. Maybe he should be Rosie and Patrick's vet?' I suggest, laughing.

'Yes! That would be funny. I can just imagine the interaction between Rosie and Cameron. Patrick wouldn't know what to make of him!' Jenny chuckles.

Pippa looks shy for a moment, as she invariably does when we talk about her writing. 'I have actually written another Rosie and Patrick story,' she says, looking almost apologetic.

'You have? Oh, that's brilliant! I can't wait to read it. I bet it's fab,' I say to a blushing Pippa.

'Yes! That's so great. You must send it to us,' Jenny adds.

Robert and John are both nodding their agreement.

'Well, my story's not quite finished, so maybe we could discuss Pippa's new story next week instead?' Robert suggests.

'Absolutely,' Jenny and I say in unison.

'Gosh! Are you sure? It doesn't really seem fair,' Pippa argues.

'Are you kidding?' I say. 'I loved your first story and it sounds as though you'd be doing a Robert a favour as he's not done killing people yet.'

'Well, okay, if you're all in agreement?' Pippa finally concedes.

Nods around the screen finalise the matter.

'Going back to your story, Amy. The other scene that really made me laugh was at the pet crematorium – all the pizza and bake off jokes.' This from Pippa, clearly eager to divert the subject away from herself.

Jenny laughs. 'Yeah, that was funny. And I liked how it

continued the chunkleberry cakes theme.'

John finally joins in. 'It was certainly very well-written, Amy. And I too could appreciate some of the black humour. Well done, indeed.'

'Thanks, John,' I say with a smile. 'Pretty different to your dark and brooding story, eh?'

'Yes, we are certainly very different writers, you and I, but that's the beauty of a group like ours, isn't it? We would probably never have crossed paths otherwise, or been exposed to each other's writing. I am very grateful for that.'

'What a lovely thing to say. I must admit, I'm very grateful Jenny and I discovered each other at the vet's that day.'

'Yep, otherwise none of these stories would exist, and it's been such a fun exercise,' Jenny agrees.

'It really has,' Pippa says. 'I feel that I'm starting to grow as a writer and have a teensy bit more confidence in my ability.'

'That's great, Pippa. You should have more self-belief – your stories are terrific,' I tell her. Fine words coming from me, the queen of low self-esteem.

The conversation drifts away from writing, and we spend the last part of the meeting talking about the Coronavirus in general, and Tom in particular, before wrapping it up for another week. As we're saying our goodbyes, I remind Pippa to email her story. I can't wait to read it.

CHAPTER 24

Pippa's second story

ROSIE AND PATRICK: RUBBISH!

'Come on, Patrick, it's almost eight.' I'm rewarded with a grunt. He doesn't look up from the copy of *The Probe* that has absorbed him for the past hour or more. I try again, a little louder. 'Patrick!' I get a 'Hm?' this time. It's progress of a sort. I'm not ready to give up. 'It's time to clap for the NHS.'

He looks up at me over his reading glasses. He looks pompous. 'Er... you go,' he says, returning immediately to his magazine.

'I will, but it would be nice if you came too – you know, to show your support for the frontline staff risking their lives every day.'

'It's not really my thing, Rosie.' He doesn't even bother to look up this time.

'For God's sake, it's not anybody's *thing* in normal circumstances, is it? But these are *not* normal circumstances, are they?'

No response.

I harrumph and head to the kitchen to collect the saucepan and wooden spoon I got out earlier. Checking the time, I see that it's seven fifty-eight; I slip on some shoes and head out the front. Some of the other residents of the Close are already standing on their doorsteps, ready to do their bit. I smile and wave my instruments at them.

Dead on eight o'clock, we all start to clap and bang our improvised drums enthusiastically. I'm not quite sure how long to go on banging, so I wait until all my neighbours have given up and gone in before I stop. Last woman standing, and all that. I hear a few fireworks going off in the distance, and tut to myself as I turn to go back in the house. I take off my shoes and head into the lounge.

'Imbeciles! Letting off fireworks! They're just supposed to clap,' I say crossly.

Nero, our ancient black Lab looks up at me, obviously in total agreement.

'Well, you didn't just clap, Rosie. You were out there banging away for England from what I could hear.'

'Chance would be a fine thing,' I mutter under my breath as thoughts of my sexless marriage intrude.

If Patrick has heard what I said, he doesn't let on, keeping his face buried behind the journal. The irony of its title is not lost on me either. Still, being married to a dentist has its advantages. Actually, scratch that: advantage. I can only think of the obvious one. An idle thought pops into my head – maybe I should cheat on him with another dentist. I don't mean have an affair; it would only be my teeth that got a jolly good seeing to.

I decide not to waste any more of my breath on trying to engage my husband in conversation. I obviously can't compete with whatever article on root canals or descaling he's so engrossed in. Heading into the kitchen, followed by my faithful hound, I return the pan and spoon to their rightful places and pour myself a large gin and tonic, adding tonic and limes to the shopping list on the fridge door. As an afterthought, I add gin. There are still two unopened bottles in the cupboard, but I'm not taking any chances in the current climate. I don't mind running out of loo rolls or hand wash, but the thought of no gin is truly terrifying.

I stay in the kitchen, sitting on one of the stools at the island unit so that poor old Nero doesn't have to get up again. My thoughts drift to our cancelled holiday – we should have been on Antigua this week. 'Not quite the island I was hoping for, boy,' I tell Nero, who looks at me adoringly. If only Patrick still looked at me like that, I think with a sigh and a big glug of gin. 'Still, at least it means you're not in kennels. Perhaps when this is all over, you and I will go away for a romantic break, Nero – strolling along a beach somewhere, enjoying a sunset or two. And all the steak you can eat. Heaven knows, you're more attentive than him,' I say, nodding in the direction of the lounge.

Nero wags his tail and I smile at him. If I'm completely honest, neither his legs nor his teeth would be up to walks on the beach and steak dinners. I dread the day, which can't be far off, when Nero wags his tail no more. At twelve, he's already been considered senior for five years. A home, a life, without him is too horrible to contemplate. I get off the stool and ease myself down onto the floor next to him, putting my arm across his neck. 'I do love you, old boy.' I lean back against the cupboard, knowing that getting up again will not be as easy as getting down here was. I sit quietly, just listening to Nero's breathing as he drifts off to sleep.

I don't know how much time passes like that before Patrick comes into the room. He pauses in the doorway and looks at me as if I'm some sort of alien. 'What on earth are you doing on the floor?' he asks, clearly bemused.

'Sitting.' I thought it was self-evident. I realise that I've well and truly seized up. Nero's muzzle is resting on my thigh and I become aware of a warm, damp patch underneath it. I can't even motivate myself to make a joke about it.

Patrick comes over and reaches out a hand. He knows full well that I won't be able to get up unaided. A part of me wants to refuse, childishly, stubbornly, but I reluctantly take his hand and let him pull me upright. I try to hang onto his hand, to pull him into a hug, but he pulls out of my grasp.

Sod you then, I think to myself.

Nero, sleep interrupted, struggles to his feet and plods off to his bed by the Aga, collapsing into it with a groan and falling asleep again almost immediately. I can feel tears pricking at the corners of my eyes and I turn away from Patrick. I don't want him to see that I'm upset. Or, worse still, to not even notice I'm upset.

I swallow the lump in my throat and shake away the tears that threaten. 'Every day with Nero is a bonus now – you do know that, don't you?' I tell Patrick. 'He's on borrowed time. I'm glad we couldn't go away. I would've hated leaving him.'

Patrick is at the counter pouring himself a whisky. 'He's had a jolly good innings though.'

'He's not a ruddy cricketer.' Patrick's words really weren't what I wanted to hear. I wanted some support. Understanding. Love. I wanted love from him. When Nero goes, there will be no affection left in the house. 'And anyway, that's not the point, I'll miss him terribly.'

Patrick doesn't respond to my concerns, instead he says,

'I'm going up to bed. To read,' he tags on as some sort of addendum not to be ignored.

Perish the thought it might be for any other reason. The tears are threatening again. I wonder if I've had too much gin? Or not enough gin? I decide it's the latter and busy myself with another drink. 'Night then,' I say as Patrick heads for the stairs.

'Goodnight.'

'Oh! Do you think you could do a food shop tomorrow?' I call out as an afterthought. 'We need gin.'

'Yup,' comes the reply, and I'm alone in the kitchen once again, except for a deeply sleeping dog. I take my drink over and slide onto the floor next to him. I'll worry about getting up later.

The next day dawns bright and sunny again – we've been blessed with some wonderful weather during lockdown. Who needs Antigua? I think, as I riffle through my wardrobe for something summery to wear; preferably something floaty, as waistbands are really not a good look on me anymore. Middle-aged spread and comfort eating are not conducive to a trim waist. As I stand in front of the full-length mirror in the bedroom, I can't help wondering if Patrick simply doesn't find me attractive any longer. I vow to do something about it.

Once the unsightly rolls are safely concealed under a suitably loose dress, I trot downstairs to the kitchen, throwing open windows as I go. The birdsong seems louder than ever since we've been in isolation. Probably my imagination. Perhaps we've simply become more aware of the stimuli around us, without all the distractions of our former busy lives.

I'm sending Patrick off to the supermarket today. He'll

grumble about it, as usual, but I know it does him good to get out of the house. I just have a couple more items to add to the list. He's sitting at the island unit with a bowl of cereal in front of him. He'll be wanting coffee. We've had the coffee machine for several years now and it's the simplest thing in the world to operate, but he refuses point blank to even attempt it.

'Sending any postcards?' I ask him, with a nod to the island I visited last night.

He frowns at me and looks confused.

'From the island,' I say, nodding again at the counter.

'Oh, I see. No.' He turns his attention back to the bowl of muesli.

And that's that, I think, as I head over to the coffee maker. While the coffee machine does its thing, I take down the shopping list and add the other bits I remembered. I'm sorely tempted to write 'Viagra Connect' on it, just to try and get a rise out of Patrick.

I take him his coffee and plonk the list down in front of him.

He glances at it. 'I thought I might go shopping this evening for a change. See if the queues are any better.'

'Oh! Well, I really need a couple of bits by seven o'clock – it's dustbin day. Could you possibly go this morning? Maybe next week you could go in the evening?'

He sighs. 'I suppose so.' He doesn't ask what I need, or why.

'Thank you.' I wish he was even a little bit interested in me, but I feel that he just puts up with me these days.

I have my coffee and some toast and marmalade, and potter about the kitchen while I wait for Patrick to get ready to go shopping. I make sure he has bags, the list and the hand sanitiser and wave him off at the front door. It's a relief to have the house to myself, even just for an hour or so. I suppose we're both feeling the effects of being confined together pretty much 24/7 these last six weeks. I will be glad when Patrick goes back to work at his private dental practice. I head back upstairs – I need to plan my outfit for tonight. I'm going out. And it's black tie. It doesn't take long to decide what I'm going to wear as my choice is limited to what I can still actually fit in to. I remind myself of my vow to lose some pounds before I change dentists.

My mobile rings after about an hour. The display shows: The Dentist. I'll have to change that, I think to myself. 'Yes, Patrick?' I can hear his exasperation before he even speaks.

'A tiara? What on earth, Rosie? Two things: Why do you want a ruddy tiara? And where do you honestly expect me to find one in Tesco's? In the tea aisle?'

'Well, to wear, obviously. And you need to look in childrenswear, in the girls' section. There'll be a stand with jewellery and hair bits and bobs. Look for pink, sparkly things. I'm sure there'll be a tiara there. Just pick the most sparkly one.'

'Oh, for God's sake,' he grumbles, hanging up the phone. Before I have a chance to remind him to use the hand sanitiser.

Patrick arrives home about forty-five minutes later, looking grumpier than ever. I should've put Viagra on the list after all – might've perked him up. He carries the shopping into the kitchen and puts it huffily on the floor for me to unpack.

'Any joy?' I ask, meaning did he get a tiara.

'Rosie, there is very little joy in going to the supermarket at the best of times. This, as you know, is most certainly not the best of times.'

'You sound like a Dickens' character,' I tell him, trying to lighten the mood. 'It was the best of times, it was the worst of times...' I pronounce solemnly.

He doesn't so much as lift the corners of his mouth. Not even one corner. My husband seems to have had a complete sense of humour failure. I wonder what I can do to cheer him up? Perhaps talking to the boys tonight will lift his flagging spirits, where I have apparently failed so spectacularly of late. Our two grown-up sons will be joining us for a family chat on the Zoom meeting app which I have managed to load onto the laptop.

I start to rummage through the shopping bags, and delightedly pull out a child's tiara. It's the cheapest, tackiest thing imaginable and will probably only last a couple of uses, but it's exactly what I wanted. 'You found one! Thank you.' I go over and give him a kiss on the cheek. He doesn't react, but at least he doesn't pull away or wipe his face afterwards. I think, had either of those things happened, my last shred of self-esteem would have disintegrated.

'I told the woman on the till it was for my granddaughter,' Patrick informs me as I attempt to put the thing on my head. 'God alone knows what you want the damn thing for,' he says scornfully, shaking his head.

'Well, you'll find out later! And we're having a conference-video-call-meeting-thing with the boys tonight at eight,' I inform him.

'Fine,' he says, turning to leave the room. 'I'll be in my office if you want me.'

I don't reply, but I think sadly that, yes, I do want you, Patrick, but do you want me? I turn my attention back to unpacking the shopping, suddenly remembering that I haven't reminded Patrick to wash his hands. I pop my head in the study and tell him, hoping that he realises I'm not nagging. I care.

After dinner that evening, I head upstairs to get changed. Patrick is sitting in the lounge catching up on the day's news. I spend time doing my hair and make-up, as if I really am going to some lavish ball or gala, and slip into a long evening dress in a deep purple. Well, if I'm being honest here, it was less of a slip and more of a wriggle and a tug. I pull on long, pink satin gloves, left over from a fancy dress party and squeeze my feet into a pair of heels, grumbling at how much they hurt. Proper shoes haven't really been a necessity during lockdown, let alone pointy high heel ones. Still, I console myself, it's not for long, and if it puts a smile on a few faces, then it will have been worth it. I'd like to think that one of the faces would be Patrick's, but I have to accept that is highly unlikely. I think all I can expect from him is a look of disbelief and perhaps a 'Good God, woman, what are you doing?' shake of the head.

Finally, I place the tiara on my head. I will admit that I'm a little nervous as I stand in front of the mirror to check my appearance. I'm determined, however, and totter downstairs, ignoring the objections from my feet. I stop at the bottom of the stairs, feeling strangely shy about my husband of a thousand years seeing me. All dressed up and nowhere to go, he'll think. Well, I do have somewhere to go, actually, Patrick, I think mutinously, and I take a deep breath before walking into the lounge. I pull myself up tall, to every last little bit of my five feet six inches, and pull my stomach in. Admittedly, this makes it difficult to speak. Patrick doesn't look up as I enter the room.

'Patrick,' I say, hoping to get his attention. 'I need you to video me putting the bins out.'

That does the trick, and he looks up at me, taking in all five feet six inches of me. Probably, actually, a little bit more thanks to the tiara. He raises his eyebrows. 'You need me to what? What on earth are you up to now, Rosie?' he asks, sounding as though he's addressing a toddler who's just crayoned all over the walls. He doesn't mention my outfit or say I look nice.

'I need you to video me putting the bins out,' I repeat, ignoring the sudden urge I have to throw myself on the floor and have a tantrum.

'I assume you're joking?' he says.

'Do I look like I'm joking,' I retort, gesturing to my outfit with both hands. 'I didn't get dressed up for nothing.'

'Er... no; so you're telling me you got dressed up like that to put the bins out? I'm afraid to ask. And I'd really rather not be involved in whatever hare-brained thing you're up to, Rosie.'

'Oh, come on, please, Patrick. I can't do this without you. You only need to film me – you don't have to be in it. No one will know. Please.'

He mutters something under his breath, but gets up from his chair. 'Christ, woman, what on earth next? Let's get this over with then.'

'Thank you! Hang on, I'll just get Nero ready. We have to go out at seven o'clock.'

Patrick just shakes his head, and stands in the hall waiting for me. He watches in disgust as I wrap a pink feather boa around Nero's neck to match the one already draped around my own.

'Come on then, let's go!' I say. 'Come on, Nero. Here, Patrick, use my phone. It's all set up ready.'

Patrick reaches out and takes the phone. 'The things I have to do for you.'

I bite my tongue and don't reply, opening the front door and calling Nero after me.

'So, if you can film me wheeling the bin down to the end of the drive, and then take some normal photos of me too. Once I've stopped walking. And make sure you get Nero in some too,' I instruct Patrick, who's looking decidedly embarrassed, and glancing round at the neighbouring properties. I pull the wheelie bin round from the side of the house. Patrick's face is a picture when he sees that it too is wearing a feather boa. I only wish I'd got a picture of him. 'Right. Ready? Go!'

I totter off down the drive, pulling the bin behind me, and calling Nero to follow. When we reach the street, I turn to Patrick and pose for the camera. 'Now come closer and take some photos, Patrick. And film the Close.'

Patrick has a face like thunder, but he does as instructed and comes down the drive, grumbling all the way. His expression turns to one of incredulity when he sees two of our neighbours also glammed-up and posing with their wheelie bins. 'What in God's name is going on? Has everyone gone completely mad?'

I turn back to the road and wave to neighbours, Judy and Sheila, and tell Patrick to film a panorama of us all. He does, before handing me my phone and stalking back to the house, muttering about 'Mad bloody middle-aged women.'

Sheila, Judy and I have a brief socially distant giggle together, and then part company, assuring each other that we'll get the photos and videos uploaded straight away.

I pat my thigh to let Nero know we're on the move again. 'Come on, boy. Well done. Want a biscuit? I know I do.' We head back indoors and through to the kitchen, where Nero's star performance is rewarded with a couple of gravy bones. Before I sit down at the laptop on the kitchen worktop, I slip my poor feet out of the killer heels, groaning with relief. Checking the videos and photos that Patrick took, I select the ones I want and load them onto the appropriate Facebook groups.

There's still a bit of time to kill before we speak to the boys, and I wonder whether I should go and change out of my evening gown ensemble. I decide, sod it, and instead busy myself making drinks and putting some nibbles in bowls. Perhaps gin and cashews will cheer Patrick up. I put everything on a tray and take it to the lounge, where Patrick has retaken his seat in front of the television.

'Nuts,' I say, putting the bowl down on the side table next to him.

'You certainly are. And getting more so by the day if that performance was anything to go by,' he mutters.

I stick my tongue out at him. And again consider a tantrum. 'Well, if it's good enough for Amanda Holden...' I say instead. Amanda had appeared looking extremely glamorous in a shimmering pink number with her wheelie bin in tow. I've yet to break it to Patrick that she also mowed the lawn in a wedding dress. I settle myself on the sofa and Nero makes himself comfortable at my feet.

'You'll have to come and sit next to me at eight o'clock,' I tell Patrick. 'When we Zoom with the boys. Patrick? Did you hear what I said?'

'Yes, I heard you.'

I turn my attention to my G&T.

Just before eight, I retrieve the laptop from the kitchen. Patrick joins me on the sofa and we join the meeting with our sons, Will and Greg. It's so wonderful to see their handsome faces grinning back at me on the screen.

'Hello, you two. We miss you!' I say.

'Hi, Mum, Dad,' they chorus. Nero looks up on hearing their voices and wags his tail.

'You look nice, Mum? What's the occasion? We haven't missed an anniversary or something, have we?' Will says.

'Dustbin day!' I tell them.

'Oh! Brilliant! Well done!' Greg says. 'Have you posted pics on Facebook?'

Patrick interrupts. 'Er... am I the only one here who thinks your mother has gone completely off her trolley? You're acting as though her behaviour is quite normal. I had to film her posing with the dustbin like Debbie McGee doing her glamorous assistant thing for Paul Daniels.'

The boys laugh. 'It is normal at the moment, Dad. This is the new normal. Get with the programme!' Greg tells him.

Patrick looks surprised at the boys' reactions. 'So, getting all dressed up in her glad rags to put the bins out is now considered normal? Really?'

'Completely normal. There are a few groups on Facebook now with thousands of members, all posting pics and vids like the ones Mum's done,' Will continues to enlighten his father.

'I've posted in two groups,' I tell them. '"Put the Bins Out in Your Ballgown" and "Getting Dressed Up to Take the Bins

Out". Sheila and Judy did it too.'

'Fantastic, Mum, just great!' Will says. Their reactions have really lifted my spirits. I raise my glass in a toast.

'Cheers, boys! It really is so lovely to see you both.'

Cries of cheers echo into the room. Even Patrick raises his glass, but he still looks too stunned to speak.

Greg pipes up again. 'Have you seen the video where several guys from the same street took their bins out and did "The Time Warp"? It was hilarious. They'd dressed up in the outfits and everything.'

'Yes, I did see that. It was wonderful. I shared it in the WhatsApp group for the Close. Thought maybe we could do something similar.' I'd done no such thing, but it was worth it to see all the colour drain out of Patrick's face.

Will and Greg have cottoned on to the wind-up and play along.

'How about "All the Single Ladies" Mum? You, Sheila and Judy could rock that in your leotards.'

Patrick's mouth has fallen open.

'Or "All About That Bass"? Plenty of booty shaking in that one.'

I know the Meghan Trainor song Greg means. 'Ooh, I like the sound of that. We're certainly not "stick figure... Barbie Dolls". Although I don't think your father would agree that I still have "all the right junk in all the right places".'

'Aw! I'm sure that's not true, Mum. Is it, Dad?' Will says.

My heart does a little wobbly thing. (A bit premature for the dance routine.) I'm holding my breath waiting for Patrick to reply.

Patrick, however, still looks stunned and has apparently

lost the power of speech. I look at my lap for a moment. I don't want my face to give my emotions away, and for the boys to see me upset. Deep breath, back in the room, Rosie.

'So, anyway, what have you two been up to?'

The next twenty minutes or so pass happily enough as the boys share their news, which, of course, isn't much as they're both working from home during lockdown. Greg lives with his girlfriend, Abbey, and he tells us about some of the Tik Tok challenges they've been doing.

'You and Dad should do some of them. Some of the couples' challenges are hilarious,' he says.

Patrick regains the ability to speak. 'What fresh hell is this, Greg? Your mother really doesn't need any encouragement, thank you very much.'

'Come on, Dad, don't be such a stick in the mud.'

'At no time, ever, will I be doing something that involves putting any part of my anatomy in a Pringles tube.'

The boys and I are in stitches at this point, my sadness temporarily forgotten. I've already made a mental note to put Pringles on the next shopping list, just to see if Patrick actually buys them.

'How's Nero doing?' Will asks, when we finally stop laughing.

I pan the laptop round so they can see him snoring on the floor at my feet. 'He's marvellous considering his age. Very slow now, but still bright and happy. He joined in with putting the bins out, in his feather boa, bless him.'

'Tell him to hang on in there until lockdown ends and we can come and see him, Mum.'

'I will, don't you worry,' I say, although it's probably not a promise I can keep.

My sadness returns when we have to say our goodbyes, but the boys both have other online events to get to. It's been so lovely having allies in the camp, even just for a little while. Patrick gets up and relocates to his armchair. I stay put on the sofa, reluctant to disturb Nero, and log onto Facebook to look at all the other pictures and videos of people putting their bins out. And I can't resist a quick peek at Olly Murs' naughty Pringles can prank.

After a while, I log out and close down my laptop, get up and prepare the house and myself for sleep. Patrick says he's staying up for a while. Before I head upstairs, I pop to the kitchen and write 'Pringles' on the shopping list, chuckling to myself as I head upstairs to bed. Alone.

THE END

CHAPTER 25

Pringles

I'm still chuckling to myself at Pippa's story as I settle down to continue with my own writing. After looking out the window for half an hour, I give up, jog upstairs to change into my bikini and head into the garden to sunbathe. I tell myself it's thinking time when the plot cooks. And I cook, because let's be honest, brown fat looks better than white fat.

As I lie there on the sun lounger, trying to focus on the book, I think to myself how much easier it would be if I was a plotter rather than a pantser. It must surely be easier if you know where you're going. For me, the writing process is like getting behind the wheel of a car (left-hand drive) with only a vague destination in mind, a schizophrenic sat. nav., frequent diversions and the occasional sinkhole. I would eventually arrive at a completely different destination, dazed and confused, but ultimately euphoric. I suppose at least it allowed me to be flexible, and the story organic. The best writing days are when the car drives itself and you're simply along for the ride. Those days are pretty amazing, when you suddenly realise hours have passed in a flash and you haven't even stopped for coffee. Today was not one of those days.

As had become the norm, I took my reference points from the Thursday night clap, and Monday's writing group. The rest of the week was just a murky lockdown blur of nothingness. I couldn't imagine life going back to normal now. I was still desperate to hug someone and had eyed the postman up more than once. I think he'd spotted me – he certainly didn't hang around after shoving my letters through the box. I wondered if perhaps brushing my hair would help? On my legs.

I was feeling slightly mad by the time the next Zoom meeting came around. Thankfully, I'd found my hairbrush. I resisted the urge to pan the camera down to show the others my legs, which I'd actually bothered to shave (mainly in case hairy legs tanned slower).

As five faces popped up on my screen, I thought about Tom. I'd give anything for him to be here, talking nineteen to the dozen and sending us to sleep. I chuckled to myself at the thought of muting him. Dear old Tom. Please get well.

'Hey, hey!' I said to the others, forcing a smile.

A chorus of greetings rang out. I couldn't help but notice that Pippa looked a little anxious. I knew she was nervous about discussing her story: a writer's confidence grows at about the same rate a glacier moves. Eager to make her feel more at ease, I dived straight in.

'Oh my goodness, Pippa, I absolutely loved your story.' It wasn't flannel. I really did. 'Honestly, you paint the characters so vividly. I really can picture Rosie and Patrick.'

Pippa blushed and smiled shyly. 'Oh Gosh! Really, Amy? Thank you. I find it terribly nerve-wracking when you're reading my work.'

I pull a face. 'I'd like to tell you that goes away, but it doesn't, not really. Not completely. I suppose it does get a bit easier with time and a bit of positive reinforcement from readers. But one bad review still affects me more than a hundred glowing ones. I can totally understand why some people don't read reviews of their work. It's hard not to take bad ones to heart.'

'Yes, I can believe that,' Pippa says. 'It is a lovely feeling when someone enjoys what you've written though.'

I nod. 'Yep, it's the best. Doesn't stop the insecurity though, not in me anyway.'

I'm conscious of the fact that the others aren't joining in with the conversation, so I throw open the floor as it were. Just don't look. I haven't hoovered. 'What did everyone else think of Pippa's story?'

'I loved it too,' Jenny says. 'One day I can imagine there being a sitcom about Rosie and Patrick.'

'Yep,' I agree. 'I think we said that after your first story too. Even more so now. You managed to get humour out of a shopping list, again. I could just see Patrick trawling round Tesco's, muttering under his breath, looking for a child's tiara.'

'I thoroughly enjoyed many aspects of your story, Pippa.' This from John, formal as ever. 'I will confess to not really understanding some of it, however. I had to search on the internet for Tik Tok. I fear I am of the wrong generation to appreciate such a thing.'

I stifle a giggle. 'I think we're all a bit old for Tik Tok really, John, but it's definitely become a big deal during lockdown as people seek out new ways of entertaining themselves and the rest of the world. I loved how Rosie embraced everything about lockdown.'

'Yeah, dragging Patrick with her, kicking and screaming,' Jenny smiles. 'You do a brilliant job of portraying their relationship; a clever mix of funny and sad.'

'I couldn't agree more. It's hilarious at times, but actually very poignant too. There's an underlying sadness to Rosie's jollity,' I nod.

'Personally, I think Rosie should bump Patrick off. Using a dentist's drill.' Robert finally joins in the conversation. I kind of wish he hadn't bothered.

I raise my eyebrows. 'She'd be killing the source of the stories then though, wouldn't she?'

Robert just shrugs. 'It's what I would do.'

I bite back a retort, and turn the discussion round again. 'So, John, when you googled Tik Tok, did you actually look at any of the videos?'

John clears his throat. 'I... um... yes...' (John rarely 'ums' and I think I know what's coming.) 'I did... I... er...'

I jump in to put him out of his misery. 'You saw the Olly Murs' one with the Pringles tube, didn't you?' I'm trying not to laugh at John's discomfort.

'Yes, Amy, indeed I did. I fail to understand why he put his... er... appendage in the tube or what was amusing when his partner put her hand in expecting to find a crisp.'

Jenny, Pippa and I are all giggling like schoolgirls now.

'Well, John, you're not the only one who didn't appreciate it. There was a big ole hoo-ha over it at the time with fans reportedly disgusted by the prank. Olly was forced to apologise publicly,' Pippa says through her giggles.

'I think it was a bit of an over-reaction to be honest,' Jenny says. 'It was just a harmless prank with his girlfriend. It's not like he flashed a stranger or something.'

'I tend to agree with you, Jenny,' I say. 'It was just a bit of fun. I totally get why it might not be to everyone's taste though.'

'Yeah, I mean not everyone likes sour cream and chive.'

Jenny can't help herself.

'Should have gone with prawn *cock*tail,' I can't help myself either, and we three get the giggles again.

Only John's stern expression stops us. He's shaking his head. 'I'm afraid I simply do not understand the younger generation, or have any appreciation of what they find amusing. Now, tell me, Pippa, are people honestly getting dressed up in ball gowns to put their dustbins out?' John was clearly keen to move onto a cleaner topic.

Pippa nodded. 'Yes, John, they really are. I think everyone's so bored and going a little stir crazy, so they're looking for ways to amuse themselves and maybe spread a bit of cheer too.'

'That's the beauty of the internet and social media at a time like this,' Jenny says.

'Yep, there's a lot of good stuff out there at the moment, in amongst the scare-mongering, fake news, conspiracy theories and absolute bollocks,' I agree. I realise I've sworn. Honestly, it's like being on a Zoom call with a disapproving parent. 'Oops, sorry.' I almost add 'Dad'.

Robert's remained silent throughout this exchange. I'd almost forgotten he was there. I glance across the screen at him. I hate the fact that you can't really look at the person you're addressing in these virtual meetings. I find my eyes wandering all over the place, which probably makes me look a bit demented. As that's how I'm feeling most of the time these days, I don't s'pose it matters. I look at him now and a shudder goes through me. It feels like he knows my eyes are on him.

We chat for a while longer about Pippa's story, encouraging her to keep writing about Rosie and Patrick. Conversation then, naturally, turns to Tom and the pandemic. As the meeting is nearing its end, I reluctantly bring the focus on to Robert's story which we should be discussing next week. At this point, I'm actually glad he's only in my dining room virtually.

'So, Robert, is your story finished and ready for us to read?'

He grins and my stomach turns over. 'Yes, it is and I'm excited for you all to read it.'

Nobody speaks. So I do.

'Um... yes, we're all excited to read it.'

There are some nods and mutters of 'yes' around the screen.

'I think you're gonna love it. I might make a few tweaks, but essentially the stories are finished.'

'Oh... stories... plural... wow... great,' I say, trying to sound enthusiastic.

'Oh yes! I told you I wanted my killer to be a big deal. You'll soon see why I needed the extra time to write. And I think you'll agree when you've read about his exploits, that he's worthy of his name. I'm not saying any more though – I don't want to spoil the surprise.'

'Great, well, I guess that wraps things up today then. Robert, don't forget to email your story... sorry... stories to us after the meeting. Take care everyone, and see you all in a week.'

I can feel a sense of relief to match my own from Pippa, Jenny and John as we call out our goodbyes and leave the meeting.

Robert's email pings up a couple of minutes later. I think about saving it until tonight, but I have a feeling his stories will not make for relaxing bedtime reading.

CHAPTER 26
Robert's stories

THE EXHIBITIONIST

It doesn't matter who I kill. I don't have some vengeful plot, or idealistic notion of ridding the world of a bad apple. I could kill anyone. It's not about the victim. It's about the art. I want the fruits of my labour to be admired, talked about, remembered for years to come. I want to be celebrated. A celebrity.

I suppose sometimes I might select a victim for aesthetic reasons. There are occasions when a corpse needs to be beautiful. They should thank me for making them famous, immortal. I'm doing them a favour, ending their pitifully small lives and transforming them into something spectacular. Was it Leonardo da Vinci who said, 'A beautiful body perishes, but a work of art dies not'?

I stumbled upon the source of potential candidates completely by accident. My mother was telling me she'd just been diagnosed with Type 2 diabetes and that she had to attend a diabetic clinic for regular check-ups. It was perfect: a walking catalogue of human subjects who came complete with their own murder weapon. Insulin. I wanted clean, unmarked corpses. No messy stabbing or slicing; no bruising or battering. (Unless it was absolutely necessary, of course.) Just a nice, clean death. They made me think of oven-ready, self-basting turkeys, all ready to go. Minimum fuss, minimum effort.

It was the easiest thing in the world to check out the local diabetic clinics in Folkestone online. I drove round and checked out the three local ones, deciding which would be most suited to staking out, and stalking patients. I decided on the Royal Victoria Hospital as it was a bigger set up and had a car park right out front. The other venues I looked at would have been tricky to lurk around and observe the comings and goings. I did a bit of reading up about the difference between Type 1 and Type 2 diabetes, and knew that it was the Type 1s who were most likely to be on insulin to treat the condition. Many of the Type 2s controlled the disease with tablets, so they were no use to me.

So, first I needed a way of identifying which patients used insulin. I figured I might be able to follow a potential victim to find out if they collected insulin from a chemist. I realised it could be time-consuming and frustrating, but I'm a patient man, and quite happy to put in some legwork for a good end result.

*

I had some leave owing from the engineering firm I worked at, so I booked two weeks off. I planned to use the time to select my subjects and do some research. This was going to be a big project and I had to get every detail right. After all, isn't that where the devil is?

On the morning of the first diabetic clinic, I arrived at the hospital about thirty minutes before the start. I needed to suss out how I was going to identify the patients – after all, people could be going into the hospital for any number of reasons. A quick look around and I struck gold: the diabetic clinic was serviced by its own door. The devil was on my side. I moved my car to a better vantage point and sat back to wait.

I didn't have to wait long as the first patient arrived at about eight forty-five for a nine o'clock start. It was a woman. I assumed she wasn't staff because she wasn't in uniform. Could've been a receptionist, I suppose. It didn't matter anyway, because she wasn't what I was looking for. A few minutes later, a scruffy, red-faced man arrived and I started to pay close attention. His clothes looked like they hadn't been washed in months, his hair was lank and un-styled, and he walked with a slight limp. I wouldn't be at all surprised to find his feet had started to go gangrenous. I know what you're thinking... he doesn't sound 'beautiful' or worthy of my artistry, but you'd be wrong. He definitely fitted the bill for one of my planned art installations. I couldn't believe my luck. I decided right away that I would follow him when he left.

I saw two more people arrive before my subject came out again. I earmarked one as a definite maybe, snapping a picture of her on my phone as she went in. I would give her serious thought and hope to see her at the next clinic. One at a time though, that was the only way I could do this. You can't rush great art.

I started up the car as soon as the scruffy man reappeared, but he headed out of the car park on foot, so I switched it off again, and followed on foot. He was carrying a white bag that he hadn't had before and I wondered if he had just picked up supplies of insulin. He limped slowly across the road and headed into Radnor Park where he sat down on a bench and proceeded to remove items from the bag. Minutes later I saw him inject himself into his abdomen. Bingo. Victim number one in the bag. Just like that. All I needed to do was find out where he lived. I was pretty sure by now that he was living on the streets. I had to hope he didn't have a place in a shelter. To be honest, he looked as though he'd been living on the streets for years. I'd be doing him a favour – putting him out of his misery. After all, it was only a matter of time before he lost his feet. Better to die with his boots on.

I walked across the park and sat down on another bench. He didn't seem to be in any hurry to leave. I wondered idly what his name was. He had quite a swarthy look about him and I thought perhaps he had some Mediterranean blood. I decided to call him by the Greek name, Ambrus, meaning immortal. I'd probably never know his real name, unless I introduced myself to him, and I wasn't planning to be his friend, but his saviour. Any introduction was going to involve me sticking a needle in him.

After a short while, Ambrus got up and headed out of the park. I followed at a safe distance, wondering where he was going to lead me next. I had all day and was actually enjoying tracking my first victim. My appetite was well and truly whetted and the muse was upon me. I couldn't wait to get started.

He was heading in the direction of the town centre and I thought perhaps he had a shop doorway with his name on it; a sleeping bag and some cardboard and not much else. His next stop, however, was a café on the High Street. I stopped on the opposite side of the road and watched, wondering if he'd go in. I couldn't imagine he was the sort of customer they'd welcome. He did go in and I saw the man behind the counter hand him a drink in one of those cardboard take-out cups. I couldn't see for sure, but I didn't think any money changed hands. I wondered if the café had one of those bleeding heart pay-it-forward-with-a-coffee schemes. A 'hanging' coffee I think it's called, where some worthy liberal pays for a stranger's drink when they buy their own. Bunch of saps.

Ambrus waved as he exited the café, and turned down the hill in the direction of the Old High Street, sipping on his drink as he walked. I followed him down the steep cobbled street. He didn't stop to look in the shop windows. No point I suppose. No bleeding liberals handing out free stuff from their arty-farty shops here. I guess Ambrus wouldn't have much use for anything they sold here anyway. He did, however, make one stop before we reached the main drag again: another café. Only this time he was handed something wrapped in paper. Ambrus clearly had a good thing going in the town. He finished his drink, chucking the empty cup into a bin as he passed it, and unwrapped his breakfast – maybe a bacon roll or something I surmised. My own stomach growled at me, reminding me that I hadn't had breakfast myself. Well, I bet no one was going to give me anything for free. It doesn't pay to work for a living. Anyway, I couldn't stop now as Ambrus was still on the move and heading across the road in the direction of the harbour. Well, it was a pretty nice day to go to the beach.

Ambrus led me through the arches and towards Sunny Sands. There still weren't that many people out and about at this time of day. It was a Monday in June, so schools hadn't broken up yet and holidaymakers hadn't hit the town. The tide was out and I could see one of Richard Woods' six holiday home art installations marooned in the harbour, surrounded by small boats and dozens of screaming seagulls. I have a begrudging admiration for the cottages that are dotted around the town, part of the Triennial artworks from 2017. They are a series of one-third size colourful cottages, plopped down in unlikely places, including the harbour, the beach, a car park and on top of a brick structure.

I admire the art, but not so much the worthy sentiment behind it. Apparently, it's a comment on the housing crisis and the social implications of multiple home ownership. And suggesting that no site is too small or unlikely or inconvenient to its neighbours, for a holiday home. Whatever.

If you don't know Folkestone, maybe I should enlighten you a little. It's developed quite a reputation as a creative town, and has art installations scattered throughout, largely due to the triennial projects. Even Antony Gormley got in on the act one year with two of his cast-iron figures. Some of the art is great. Some is pretentious crap. I plan to enhance it.

Back to the meandering Ambrus. He's carried on past the harbour and taken the path above the beach. Just as I think we're running out of path, he climbs over the fence onto the grassy bank behind. I can't stop without looking suspicious, so I walk past the spot, glancing round as I pass to see a small two-man tent squashed into the space behind the wall. Home sweet home. They say location is everything. Well, Ambrus had picked a pretty nice spot for his summer home, and he'd also made things pretty convenient for me. The plan for exhibit number one was coming together nicely.

*

I turned back the way we'd come, and started the trek to my car. Checking my watch, I was surprised to see it was only ten twenty. If I hurried, I might be able to get back to the clinic before it finished, and potentially get a head start on a second victim. No, not victim, subject. Victim implied something bad was going to happen to them.

I walked briskly and made it back to the hospital in about twenty minutes. I got back into my car and immediately checked the glovebox for something to eat. I found a Snickers Bar I'd stashed there and ate it gratefully. It was soft, but edible. Next time I did this I'd bring supplies. I thought about popping into the main hospital and grabbing a drink from a vending machine, but the diabetic clinic would be finishing soon and I didn't want to risk missing a possible candidate.

Swallowing the last of the chocolate, I sat back in my seat and watched the door. After a few minutes, a besuited but overweight man came out. I cocked my head to one side as I assessed him. Type 1 or Type 2, I wondered. He did fit the requirements for something I had in mind for July. As I watched him climb behind the wheel of a dark grey Audi, I decided he was worth further consideration, and a minute later I was following him out of the car park. He drove west to the 'nice' side of town. No homeless people sleeping in tents here. He pulled onto the drive of a large detached house with manicured gardens and a double garage, and I carried on driving. Food for thought, but I still needed to find out if he used insulin, and he wasn't going to be as accessible as Ambrus. His house was probably alarmed, for starters.

With nothing more to be done, I headed home, thinking about the excellent progress I'd made in just one morning. As I was locking the car and walking to my front door, I had a sudden thought: did subject number two need his own insulin? Did he even need to be a diabetic? Once I'd killed Ambrus I could take all his insulin and syringes and use them. On anyone I wanted. This realisation would make life a whole lot easier. I'd got my mind so set on killing diabetics with their own insulin that I hadn't really thought it through. As much as I liked my original concept, it was fraught with difficulties.

I made myself an early lunch and sat down to think about Ambrus. He was like a gift from the Gods, and a perfect place to start. I had to give serious consideration to the logistics now though. The first thing I needed to do was check out the tide times. I needed low tide after dark. A quick search on the internet told me what I needed to know. Next, I set about making a label. Every art exhibit needs a label. I laminated this one as it needed to be waterproof. I was pretty sure I had everything else I would need in my workshop, except for some chains and padlocks. As I planned the details, my excitement grew. I couldn't wait for people to see my first piece, to witness their reactions, and begin my journey to celebrity.

*

The following morning, I set off early for a quick shopping trip to a big DIY store in a neighbouring town. I was wearing a baseball cap over my dark blonde hair, and keeping my head down as I pushed my trolley up and down the aisles, looking for the items I knew I needed, and some I thought might come in handy. I picked out some sturdy lengths of chain and substantial padlocks, and a big roll of chicken wire. Then I went in search of sacks of builder's sand, quick drying cement and builder's glue. I added a big roll of heavy duty polythene as an afterthought and headed for the checkout. My head was buzzing with my plans for Ambrus, and thinking ahead to my next project.

The woman on the checkout tried to engage me in conversation. I just told her I had a big project for my garden and left it at that. I didn't want her to remember me. I paid with cash and headed out to my car. As I loaded my purchases into the boot, I wondered to myself if it was time to trade my estate in for a van. I made a mental note to look into it tomorrow. I had to put the roll of chicken wire and the polythene on the back seat to get everything in. I drove home with the windows down, taking my cap off and running my fingers through my hair as the wind whipped into the car. I was feeling more alive than I could remember feeling for a long time. This was my destiny, and I was hyped to be a step closer to fulfilling it. I turned up the radio as 'Highway to Hell' came on and drummed out the beat on the steering wheel, singing along to the chorus at the top of my voice. Life was good.

I arrived back at my house about thirty minutes later and drove round to the parking space at the back of the property, behind the garage and workshop. I'd always liked my privacy and when the dilapidated cottage had come on the market a few years back I'd snapped it up, gradually doing all the renovations myself. I was handy with a power tool and a plastering trowel, skills which were soon going to come in very useful. I unloaded everything into the garage – I didn't often put the car in there, instead using it for storage. I needed space in the workshop for my practice pieces.

After I'd closed and locked the garage, I headed up the garden and let myself in through the back door. Chucking my keys on the side, I set about making myself a pot of coffee. I poured myself a mug and took it outside, sitting on the bench outside the back door and putting my feet up on the low wall that edged the lawn. The June sun was hot even now at ten thirty in the morning. It would've been nice to work in the sun, but I couldn't risk prying eyes seeing what I was doing. I didn't want to spoil the surprise, the unveiling. It would be a general admission event, not one of those poncey exclusive invitation-only events, but even so, I didn't want anyone getting a sneak preview.

I finished my coffee and popped back into the kitchen, pouring myself a second and grabbing my keys again, before heading back up the garden. Unlocking the garage, I hoisted up the roll of polythene and took it into the workshop, where I cut a length that covered the middle of the floor. Next I retrieved a bag of sand, the chicken wire, cement and glue, moving them into the workshop. It was time to experiment. I then spent a pretty enjoyable couple of hours experimenting with different mixes of sand, cement, water and glue until I hit on the perfect one; it gave me time to work and shape, but dried to the colour of beach sand. I then made a shape out of chicken wire to see if I could use it as a mould. Success. Project number two was taking shape beautifully. I still needed to decide what that shape would be.

While I worked I was thinking about my plans for Ambrus, and had a flash of inspiration. It would make things a bit more complicated, and messier, but I decided it would be worth it. My pulse quickened as I thought about the impact of the piece. This was a better high than drugs or alcohol, and I could almost feel the rush I knew I would experience when my exhibition opened. My impatience was growing, but I had to wait for the right low tide. I made a mental note of what I needed to take with me, and added a note on my phone to buy some super strength cans of lager when I did my usual food shop.

Happy with my progress, I cleared up the mess I'd made in the workshop, locked up and went back into the house. While the idea was fresh in my mind, I printed off and laminated a second exhibit label, grinning to myself all the while.

The only other thing I wanted to tick off my list today was get a less, shall we say, documented, car. I'd spotted a group of travellers camped up a few miles away, with several vehicles on site. I was pretty sure I could persuade them to part company with one for cash, no papers exchanged, no questions asked.

An hour or so later, I was home again, driving a slightly shabby, silver Ford Focus Estate. I reckoned it would look alright with a little bit of TLC. I'd been right that the pikeys would be happy to part with one of their cars. They'd only agreed to a straight swap for my own car though. I'd gritted my teeth and agreed. They weren't stupid – they knew there must be something dodgy going on and took full advantage of having the upper hand. I hated them getting one over on me, but needs must as the devil drives. I reported my car stolen.

A couple of days later, the police called to say my car had been found burnt out at a travellers' site. The whole place had been razed to the ground. Funny that.

*

Finally, after an impatient wait, the twenty ninth of June arrived, bringing with it the perfect tide. The weather was dry, the air still and the moon nowhere near full. As I packed the car with everything I'd need in a giant rucksack, along with two folding deckchairs, the adrenaline started to kick in. It was a heady mix of excitement and anticipation. Was I scared? I suppose I should have been, so much could go wrong, but I felt invincible. This was my destiny, so why would anything go wrong? The Gods were on my side. They'd brought me Ambrus after all. I wondered idly as I got into the car what his real name was. Maybe I'd ask him.

It was gone eleven p.m. when I arrived at the beach. I was fully aware that this might be a false start: there was a lot of stuff outside of my control. I was gambling on Ambrus being there, being alone and being amenable to my suggestions. Deep down though, I believed everything would go to plan. It had been ordained. The signs were good and there was no one about.

I walked briskly along the path, just close enough to see a lone figure sitting on the bench next to the spot I knew Ambrus had his tent. I knew instinctively it was him, even without good light or approaching too near. The adrenaline kicked up another level. I retraced my steps back to the small harbour, where I could just make out the shapes of boats and the outline of the pale pink 'holiday home' which was to be the stage of this piece. I tramped across the still-damp sand and gratefully dumped the rucksack off my back onto the ground behind the cottage, unpacking everything I'd be needing, before setting up the two deckchairs in front of the miniature bungalow. I broke off a couple of cans of the strong lager I'd brought and headed back up to the concrete path above the beach.

I knew this part of the plan was another huge gamble, but

it would make everything else so much easier if I could pull it off. Anyway, I liked a flutter, I thought as my pounding heart reminded me. I felt a satisfied smile cross my face as I neared Ambrus.

'Hey, mind if I sit?' I asked as I neared him.

The homeless man looked up at me, focusing slowly before he shrugged and gestured to the seat next to him. 'Sure. It's a free country,' he said, his words slurring a little. I got the distinct impression he'd beaten me to it with the booze. Hopefully that would make him more pliable.

'Beautiful night,' I said. 'You live around here?'

Again he gestured, tipping his head back towards the tent and pointing a shaky hand.

'You picked a good spot.'

'Until I get moved on again when the place starts to fill up.'

'That's a shame. Enjoy it while it lasts then I guess,' I say. 'I'm Robert, by the way. What's your name?'

'Peter. My name's Peter. Nobody's asked me my name in a long time. Nice to meet you, Robert.'

'Good to meet you too, Peter.' I didn't tell him he'd always be Ambrus to me. I pulled a can of beer from each of my coat pockets and held one out to him. 'Join me?'

He looked surprised, but nodded his thanks and took the proffered drink, pulling the tab and downing most of it in one.

'Take a walk with me, Peter. I've got more beers down in the harbour.'

If he was surprised, he didn't show it this time, but simply shrugged and shuffled to his feet. I couldn't believe how smoothly it was all going.

'You got a blanket or something I can borrow, man? Gettin'

kinda chilly now. I guess you don't feel the cold so much. Maybe in your tent?' I ask him.

'Sure – inside,' he nodded to the tent again. 'Don't mind the smell.'

I climbed easily over the fence and stuck my head and arms into the small tent, recoiling as the stale odours hit me. Holding my breath, I rummaged around in what looked like a pile of rags until I found the white bag I recognised from the hospital. I wrapped it in a smelly old blanket and backed out of the tent.

We took a slow walk to the harbour and in a few minutes, Peter was seated in one of the deck chairs in front of the bungalow, swigging from another can. He didn't seem at all phased by the strangeness of the situation, which I took as a sign that it was all meant to be.

'So, Peter, where are you from originally? You don't look as though you're from round here.'

He looks sad for a moment. 'I am of Greek descent. Roma. A gypsy, you would say. My name is Petros, but here people prefer Peter. They treat me a little better as Peter.'

I nodded. I was right about him being Greek.

'I'm sorry if my kinsmen have treated you badly, Petros,' I tell him. 'We're not all bad.'

He nods, and his head stays lowered for a few moments, as if he's fighting sleep. 'I know, I know. There are good people here too, kind people.'

I thought about the places in the town he'd got free food and drink from.

He downed the remainder of the can.

'Let me get you another one. I need to take a piss, too.' I got up from my deckchair and went round the back of the bungalow, out of sight. I switched on the head torch I'd brought with me and quickly located a vial of insulin and a syringe from Peter's bag. I didn't know how much insulin would be fatal, so I just drew up a full syringe. Grabbing another can I returned to Peter. His head had dropped again, and it looked as though he'd fallen asleep. I put the beer down on the sand and waited a minute or two. He didn't stir. Shit, he was making this too easy for me. I shrugged as I stuck the needle in his chest and pressed the plunger. His body jerked upright as the needle penetrated his skin. He looked round at me, confused and unsure what had happened.

'You okay, Petros?' I asked calmly. 'I think you were dreaming, mate.'

'I don't feel so good,' he said. 'I can't remember if I took my insulin. I'm a diabetic, you see.' Even as he spoke, I could see he was already fading.

'Don't worry, my friend,' I reassured him. 'I'll sort it. Nothing to worry about. Just wait here.' I got up and started to head away from him, as if I was going to the tent, but instead I doubled back and quietly retrieved the insulin and syringe from the sand. 'Here you go,' I said, returning to Peter. He muttered something unintelligible and flapped his hand in the vicinity of his abdomen. 'You want me to inject you? In your stomach?' I asked, only too happy to oblige. I lifted his filthy jumper and injected more insulin. He sort of grunted and then went quiet. I sat back in my chair and waited. It wasn't many minutes before all I could hear was silence. I checked for a pulse, but found none.

'Right, Peter, me old mucker. Time for the next bit. You'll

like this.' I grab all my stuff from behind the bungalow, slipping on a disposable coverall over my clothes and putting the head torch on. I was going to need more light for this bit.

I laid Peter's now lifeless body on the sand. Taking up the Stanley knife I'd brought, I cut through his stinking jumper before sinking the blade into his chest and cutting down towards his belly. The blood and stench almost overpowered me and I wished I'd worn a mask. I looked away and took a breath. Next, I started up my cordless oscillating saw and cut through his sternum. I almost retched, but I held my breath and forced myself to continue. I just needed to get this done.

Once I'd cracked his chest, I made short work of removing his heart. It wasn't surgical, but that didn't matter. I slipped the bloody organ into a plastic zip lock bag and put it in the rucksack. The blood was now running in rivulets, finding its way to the channels in the sand and making for the sea. The mess didn't matter – the sea would be cleaning up after me, before the big reveal after the next high tide.

I chained his chair to the pontoon on which the bungalow rested, securing it with one of the padlocks. I gave it a really good tug; it wasn't going anywhere anytime soon. Manhandling Peter's corpse back into the deckchair took some doing, but finally he was seated once more. I then chained him securely to the chair. He had to survive high tide coming in over him. Last, but not least, I nailed the exhibit label on the door of the bungalow. It read:

AMBRUS: Just Visiting: Home is Where the Heart is.

I hoped that people would appreciate the social commentary bollocks and the irony of a homeless man being found at one of the holiday homes.

There wasn't time to stop and admire my handiwork. I quickly stripped off the overalls, turning them inside out as I did so, packed everything up into the rucksack and headed out of the harbour and back to my car which was parked on a quiet residential street a few minutes' walk away. I just had one more stop to make before I could call it a night. And what a night.

I drove to the location of one of the other holiday homes, situated next to a path up on the cliffs above the town. I parked as close as possible and then walked the short distance to the little yellow bungalow. Removing Peter's manky old blanket from my rucksack, I nailed it over the front door. It was a ratty old patchwork thing of reds and purples, and looked pretty pitiful against the smart yellow paintwork. Then I nailed the plastic bag containing his heart on the blanket. Finally, I took my second laminated exhibit label and secured it above the piece. This one simply read:

PICNIC: Home is Where the Art is.

I stood back to admire my creation, wondering which would be discovered first. More than satisfied, I jogged back to the car and headed home.

*

I was asleep the second my head hit the pillow and slept the sleep of the dead that night. I'd thought that it would take me hours to come down from the night's excitement and for the adrenaline buzz to dissipate. My dreams were filled with the rush of the incoming tide, and the thought of Peter's body waiting there to be discovered.

I woke the next morning feeling refreshed. I lay in bed

looking at the ceiling and recalling the events of the night. Grabbing my mobile from the bedside table, I scrolled through the photos I'd religiously taken at all stages of the kill and display. A little while later, I put on a Within Temptation CD really loud and made coffee which I took out into the garden. I'd showered after I'd got home the night before and removed all traces of Peter. I still needed to deal with the stuff from the rucksack, but before I did that, I wanted to head to the harbour to see what was happening. Maybe it was a bad idea – the police would probably want to question anyone in the vicinity. But that old cliché about returning to the scene of your crime is a cliché for a reason. The draw was irresistible.

I finished my coffee, quickly changed my clothes for running gear, laced up my trainers and set off. I hated jogging, but with the destination in mind, it wasn't so bad. I could feel the adrenaline rising again, and the anticipation building at the prospect of the first unveiling; my first exhibition piece on view to the public. I hoped there would be screaming. I really hoped I hadn't missed it all. As I ran, I thought about the police investigation which would begin; the crime scene photographs on a white board, spreading my art, disseminating it. They'd think it was a one off crime. But not for long. Exhibit number two wouldn't be far behind. I wondered if they'd give me a name once they realised this was only the beginning? I decided I'd like to be called the Exhibitionist. Maybe the press would be there. They might come up with a name for me too. I couldn't wait to see my work emblazoned across the media.

I barely noticed the next couple of miles and before I knew it, I was approaching the harbour. I ran under the arch and slowed my pace until I could just see ahead to the harbour itself. I checked my watch: I knew the tide would still be going out, but Peter should, in theory, be visible to some degree. If they wanted to get to him, they'd have to take a boat out, or wait for the tide to go out further and the water to be shallow enough to wade through. I stood with my hands on my hips, as if I was just a jogger getting his breath back.

I desperately wanted to go closer, to witness the spectacle unfold, to revel in the glory, but my rational side told me I couldn't risk it. I couldn't get caught now, not when there was still so much to do. I decided instead to head back the way I came and watch from the road above the beach, so I took the shortcut up a steep flight of steps and jogged up the road until I found the best vantage point. It wasn't ideal as I was quite a way from the action, but it was better than nothing.

Looking down on the scene, I could now make out a small boat by the bungalow. It didn't look like a police craft – more like a private fishing boat. I couldn't tell who was on board, but I could see a couple of police cars parked by the harbour wall. I suspected that the police had hitched a ride with a local to check things out. They were probably hoping it would prove to be a dummy, a prank by the local kids. So, it hadn't turned into the full police and media circus yet. I was here for the big reveal. I sat down on the grassy bank and made myself comfortable to watch events unfold. I wished I'd brought a drink with me. Must get better at this planning lark, I thought to myself. It was like the hospital car park all over again.

It didn't take long for them to realise that this was indeed for real, and the boat to make back to the harbour wall. I saw a uniformed copper get into one of the cars, presumably to get on the radio to request SOCO and the coroner and whoever else needed to be present at a suspicious death. I chuckled as I thought that they didn't yet know the half of it. I wondered if they'd discovered the other Ambrus exhibit on the cliff path, and how quickly they'd join the dots and make the association. It wasn't rocket science.

In a matter of about ten minutes, more cars and vans arrived on the scene, and the business of sealing the crime scene began. They couldn't erect the usual tent over the body, so they did the next best thing and put a screen up along the harbour wall, blocking the view across the harbour to the bungalow. They cleared all the bystanders back behind the tape which now stretched across the entrance to the harbour. Spoilsports.

I assumed that they would have to examine the body in situ, although, of course, the sea would very kindly have washed away any useful forensic evidence. The next people to arrive were the press and my heart rate quickened as I thought about my impending fame. Maybe I should find a way of communicating my desired name to them? Perhaps I should sign my next piece? Otherwise I ran the risk of being called something naff or objectionable, like – I don't know – the Art Attacker, or the Folkestone Filleter. Ugh. Yes, I would definitely have to sign the next installation. Or maybe I could send an anonymous note to the press? They loved that sort of thing. I'd have to give it some thought.

It was getting pretty boring sitting on the bank now. The screen blocked off my view of the body, and it was going to be some time before low tide allowed a forensic team to reach the body. I decided to jog up to the second site and see what was happening there. It took about ten minutes to get to the entrance of the cliff path, and I jogged slowly towards the bungalow. As soon as it came into sight, I saw that the police were already there and a white tent had been erected over the bungalow. There were a handful of people in white coveralls, similar to the one I'd been wearing when I cut out Peter's heart last night, milling about. I guess they'd already determined it was a human heart. I wondered if they knew about the body in the harbour.

With nothing to be gained by hanging around, I decided to head home. I'd probably be better off watching events unfold on the local news channel.

Arriving home about twenty minutes later, I kicked off my trainers, grabbed a bottle of beer from the fridge and settled down in front of the TV. I didn't have to wait long before a news reporter gave a brief commentary from the scene at the harbour. They didn't have details, only that a man's body had been discovered in suspicious circumstances. I was guessing that even when the police did speak to the press, they would hold back some details. They'd be kept between them and me. It was just the very start of our relationship.

*

I was pretty sure there'd be no real news about Ambrus for some time, so I headed up to my workshop to make a start on my next piece. I wasn't relying on anyone else's art for this one, although it would be displayed in a gallery of sorts.

The first thing I needed to do was make a frame out of chicken wire. Thankfully, I'm pretty handy with a pair of pliers and wire cutters. Not just a result of a misspent youth, but years of constructing engineering design models. The frame was going to be the easy part. The rest of the construction was going to test my artistic skills to the limit. Most of my drawing was of the technical variety. I wasn't too stressed though – if this design didn't work out, I would simply go to plan B.

I decided to make the model in sections and spent some tedious time cutting suitable lengths of chicken wire from the roll. It was painstakingly slow, but it gave me time to think, and plan. I was trying to decide who should be the centrepiece of this installation. I couldn't decide whether to try and be clever with my choice, or just go with easy. I reprimanded myself. I shouldn't be getting lazy already. The truth was, I was impatient to build my collection, but that was no excuse for sloppiness. Everything had to be right.

In an attempt to distract my brain for a while, I put some music on my phone and focused my full attention on the job at hand. I started on the legs. I had a piece of paper on the floor next to me with various measurements scrawled on it: leg length, arm length, waist, chest, etc. They were my measurements. I also had a full length photo of myself and an assortment of headshots from front and sides.

I knew the frame didn't have to be perfect, and I could only realistically estimate the lengths of each piece I made, knowing I had to allow for the layers which would go over it. But, my technical eye was pretty reliable. My hands were sore by the time I'd made the legs, arms and torso. I probably should've worn gloves, but I'd decided they'd be too restrictive. Besides, I kind of liked the discomfort; it felt like I was making a memory with my hands.

I took my time over the hands and feet, leaving the head

until last. By the time I joined the pieces together, my back was aching and I had blisters on my hands. I checked to make sure I hadn't broken the skin anywhere. Didn't want any pesky DNA left on the chicken wire. I wasn't worried about finger-prints as there wasn't a big enough surface to leave even a partial. I was pretty satisfied though and excited to start the next phase. First I needed to eat. I sauntered back up to the house, rubbing my sore hands as I went, and smiling to myself. I switched the radio on in the kitchen, selecting the local station and hoping to catch a news bulletin. I washed my hands and collected up the necessary items to make a sandwich, which I ate in the kitchen. The news came on and I stopped chewing to listen, but they just said the same as before: the body of an unidentified male was found in the harbour. Checking the kitchen clock, I knew the tide would be well out now and they would be examining the scene at the bungalow. It gave me a real buzz thinking about it. All those people talking about me, marvelling at me and what I'd done. It made me even more eager to crack on with the next one, and I swallowed the last of the sandwich, grabbed a bottle of water and headed back to my workshop.

The first thing I needed to do was make up the mix of builder's sand, cement and glue, so I filled a bucket of water from the outside tap and followed the ratios I'd perfected previously. I didn't make up too much in one go as it was obviously time-sensitive. I started to apply the first batch to the wire frame, starting at the feet and working my way up. I used a plasterer's trowel, having experimented with a few different tools. This first layer was simply a base and, as such, just needed to echo the shape of the mould. The detail would all be added to the final, top, layer.

It was time-consuming work, but after about ninety minutes, I had a satisfactory first layer and my model was starting to look more human. It actually made me think of one of Gormley's iron men, and triggered thoughts of another possible piece. I didn't want to be accused of copying though; it was important to me to be original, so I dismissed the idea.

I sat in the garden while I waited for the sand to dry. I closed my eyes and let my thoughts drift. The warmth of the sun was soporific and I must've nodded off. When I opened my eyes again, I grabbed onto to the tail of a dream and realised I had the body of another idea. I would let it develop in my brain as I continued working on my sculpture.

The rest of the day was spent in the workshop. First, I scored the now almost six-foot sandy body and applied a layer of glue to ensure the next application adhered properly. I'd decided that actually two layers would be sufficient – the first one was pretty thick. So, I worked on the second layer in much smaller sections, allowing myself time to apply detail as I went. I had a selection of tools to hand, from brushes, to trowels, to a bradawl for the finer work.

It wasn't an easy process. I had to work quite fast, using a medium with which I had little experience, and artistic skills above my paygrade. I started at the feet, figuring I'd need all the practice I could get before tackling the head. It took ages, but I finally had a pair of recognisable converse trainers. The legs were a lot easier: my trademark Levi's didn't need too much detail, just the stitching, fly and pocket details. The bradawl came into its own for these. As I scratched out the finer details, I used a soft brush to dust away the sand. With the legs done, I started to feel better about things, and tackled the torso with more enthusiasm.

I dressed my sandman in a T-shirt, which was easy enough to mould. I had toyed back and forth over the slogan to put on the T. I'd eventually settled on the words 'Bring me a dream'. My reckless side had wanted to use an example of one of my own shirts: The Killers, or Engineers are all Torque, but I knew that was a stupid risk. I initialled 'T.E.' on the shirt. I still hadn't decided how I would make my moniker known to the world, but I couldn't resist a little nod to it here.

I took a much-needed break before tackling the hands and head, refuelling and stretching my aching back. I was pretty happy with my progress and feeling a bit more confident about sculpting the sand.

The hands didn't turn out too bad – far from perfect, but I didn't think people would be looking too closely at them anyway. I'd learnt another little trick as I was working on the knuckles and nails: using a spray bottle of water to give me a slightly longer window of time in which to work.

Last, but definitely not least, was the head. I wasn't looking forward to tackling this, but I faced the challenge head on. I spent a few minutes studying the photographs I'd taken of my head, and then dived in. After a few false starts, when I actually removed the entire new layer, I began to see something starting to resemble my face shape. I had thought about putting sunglasses on it, but that wouldn't have fitted with the theme I had firmly in my brain. I just hoped my efforts would be appreciated by my audience. Doubtless it would be too subtle for some, but I reckoned plod would get there.

Finally happy with Mr. Sandman's face, I made a start

on the hair, which proved to be bloody difficult. I seriously thought about giving him a shaved head, but I persevered and ended up with a tousled mop that looked a bit like my own.

I stood up, stretched my back and stepped away to look at the sculpture. I was happy. It definitely bore a resemblance to me. Obviously, without colour and definition and detail, it also looked like a million other guys, but it was good enough. I cleared up my tools and left him to dry. I just had one more prop to prepare, but I couldn't progress that just yet. Not until I had more photographs.

*

With more time to kill before the Sandman could enter proceedings, I turned my attention back to the town's art installations. I was looking for inspiration, pieces I felt I could enhance. Or maybe ruin. I wasn't sure yet. Sometimes, the pretentious bollocks behind the pieces made me want to vomit. Oftentimes I could appreciate the physical art though. Other times I thought it was crap. Scrolling through the art from the 2017 Triennial, which was entitled 'double edge', I came across a 'sound work'. It was called 'Halfway to Heaven' and it had just given me a cracking idea.

'Halfway to Heaven' was an interactive sound installation that had been set up in an old Baptist burial ground in the town. The main speaker was one of those flower holders you see on graves, the ones with the holes in the top, and sometimes an inscription on. This one had 'we gather together' engraved on it. It linked in to several other similar speakers around the graveyard, with stuff like 'close your eyes and see' and 'where you are is where I'll be' inscribed. I reckoned I could improve it with very little effort, and set about planning.

I have to say I really loved the planning process. After the initial idea came to me, it was amazing how it took on a life of its own, one thought triggering another like a row of dominoes falling. I'd listened to a snippet of the actual sound recording – not the whole seventeen minutes, life was too short for that – and it was a churchy choral thing. Not my cup of tea at all.

That night, I paid a visit to the graveyard after dark. It hadn't been in use since the 1850s – something to do with Baptists not being allowed to be buried on Anglican ground prior to that. It crossed my mind that it might not be a suitable location for one of my pieces, with it being disused, but you could always count on a dog walker or a jogger to stumble across a body, couldn't you?

I found the main speaker, next to the war memorial, just as it had been in the photos online. To anyone passing who didn't know otherwise, it looked just like any other flower holder. I carefully removed it from the site, slipped it in my rucksack and headed home to examine it.

Unscrewing the baseplate, I was relieved to find the workings were pretty simple. I had enough technical ability to replace the music track with one of my own. I wasn't a hundred percent sure how it linked to the other speakers in the graveyard, but I wasn't really that bothered. I only needed one. If my chosen song blasted out through more speakers, that would just be an added bonus. I couldn't find a way of increasing the volume, but I was happy enough. I added a motion sensor that I removed from a garden light, and tested it over and again to make sure it worked. As soon as I activated the sensor, the strains of AC/DC's 'Highway to Hell' started up. No longer halfway to heaven, but all the way to the pit of hell. I just had to hope nobody missed the speaker for now. They'd probably just think it was vandals anyway. I s'pose they'd be right, in a way. Can't make an omelette with breaking eggs. Can't create art without cracking a skull or two.

I had an image in my head of what my victim and centrepiece should look like. I just had to find her. Summer in a seaside town is pretty much perfect hunting season. Teenaged girls were out in their droves, scantily dressed and just asking to attract the wrong sort of attention. They made it too easy for me. I spent a few happy hours mooching round the town and down to the beach, observing groups of girls who looked to be about fourteen or fifteen. I had a very specific type in mind. I saw a couple of possibles, but they weren't quite right. I wanted a girl who still had a look of innocence about her; none of those ridiculous eyebrows and heavy make-up that girls seem to favour nowadays.

I was sitting on a low wall opposite an ice cream parlour when I saw her. She came out with a couple of other girls, all holding ice cream cones, and looking happy to be alive. I focused all my attention on her, sizing her up, picturing her in my piece. That brought other pictures to mind and I felt myself getting aroused. I forced the pictures out of my head and looked her up and down. I guessed her to be fourteen; slim, limbs tanned to a golden-brown, with the palest blonde hair which hung straight and almost to her waist. And her face... she had the face of an angel. She was perfect.

I spent much of the day following the three girls, and eventually followed the angelic one home. Although I was pretty sure I'd be able to find them again – teenagers are pretty predictable during the summer holidays – it didn't hurt to know where she lived. I also wanted to check out possible places I could take her unawares. I groaned at the thought. The images were back. I'd never thought I was interested in young girls before now. My appetites were changing. I hadn't decided whether or not I was going to give in to them and eat my fill. I'd heard the other two girls call her Daisy. It suited her. It smacked of innocence and simplicity. And it made me want to deflower her even more.

I wanted to get my hands on some chloroform. I'd watched a couple of YouTube videos on how to make it, and it wasn't that hard with the right equipment. You only needed bleach and acetone for the reaction, but it looked like a pain in the arse, even for a science nerd like me. In the end, I'd ordered some online and had it sent to my work address. I was still on annual leave, but I could let myself in after hours and collect it. I knew there was a bit of a risk attached, but hopefully it wouldn't raise suspicion as the firm could easily be using it for lawful reasons, and not knocking out a young girl, with a view to killing her. And possibly worse.

I had a couple of other bits I needed and checked out the local charity shops until I found what I was looking for. I bought a reel of white cotton in one of the pound shops. A few easy alterations – although I'd never done more than sew on a button before now – and I'd have my angel's final outfit. The thought of undressing her sent my thoughts into overdrive again.

I just needed opportunity now. And for the bunch of Oxeye Daisies I'd picked from a field near my house to die. I hadn't put them in water when I'd brought them in, and they were withering nicely. I thought they'd be a nice touch in the flower vase speaker. It's all about the detail. I wanted people to appreciate the amount of thought and effort that went into my exhibits. I wasn't doing all this just for my own enjoyment, after all. Although, I will admit, I was getting a hell of a kick out of it all.

I found Daisy and the same two friends easily enough. She was never on her own though that second day, with all three girls going back to her house after they left the town. I wasn't too worried though. I knew I'd have my chance and anyway, the anticipation was a huge turn on. The next day I found Daisy and her friends at the beach. I found a spot on the bank above the beach where I could watch them from. I could see that all traces of Ambrus's tent had been removed from further down the path. Ah! Ambrus! You'll always be my first. You will always have that honour. Always have my heart. I couldn't help laughing at my own joke as I thought of the homeless man's heart hanging in a bag from the holiday home. I still had the rest of his insulin and needles stashed at home.

The girls stayed on the beach most of the day, only leaving to get drinks and snacks and use the public toilets. It was fine. There were worse ways to spend a summer's day. Finally, they all got up to leave at just gone four thirty. As I watched them pack up their stuff, I hoped they were going home separately, guessing that they probably had to go home for dinner. As I watched Daisy standing on the sand, lithe and untouched in her white bikini, I felt the familiar arousal she brought about in me. I still couldn't quite work out if it was purely sexual, or more the thought of completing my next exhibit.

I trailed after the three girls as they headed away from the beach and the adrenaline kicked in when they stopped, shared goodbye hugs and set off in different directions. Assuming Daisy was going home, I jogged to my car and drove back to the route she'd be walking. I had removed the small bottle of chloroform from my pocket and poured some onto a cloth, trying not to breathe in as I did so. I could see Daisy up ahead.

I had an idea. It was riskier in some ways, but definitely worth a shot. If it failed, I would just go back to my original plan. I rolled down the passenger window, which was on the side Daisy was walking, and slowed down as I approached her.

'Hi! Daisy!' I leaned towards the window and called out. There was no response from her initially, and I realised she had earbuds in. I looked around to make sure there was no one else around and pulled the car to a stop a few feet in front of her. I waved my hand and called out again. 'Daisy! Hello!' She stopped and leaned down to look in the car. 'Hi, it is Daisy isn't it?'

I could see her mind working as she weighed me up. I had on my best smile, and I knew her name. How bad could I be? 'Um... hello,' she said, trying to place me, wondering if she should know me.

I took another gamble. 'I'm Nick. I work with your Dad.' I don't know why I used a fake name and had no idea if she even had a dad. She looked kind of relieved and smiled at me. I felt a lurch in my groin. 'Jump in, I'll give you a lift.' I could see her hesitating; going over in her head all the things she'd been told about not getting into a car with a stranger. But it was a hot afternoon and she was probably tired and anyway, I wasn't a stranger, was I? Not really. I knew her dad.

She shrugged and opened the passenger door. I couldn't

believe my luck. It was just too easy. She half turned and reached back for her seatbelt. As she turned back to the front, I shoved the chloroform-soaked cloth over her mouth and nose, using my free arm to hold her back against the seat as she struggled briefly.

I glanced round again, but there was still no one in sight, and quickly pulled away from the kerb. Daisy lolled against the passenger door, but she was out for the count. I didn't know how long the effects of the chloroform would last though, and I was anxious to get her home and secured.

Arriving home about ten minutes later, I parked behind the cottage and carried Daisy into the workshop. I'd left a chair ready for her, and I secured her arms and legs to it with cable ties. I gagged her too. Didn't want her coming round and alerting the neighbours. I rummaged in her bag and took out her mobile phone, switching it off. I wasn't taking any chances on her parents having one of those tracking apps on it. I was still undecided about what to do next. It was most unlike me. I was usually so decisive and in control. Daisy had an unfortunate effect on me. I could've just injected her with a huge dose of insulin while she was still unconscious, but there was a big part of me that wanted to see her open her eyes and see me. Really see me. And know that I could do whatever I wanted with her. To her.

I locked up the workshop and went into the house. I needed a bit of distance from the sight of her, and time to think.

Three beers later and I was feeling a little more relaxed about the situation. I knew that I had to take back control. I would not allow myself to be seduced by her. I was stronger than that. I had all the power. Figuring she may well have come around by this time, I went back to the workshop. I could hear faint moans coming from inside.

I opened the door and a pair of terrified blue eyes looked up at me. She was struggling against the ties and I could see livid marks on her wrists and ankles. She'd obviously been struggling for some time. I didn't want her ruining her pure beauty anymore, so I went in and grabbed both her arms.

'Keep still!' I instructed her, my eyes boring into hers. I could almost smell the fear on her. Then I realised what the smell was. She'd wet herself. I turned my nose up in disgust, and any animal attraction I'd felt for her evaporated. I just needed to finish the job. I reached for the syringe I'd left prepared on the work bench and plunged the needle into her flesh. I felt her body flinch and heard a gasp of pain through the gag. And then I just sat back in another chair and watched. Watched as she gradually began to slip away. Her eyes drooped and she slumped into the seat. Then, suddenly, her body started to shake and she went into some kind of seizure. It seemed to go on for ages, and then, it stopped as quickly as it had started and she was gone. The blue eyes were lifeless and her body limp. The convulsions had made even more of a mess as she jerked against the cable ties, and I was pretty pissed off. I soon shrugged it off, figuring maybe it would add to the drama of the finished piece after all.

I cut the ties and lowered her body onto the polythene I'd spread on the floor. I wrinkled my nose at the smell of her and tried not to breathe too deeply. I cut off her clothes – she still had on the white bikini underneath her dress. I wondered about leaving it on her. Making up my mind, I cut through the straps and sides and removed it, tossing it in the heap of clothes and her bag to be burned later.

Once she was naked, I marked out a pattern on her chest. It was an inverted pentagram circumscribed by a circle: a sign of Satan. I then proceeded to prick the skin with a needle, over and over again, following the pattern I'd drawn. It seemed to take ages – I had no experiencing of tattooing. Eventually, I figured I'd pierced the skin sufficiently and I proceeded to apply black ink all around the shape, before wiping off the excess. It was pretty crude as tattoos go, but it was good enough. I then added my signature 'TE', which was pretty quick and easy after the main tattoo. My angel was well and truly defaced. The devil, old Nick, had claimed her. She was lucky he hadn't done more to her.

Next, I dressed her in the flowing white creation I'd made from the charity shop purchases, and she began to look angelic again. I'd even made her a pair of wings, which I secured to her back after rolling her over awkwardly. As I was discovering, corpses are not the easiest things to deal with.

When I was satisfied with my work, I left Daisy safely locked in the shed, and went back indoors to take a long hot shower. All I had to do now was wait until after dark to transport Daisy to her final resting place.

After I'd showered I made myself something to eat, realising I hadn't eaten all day. I stuck some rubbish on the TV to pass the time, and printed off the exhibit label which I laminated. Rain wasn't forecast, but I wasn't taking any chances. It was England in the summertime, after all.

I set an alarm on my phone for one thirty a.m. in case I fell asleep, but I was too wired for that. I shrugged into a dark jacket and left out the back door. In a few minutes, with Daisy safely in the boot, I set off for the graveyard.

As ever, luck was on my side and I saw no one on the drive to or in the vicinity of the cemetery. I parked as close as possible and got out of the car, put my rucksack on my back, scooped Daisy up and walked the short distance up the hill. As slight as she was, Daisy was still heavy enough that I was out of breath when I reached the war memorial. I lay her on the path in front of the stone cross, straightening her limbs and arranging her hair blonde hair in a halo around her face. I pegged the exhibition label next to her. It read: 'Pushing up the Daisies', and this time I signed it The Exhibitionist. I placed the speaker on the ground and filled the flower holes with the dead daisies. The trickiest bit was switching on the motion sensor without activating it. The last thing I needed was the dulcet tones of Bon Scott blasting out 'Highway to Hell' at two a.m.

Silence prevailed and I walked quickly and quietly back to my car. Fingers crossed, whoever discovered the body would trigger the sensor and the AC/DC song would play. Part of me wanted to rig up a camera feed somewhere so I could watch the unveiling, but I couldn't take the risk. I was gutted though. This must be what Banksy feels like, I thought. I didn't understand why he didn't want people to know who he was, to take the credit and revel in the adoration.

I was too wired to sleep. I sat on the sofa looking through the many photos and videos I'd taken at all stages of my Daisy project. I found myself regretting the fact that I didn't give in to my animal lust before she'd made a mess of herself. I wondered if this was a need I'd have to satisfy sometime soon. I was pretty sure it was going to nag at me until I did something about it. I thought about Daisy's friends and the veritable walking buffet in the town on sunny days. I shrugged. If the desire got the better of me, I'd just take my pick. All you can eat. I had a flash of inspiration then, about recreating 'The Last Supper' which made me chuckle.

I finally fell asleep just before dawn, wondering about when Daisy would be discovered. She would've been reported missing by now, presumably, and a search would be underway. I made a mental note that I still had some stuff to burn in the morning – Daisy's clothes and bag, the remnants from her angel outfit, my gloves and so on. I couldn't get sloppy now. I was having way too much fun.

*

The day I'd waited so impatiently for, July twenty-first, dawned bright and sunny. The sandcastle competition started at ten a.m. and ran until one. I showered and had a quick breakfast before heading to Sunny Sands. I drove some of the way, parking on a residential street, and walking briskly the last half mile or so. I knew there was no point trying to park any closer on a day like this.

I needed to get there early, and was anxious about what I would find. I was just praying that my gamble had paid off. As I walked down the slope to the beach and looked across the high tide line, I heaved a sigh of relief. My early entry to the competition was still intact, undisturbed. I'd made a visit to the beach just before dawn when the tide was still going out, and left my sand sculpture in place. I'd swept sand around the edges of the figure so that it blended with the beach a little better. My heart rate quickened as I thought of the hidden treasure that lay inside. My little Russian doll. I was also gratified to see that the umbrella I'd positioned over the head of my sculpture, pegging it deep into the sand to secure it, was still in place.

I didn't approach my piece, but instead found a good vantage point in one of the arches at the back of the beach, settling myself in for the duration. I had my cap and sunglasses on, and a small rucksack with snacks and water in. I was learning. From where I was sitting, it would also be relatively easy to slip away unnoticed up a flight of stone steps to the path above when it all kicked off.

The beach filled up rapidly and by ten o'clock about a dozen teams set about building their sand sculptures. I'd seen a few people walk over and check mine out. There was obvious curiosity at this finished piece, apparently abandoned by its creator. I held my breath and hoped that no one paid too close attention. Whilst I'd got the colour match pretty damn accurate, it probably wouldn't bear too close an examination. Thankfully, none of the onlookers got down and looked inside the umbrella either, for inside it were stuck photographs from my other kills. Okay, so I'd totally nicked the idea from the legend of the Sandman, but I'd gone one better. The Danish legend has it that the Sandman carried an umbrella under each arm; one of them, with pictures on the inside, he spreads over the good children who dream the most beautiful stories all night through. But the other umbrella has no pictures, and this he opens over the naughty children so that they sleep heavily, and wake in the morning without having dreamed at all.

My umbrella had beautiful pictures of my works of art

which I was sure would give me the most vivid and pleasurable dreams. Some of those pictures were of the little Russian doll hidden under my double's sandy exterior. She was certainly naughty when I took her home from the pub two nights ago. She'd died with a smile on her face alright. It was a shame to have to douse her in bleach, but I couldn't risk my DNA being found on or in her. I'd used a condom – not just for reasons of anonymity, but also because she'd probably fucked half of Folkestone. I guess that's the closest I'd ever come to necrophilia. Wasn't my bag. I'd leave that to the sickos. I couldn't risk being caught yet; I still had work to do as I built towards my grand finale. I smiled to myself at the irony that I had been inside her and now she was inside me.

I sat back and allowed myself to soak up the holiday atmosphere, the excitement; watch the happy smiling faces of locals and holidaymakers alike, as they played on the sand. I'd wipe the smiles off their faces. When the waves came rushing back over the sand, I'd watch the tide turn on their happiness. I felt aroused at the thought, and remembered my night with the young woman who barely spoke English. She might not have been Russian, but she was definitely Eastern European. I guessed her to be in her early twenties. She was no Daisy: no angel. She'd barely noticed when I stuck her with the needle full of insulin. She'd been too preoccupied with what else I was sticking in her. I could've just increased the pressure on her throat as I semi-choked her, but insulin was part of my trademark now, my modus operandi.

I'd stored her in the cool, dark garage, doused in a gallon of bleach and wrapped in some of the plastic sheeting I'd bought. I figured the bleach might keep the smell down as her body started to decompose too. She wouldn't have to wait long until she went on display anyway. I'd thought about shoving a doll up inside her when I was done with her, but decided it was just too obvious. Let them work out Babushka and the Sandman for themselves.

By midday, with the sun at its zenith, the creations on the sand were really taking shape. There was a turtle, a Disney-style castle, an octopus, and a crown, amongst others. From time to time someone would amble over to my lonely man. They weren't to know about the company he kept inside. Not yet anyway. I could tell from their gestures and shrugs and the way they looked around that they were wondering who the mystery builder was, and if he or she was going to put in an appearance. Thankfully, good gamesmanship and the spirit of the competition kept anyone from interfering with my sculpture.

The tide had turned and was creeping back up the beach; it would be another couple of hours before the waves started to tickle the toes of my man. I wondered how long it would be before people started to notice that the sand wasn't washing away the way it ought to. Excitement gripped my gut as I thought about the unveiling, when Babushka (or Ludmila, or whatever the fuck her name was – I hadn't bothered asking) would get her moment in the sun.

One o'clock arrived and brought with it the judges of the sandcastle competition. I watched as they made their way across the beach, making notes on clipboards and talking in whispers behind their hands. Self-important asses. Probably local dignitaries who thought they mattered. When they reached my sculpture, they looked around, obviously looking for the artist, or artists. They spoke to the other contestants nearby, who I could imagine informing the judges that no one knew the identity of the mysterious sculptor. Banksy popped into my head. I had a lot of respect for Banksy.

The judges shrugged, clearly having no choice but to eliminate Sandman from the competition. Fine by me, I thought. I don't need your approval. First prize was awarded to a replica of Dover Castle; it was actually pretty impressive and I agreed with the decision. When the trophy had been awarded and photos taken for the local newspapers, the judges left and everyone got back to just enjoying their day. Only one photographer had bothered capturing an image of the Sandman as far as I could tell. He'd be pretty chuffed later when he realised what a scoop he had, I thought with a chuckle.

As the afternoon wore on, and the sea gradually began to reclaim the beach, my excitement built. I had deliberately deposited my sculpture a little closer to the water than the designated competition area. I wanted it to be reached first, in an effort to ensure discovery before everyone left the beach. I wanted witnesses.

As the first waves touched the Sandman's feet, I sat forward, fully alert. It was an instinctive movement and I made myself sit back again as soon as I realised what I'd done. I realised I was holding my breath too: the big reveal would be soon, I was sure. But I didn't want the quiet 'oohs' and 'ahs' of a calm gallery, I wanted screams and crying and disarray.

It wasn't long before the shallow incoming waves lapped around the feet and crept up the legs. Everyone had begun to move their stuff further up the beach, and some were packing up to leave. I willed them to stay a little longer, to be part of my audience. I'd make it worth their while and they'd really be missing out otherwise.

As I sat and waited, trying to control my impatience, I wondered who, if anyone, would notice that the mystery, unattended sculpture was not washing away. It turned out to be a couple of boys of about ten. They ambled over and stood looking down at the Sandman. I started filming them, surreptitiously, on my mobile. I could almost read their minds – after all, I was ten years old once. They wanted to kick the sand and speed up the demolition process. They probably wanted to remove the umbrella too, and maybe toss it upside down in the sea. I chuckled to myself at the thought of the umbrella bobbing across the Channel to France, and some poor unsuspecting French kid getting a slightly more graphic bedtime story than usual.

I watched and waited while they tried to decide what to do. Eventually, their natures got the better of them and they kicked Sandman's legs, one on either side. I stifled a laugh as they both cried out in pain at their stubbed toes, as their feet met with something other than simple compacted beach sand. People looked over on hearing their shouts. One of the boys ran back to his family group and pulled someone I assumed to be his father back to the Sandman. I could see the boy jabbering and gesticulating as they went.

By this time, a small crowd had gathered and some people had reached down and touched the sculpture, as if needing to confirm what they were hearing. I watched their faces, trying to read their thoughts. At this point, they probably still just assumed it was nothing more than a sculpture, albeit a much more solid one.

It was the boy's father who finally got down on his knees to examine it more closely. As he shoved at the torso, the body budged sideways a fraction. I could sense realisation dawning that his was actually a solid piece. He shoved it again, harder, with two hands. It moved far enough this time to knock against the surprise inside: the Sandman's final meal.

Feeling the resistance, the man looked to the crowd: 'Help me get this thing up,' he said.

Two more men joined him down on the sand, and six hands tried to lever their fingers under the edges. My heart was beating double-time by now and I had to remind myself to breathe. It was just a matter of seconds.

It took a little effort to prise the Sandman from the beach. I figured a slight suction had stuck him fast. But, all of a sudden, he flipped, and there she was in all her glorious bleachy beauty: my Babushka.

The scene quickly became chaotic. People were screaming and pulling their children away. One of the three men launched himself a few feet from the body and threw up. I appreciated the fact that he didn't spoil the art.

'Someone call 999!' a voice yelled.

I knew I should probably leave at this point, slip away unnoticed while everyone's attention was directed elsewhere. But I couldn't resist staying a little longer to revel in the reaction to my piece. I wondered what they would do, bearing in mind that the tide was now coming in fast.

One man, an older guy who looked to be in his fifties, seemed to take charge then. He instructed someone to take photographs on their mobile phone; to capture everything in situ and continue snapping away as they moved the body above the high tide line.

I knew this was my cue to leave, reluctantly. Attention would be redirected towards the back of the beach and someone might just pick me out later in their recall of the situation. Certainly, I hadn't reacted to the horror the way everyone else had. I stopped the recording on my phone, quietly got up and walked calmly up the stone steps, out onto the concrete walkway, and then up the cliff path to the road above. Only then did I allow myself to look back, but from this angle, the scene was hidden. I was more than satisfied anyway. As I made my way home, I thought I'd have a celebratory beer when I got in. It should be champagne really, I suppose, to celebrate the success of my latest exhibit, but I couldn't stand the stuff. Or maybe vodka, in a toast of thanks to my little Russian whore, who'd made it all so easy for me, before and after death.

Beer in hand, I sat down in front of the television so I could keep an eye on the news. I opened my laptop too to check out all the social media platforms. In this day and age, I would bet my life on the fact that the 'official' photographer was not the only one taking photos of the exhibit. And, knowing human nature, at least some of those photos, and probably videos, would find their way onto people's social media pages. Others would probably be sold or sent to TV and print media. My work and my notoriety would spread beautifully. I mentally gave thanks for the way people had evolved into these attention-seeking freaks, desperate for their fifteen minutes of fame and approval from their peers. Sad wankers.

I didn't have to wait long for the local news to come on and was delighted to be the opening story. I was really hoping to hit the nationals too. A reporter was live at the scene.

'A fun day at the beach here in Folkestone turned into a nightmare today, when beachgoers were horrified to discover the body of a woman concealed under what had been thought to be an entry in today's sandcastle competition.'

The reporter then went on to interview one of the men who'd flipped the Sandman. He was now dressed in shorts and shirt, but still looked pretty grey around the gills. He recounted the story pretty accurately, except for the part when he'd chucked his guts up, which he omitted, no doubt out of male pride.

Next came a poorly shot video of the drama as they moved the body and sculpture to safety. The reporter spoke over the video.

'Thankfully, witnesses quickly realised they had to move the body to safety, and to protect any evidence from the incoming tide. One man I spoke to said he knew in normal circumstances they should not have touched anything, but realised otherwise everything would be washed out to sea. He said they believed this was the only sensible course of action and that it stood the best chance of preserving vital clues for the police. The police have now cordoned off the area and a murder investigation has begun. We have no more details of the victim at this time.'

There was no mention of the umbrella with its gory story emblazoned on the inside, or any other details, like the words on the T-shirt. I wondered if the police had warned the media off. I knew it was in their best interests to keep certain details back. It helped them rule out the psychos and attention-seeking copycats.

I didn't know how I felt about being imitated. Would I be flattered? Maybe. One day. But not yet. Not until I'd finished my final exhibit. Until then, I had no desire to share the stage or the limelight.

I thought again about the umbrella. I hoped they'd removed it to safety. The story didn't make sense otherwise. Of course I had my own photographs: I documented all my work as I went, capturing every detail, not just for my own future pleasure, but for posterity and to be enjoyed by an audience.

I didn't budge off the sofa for the rest of the day, apart from popping to the kitchen for sustenance, or to use the bathroom. I joyfully soaked up the news as more and more details came to light. The umbrella got a mention – it had been retrieved, but still nothing was said about the photo-story within, which recorded Babushka's final hours. She hadn't objected when I'd taken intimate and downright degrading pictures of her. It seemed to me that she had no inhibitions and no shame. She was a slut, and the world had no need of her alive. Dead, she mattered much more. Dead, she would live forever.

*

I had one more exhibit in mind before my grand finale. The idea had come to me that day I'd fallen asleep in the garden. Since then, it had blossomed into something beautiful. I'd driven round the town, picking up sightings of the five parts of the 2017 exhibit I had in mind, and done my research online. This was going to happen, and fast, as the final exhibit was only a week away. I wasn't worried. Once I had the plan in my head, the rest was child's play.

The next installation that had the honour of receiving the

attention of the Exhibitionist was entitled 'Pent Houses', and consisted of five water towers, like the ones that used to appear above the streets of New York, placed along the lines of the hidden waterways of the Pent Stream. I had great respect and admiration for this particular piece – I could appreciate the thought and ingenuity that had gone into it. I felt I could relate to these two artists, and I loved the clever connections they formed.

The water towers mapped the course of the waterway, now hidden under the streets of Folkestone, that had helped bring prosperity to the town and created the harbour. One of the towers had a Plimsoll line marking, which was a nice little nod to Samuel Plimsoll who'd died in Folkestone. Details like that pleased me. I also liked the link to the harbour and beach, where Ambrus and my Babushka had been displayed. It had a kind of fluid connectivity that tied it all together somehow. Daisy was different, special, displayed above, on higher ground, as befitted her purity.

As brilliant as the 'Pent Houses' were, I knew I could take the story to the next level. Cue Eanswythe, patron saint of Folkestone; a seventh century Anglo Saxon princess, daughter of Edbald, one-time King of Kent. Refusing to marry a visiting Pagan prince, the princess became a nun, spending the rest of life in the nunnery she built – said to be the first in the country. It was common for unmarried princesses to be made saints, but saints needed miracles, and Eanswythe was said to have made water flow uphill when the contour aqueduct St. Eanswythe Water was created from the Pent Stream to supply the priory.

In stained-glass windows Saint Eanswythe was portrayed

holding an abbess's staff, wearing a crown, and holding a book. Some pictures added a fish to the items she held. Who knows what the truth is? It was all a bloody long time ago, and much of what's been written is probably bollocks. I decided to ignore the fish, and turned my attention to creating or locating the other items.

The simple Anglo Saxon crown was easy enough to fashion in my workshop, as was the staff. Thank God for basic seventh century decoration. I gave serious thought to what book she should be holding. Thank God I wasn't restricted to authentic texts from the period. I settled on a copy of *Hamlet*. Get thee to a nunnery, Eanswythe. The one thing I couldn't decide on was her costume. I toyed with the idea of making her a robe and cloak but decided I preferred the juxtaposition of ancient and modern. With a little bit of Shakespeare in between for good measure. For measure. I laughed at my own joke.

I'd studied the map of the Pent Stream, and found one section that was still visible above the ground, forming a gently winding stream flowing through the grounds of Folkestone Sports Centre. It was pretty easily accessible from Cornwallis Avenue.

I'd got it into my head that I wanted my Eanswythe to have flowing red hair. I think I was being influenced by Millais' 'Ophelia', which was no bad thing I s'pose. She needed to be about twenty – the age the saint was when she died. Time to go hunting, one of my new favourite pastimes.

Late evening was the best time for this particular hunting party. I wasn't interested in the young girls who roamed the town during the day, but the slightly older ones who took to the streets at night, equally scantily clad a lot of the time.

They didn't seem to have any respect for their bodies, leaving very little to the imagination. Still, I suppose, at least you knew what you were getting. As I trawled around the pubs and saw all the bare flesh on display, I wondered if I'd made a mistake in not making a costume. Too late now though. I was ready, and hungry for the kill.

Round about closing time, I parked the car I'd 'borrowed' close to a taxi rank, and waited. I'd made a fake driver ID which was now hanging in the front of the car. (I'd thought about stealing an actual taxi, and killing the driver if need be. But I wasn't some psycho who killed for the sake of it.) I was taking another gamble but, after the one with Daisy had worked out so well, I was feeling lucky. Fortune favours the bold, doesn't it? Although I preferred Andy Warhol's 'Art is anything you can get away with'. I was getting away with murder.

I bided my time. There were plenty of pissed girls, staggering up and ordering taxis. I just had to follow my instincts. I'd know when the right one came along. After about twenty-five minutes, I saw her. Fuck, she was perfect. Round about twenty, slim, not too tall and with auburn hair flowing over her shoulders in loose curls. She was swaying all over the place as she went up to the taxi window. She then went and stood away from the rank to wait. I took my chance. In order to pull up next to her, I had to drive round the block due to the one-way system. I silently prayed a genuine taxi wouldn't get to her before me.

'Where to, darlin'?' I said as I pulled the car up beside the kerb.

I could tell she was barely able to focus. She half tripped

over to the car and went to open the back door. I'd locked the doors.

'Hop in the front, door sticks,' I said, leaning over and opening the passenger door. Alcohol had stripped her of all sense and she practically fell into the front seat next to me. I could smell booze and a sickly sweet perfume mixed with sweat. I quickly pulled away from the kerb and drove off. My heart was pounding. I couldn't believe I'd done it again. Risking a glance round at her, I saw that she was fighting to keep her eyes open. I wondered where the fuck her friends were, and what sort of friends would let her leave on her own in this state. I shrugged. Win for me.

'Where to?' I said, feeling like I should keep up the pretence for now.

She mumbled an address on the east side of town.

I drove in the general direction until I found a quiet place to pull up. Before she had time to even think about reacting, I'd smothered her mouth and nose with a chloroform-soaked cloth. She put up less of a struggle than Daisy. Once she was out, I drove to Cornwallis Avenue, past the houses, and parked up on a deserted stretch.

She weighed next to nothing as I scooped her into my arms and carried her to the stream. Her legs bounced up and down, and her long hair felt soft as it brushed against my arm. My Eanswythe. My Ophelia. I was about to break with tradition as far as my M.O. went. There was no syringe full of insulin for this one. I wanted water in her lungs which meant she had to go in breathing. I lowered her gently into the stream.

The water wasn't very deep, and I had to push her right to the bottom to submerge her face. I held one hand on her head and the other at the tops of her legs. I had no real idea what happened when an unconscious person drowned. I'd read up a little bit about passive drowning victims and I wondered if I should flip her over so her face was uppermost in the water. I needn't have worried. It all happened pretty quickly as she kept on breathing and her lungs filled with water.

She was heavier when I carried her back to the car, 'her garments, heavy with their drink'. I'd lined the boot of the car with more plastic sheeting and, as I lay her gently down on it, I thought how useful the purchase had been that day at the DIY shop. I couldn't take her to her final resting place, not yet, so I took her home with me and transferred her to the workshop, lying her down on a bed of newspaper and old towels.

Her red curls were now long and lank which was disappointing, but once she'd dried out she'd do the job. I don't s'pose seventh century nuns paid their hair much attention anyway. Maybe they cut it short, or even shaved it off? I shrugged the thoughts off – I had an image in my mind of the exhibit and I wasn't going to change it now. That's the beauty of artistic licence anyway.

I felt the adrenaline ebbing away and felt suddenly exhausted. I guess I'd had a busy few weeks. I locked up the shed and headed to the house. It had been a good night, but now I needed to sleep.

The next morning I woke early, stretching and hanging on to fragments of a beautiful dream. The Sandman had obviously visited with his umbrella. I jumped in the shower with thoughts of Daisy for company, before pulling on jeans and a Tee and going downstairs to make coffee. I took the drink up to the workshop, eager to see how Ophelia had dried out.

She didn't look too bad at all. She hadn't been in the water for long, so I guess that helped. I was gratified to see her hair had sprung back to curls as it dried too. Nice. I took in her outfit. I hadn't really had time to stop and appreciate it last night. She was wearing a short denim skirt and a blouse that was pretty much see through, over a black lacy bra. On her feet she wore high wedge sandals – those ones with the raffia heels –and her toe nails were painted a bright orangey-red. It was pretty tarty, to be honest, and far from ideal. I wondered again if I should have made her an alternative costume, more befitting of the piece. I talked myself out of it, deciding that the juxtaposition of tart and nun could work well.

I practised the piece there on the workshop floor, placing the crown atop her flaming head. Then I hit a bit of a stumbling block as I tried to put the abbess's staff in her hand and was met with the stiffness of rigor mortis. Damn. I should've positioned the staff and the book last night while she was still pliable. I'd make it work, but I was pissed off not to have thought of this until it was too late. I prided myself on attention to detail. I suppose I was still a relative beginner at handling corpses. I'd get better.

The day stretched emptily ahead of me. I couldn't complete my latest exhibit until well after dark. As impatient as I was to advance my art, I forced myself to tackle some long overdue chores in the house and garden. This included clearing out the fire pit, which now contained the charred remains of Babushka's and Daisy's belongings. I bagged it all up and wondered how best to dispose of it. Obviously there was no DNA evidence to be got from any of it, but it could still cause questions if found. You could still make out what some of the bits were, including the metal rings from the sides of Daisy's bikini bottom, and a metal compact case from the Russian's bag. I wondered whether I should chuck it off a cliff somewhere, to be swallowed up by the sea, or put it in a random bin somewhere in the town. In the end, I decided to take it to the tip and chuck the bag into a huge general rubbish skip.

I made myself a bowl of pasta that night, washed down with a bottle of beer. While I ate, I looked at the locations of the five water tower 'Pent Houses' on a map, and tried to decide which was the best one. Two were inaccessible and easily eliminated. It was a shame there wasn't one closer to the Benedictine Priory, now The Parish Church of St. Mary and St. Eanswythe. The police would just have to work a bit harder to make all the connections. I finally selected the one off Tontine Street. It was a bit risky, close to the centre of town, but it would be easy to stop the car there and I reckoned I could be done and gone in under a minute.

After I'd eaten, I put the television on and sat on the sofa to wait. I flicked between news channels, eager for any mention of my exhibition. It gave me such a buzz listening to them talking about the Folkestone murders, which were now being described as the work of a serial killer. I was desperate for everyone to know my identity, and I had to remind myself that once that happened, the fun was over. I just had to grin and bear the anonymity until I was ready to stop; until the inspiration stopped coming. Then, and only then, would I reveal myself to the world. I set an alarm on my phone in case I fell asleep. I didn't think I'd need it though, as the adrenaline was starting to kick in.

My alarm went off at two a.m., waking me from an

unexpected sleep, and another delightful dream about Daisy. I yawned and stretched, before donning my dark jacket and black baseball cap, grabbing my keys and heading to the workshop. I'd already taken loads of photos of the redhead, but I took a few more before loading her in the boot along with her new belongings. I photographed her in the boot too. I knew it was important to document absolutely every detail of the making of each piece; one day they'd feature in a book. Or maybe even books. I could imagine a big glossy coffee-table book of my greatest works.

I drove the ten minutes to town and parked on the road behind the water tower. The area was deserted, luck being on my side as ever. Another quote popped into my head: 'Creativity takes courage'. I think that was Matisse. Well, I was proving I had no shortage of courage. It took only seconds to place Ophelia's body under the water tower, and to position her crown, staff and the copy of Hamlet. I had to just lean the book and staff because of her stupid stiff hands, and experienced a moment of angry frustration. I took it out on the body, ripping open the sheer black blouse to reveal the pale skin underneath. I quickly snapped a few more pics and left. My heart was pounding as I peeled off my gloves, got into the car and drove off.

As I drove home, feeling my heart rate gradually return to normal, I thought about the clues I'd left. If they flicked through the copy of *Hamlet*, they would find just one sentence underlined in Act 4, Scene 7 when Laertes says of Ophelia, "Alas, then she is drowned". I'd also signed the inside cover with my chosen artist name, just in case they were in any doubt. Undoubtedly, the post mortem would find that she actually drowned. I hoped they would go one step further and identify the water in her lungs as having come from the Pent Stream, and some bright spark would make the link with St. Eanswythe. My version of mixed medium art.

*

Preparations for the final exhibit, my grand finale, were well underway. It was a massive turn on to imagine the reaction of the audience to my final showpiece. In my mind, following an initial deathly hush as they tried to process what they were seeing, I could hear screams and chairs being tipped over; see people running for the exits, or struck dumb in their seats. Order turned to chaos. Beautiful.

I didn't have too long to wait until my chosen date of Saturday July 29. The weather forecast was looking favourable – it was an outdoor event and I wanted a packed house, so it had to be dry. I reckoned the venue seated around 250: my biggest audience yet. I knew there would undoubtedly be kids present. Well this was my gift to them. They'd witness something truly memorable. Okay, so they'd probably be fucked up by it for a while, I thought with a shrug. Not my problem. My circus. Not my monkeys. Anyway, they should thank me for letting them be part of something so special.

As promised by the Met. Office, show day dawned with blue skies and sunshine. Temperatures were predicted to reach the high twenties, which boded well for the eight p.m. start. The game was on.

I couldn't settle to anything much during the day, impatient as I was to get started. I spent a lot of time surfing the internet, rereading some of the many stories that had been posted about my achievements. I revelled in the atmosphere of fear I'd brought to the seaside town. Atmosfear. That would have been a cool name for tonight's show. I typed it into Google, but of course someone had got to it first – some undoubtedly dumb Australian video board game.

I had a soundtrack to go along with tonight's exhibit. I'd toyed with Marc Almond's 'The Exhibitionist', but it was just too slow to create the right atmosfear. Damn, I love that word. I'd settled on Metallica's 'Enter Sandman' as being appropriate and having the right level of menace. It would be the stuff of nightmares. Sleep with one eye open... Fuck. I couldn't wait.

Finally, it was time to leave the house. I didn't need to take much with me for this final installation; the tools of my trade fitted in my pockets. I was wearing my usual jeans, a dark-coloured T-shirt and baseball cap. They seemed to render me all but invisible. Nondescript. Unremarkable. If only they knew. I slipped on a lightweight black jacket, and pocketed the things I'd need.

I drove some of the way to the Harbour Arm, but didn't use the pay and display car park there. I didn't want the risk and inconvenience of having to queue up to pay and get out at the barrier, with the car park attendant looking on and wondering why I hadn't stayed for the show. I parked on the street and walked the rest of the way to the venue. I'd booked my ticket online; seemed a bit crap to have to pay to see my own show, but it was by far the easiest way to gain entry. It was still daylight and I wasn't chancing someone seeing me slipping in through the wire fence that surrounded the area. I was counting on there being no one around in the car park when I made my getaway later. I'd already found the best spot to get out, and had cut the wire in the middle of the night before. You couldn't tell at a glance that the wire had been snipped down the length of a post. From there I could gain access to the beach and slip away unnoticed.

I joined the queue to get in and showed the ticket on my phone, careful not to make eye contact with the guy on the gate. I just looked at my phone the whole time and nodded my thanks. Unremarkable. Invisible. The place was filling up already, people queuing at the food and drink vendors, buying chips and beers before the show started at eight. I lurked on the edge of the scene, biding my time. I watched the smiling faces, and listened to the happy chatter of people just out to enjoy themselves. I couldn't wait to wipe the smiles off their stupid faces. They were here at the Harbour Arm outdoor cinema to watch *The Greatest Showman*. It had made me chuckle when I'd looked through the summer programme for the cinema. This film was the obvious choice. Gradually, the seats filled up; the cheap plastic seats at the back, and the more expensive striped deckchairs at the front. Lucky things – they'd get the best view. I imagined them struggling to get out of the chairs when the action started, and smirked.

With about ten minutes to go until the film started, I snuck quietly to the projectionist's hut. Before I opened the door, I put on the pair of Nitrile gloves from my jacket pocket and took out my Stanley knife, pushing up the blades with my thumb. I will admit to having a moment's anxiety. This was completely different to anything I'd done before. This wasn't going to be a clean kill like the others. It had to be quick and dirty.

As I opened the door, the adrenaline kicked in big time. The guy on the swivel chair started to turn.

'Hey, you can't be in...'

He never finished the sentence as I grabbed his head and slashed into the soft, fleshy part of his throat where I knew the carotid artery was situated. He was bled out and dead in about thirty seconds. I pushed the chair away from the computer desk. I had to work fast. I'd prepared for what I hoped was every eventuality. I'd burned my film onto a DVD, a Blu-ray and a USB memory stick. I quickly sussed out the situation, and inserted the memory stick into one of the ports on the computer and watched it load. All I had to do at eight p.m. was press play.

Showtime! At eight o'clock on the dot, I hit play and I got out. Fast. I was through the fence and down onto the beach in about thirty seconds. I could hear 'Enter Sandman' playing. I was gutted I couldn't be in there to witness the spectacle, see the horror unfold as the audience realised what they were seeing on the screen. I wished it was dark too. The images on the screen would have been so much more vivid then, and I could maybe have risked staying on the beach to listen. I'd watched the film many times, of course, but never on the big screen. The audience was enjoying all my greatest hits: photographs and videos of all my kills and my beautiful art installations.

The screams started as I was walking to my car, pulling my gloves off inside out as I went. The feeling it gave me was the biggest thrill. Even better than the actual kills. It was never really about the killing anyway. It was about what came afterwards. And this, this was what it had all been building towards. Fuck Hugh Jackman. I was the greatest showman.

Arriving back at my car, I was still on a high. I was too hyped to drive and sat for a few minutes with the window down, straining to hear anything coming from the Harbour Arm. I must've been out of earshot though. I wondered if they'd managed to stop the film, and discovered the body of the projectionist.

I sat there long enough to hear the first sirens and then I drove home, careful to obey the speed limit and not do anything that might draw attention to me or my car.

Arriving home a few minutes later, I parked at the back of the house. I unlocked my workshop and quickly stripped off my clothes, changing into the spares I had stashed on my workbench. I chucked everything in the bonfire bin by my workshop, poured a whole load of lighter fluid on them and lit it, adding the gloves, DVD and Blu-ray. The USB stick back at the cinema had only ever been handled when I was wearing the gloves. Then I let myself into the house. The next thing I did was to chuck my knife in the sink and scrub it with bleach, before drying it and putting it back in my tool box.

Back indoors, I sat down at my laptop to make sure the emails I'd timed to send at eight p.m. had sent successfully. They were mailed from a burner email using a VPN, and included a copy of tonight's show. I had sent emails to every major news network, and a whole host of minor ones too. I was counting on them being monitored 24/7. So, I wasn't worried about my audience running screaming from the cinema; there was an even bigger one out there, just waiting.

I got a beer from the fridge and took up my usual position on the bench by the back door. I was thinking about what came next. I was undecided. I wanted the world to know the identity of the Exhibitionist; I wanted to be famous, infamous. I wanted celebrity, notoriety. But I wanted it on my terms, when I was ready. I didn't want to be found out by the police. I was smarter than them. I didn't know if I was done killing yet either. Maybe I'd move to another seaside town; work my way around the country. The greatest showman goes on tour. Summer seasons from Bournemouth to Blackpool and beyond. I found the idea appealing. Fear would spread around the country as people wondered if their town would be next. The Exhibitionist would be a household name. Yes! That was what I wanted. That was true fame, celebrity.

THE END

CHAPTER 27

Sick

I message Jenny as soon as I finish reading Robert's story. I actually feel physically sick.

You read it? I typed. *What the fuck?!*

As usual, she replies promptly. *I know! Sick fuck! What the hell?!* She's clearly reacting in the same way as me.

I'm not overreacting then? That story is not the product of a normal mind?

Er, no! I really think he's sick in the head. God knows what Pippa are John will make of it – they're even straighter than we are.

I don't think I want to be around him anymore.

You and me both. I'll have to ask him to leave the group. Not sure how though – I actually feel pretty intimidated by him now.

I agree. Well, at least we're safe for now. All the time we're only meeting online, it's not such a problem.

No, I s'pose. To be honest, I'd rather not see his face again, even on screen. And I definitely don't want to discuss his story with the group.

Me neither. What do we do?

Jenny sends the shrugging emoji.

We could say that the group is cancelled for the foreseeable future, due to Covid and the fact that Tom's in hospital, I suggest.

I guess. Tell Pippa and John privately what's happening.

Yeah, and then when this all blows over, we could start up again – different time and place, so Robert can't invite himself to join again.

I think we might have to. Looking back now, it was a bit weird how he joined the group in the first place.

I know. Seemed funny at the time, but it was a bit stalker-ish, wasn't it?

How do you think he'll take it if we don't have a meeting to discuss his story?

Hmm... don't know. What do you think?

Maybe we just have to blag our way through one last meeting? I don't know if I can face it.

How about asking the other two what they think and making it a group decision?

Sounds like a plan. I'll contact them and get back to you.

We say our goodbyes, and I put down my phone. I can't shake the unsettling feeling that Robert's story's triggered. Okay, so we'd all written our own murder stories, but none were so graphic or grisly. Like Robert, I too had written my story in the first person, but my 'murder' had been a tragic accident and I'd been eaten up with remorse. Robert as a killer was a complete psychopath. And maybe a narcissist. Reading his story had really felt as though he relished every second of it. He gloried in the killing and thought it art. I shudder as I remember some of the details. We definitely need him out of the group.

I struggle to get Robert's grisly story out of my head, and can't really settle to anything for the rest of the day. I'm relieved when I finally hear back from Jenny.

Soo... John and Pippa are in total agreement – Robert's a sick fuck and has to go.

I bet neither of them used that expression though!

And you'd be right. They were much more restrained in their turn of phrase, but the outcome's the same.

What about a final meeting to discuss his bloody story and officially close the group?

I think we have to have it. I told Pippa and John that they could skip if it they wanted. You and I would handle it. Although the thought actually makes me want to vomit.

I agree. We'll be okay. We'll get through it together, and then we never have to see him again.

Amen to that.

Okay, sorted. Right, catch up soon. I'm going to attempt to get some writing done.

All rainbows and unicorns please. No more murder.

No more murder. I promise. I didn't tell Jenny that I was actually about to kill off a character in my new novel. It was a car accident, anyway, so not exactly murder.

The rest of the week passed in the usual blur of writing, sunbathing, and shouting at the television when the daily government briefing was on. If I did murder anyone in my book, they'd either be a politician or a journalist. Maybe both. Every now and then an unwanted thought would creep up on me about the impending meeting with Robert, which I squashed back down as best I could, but it was never far from the surface. The logical part of me tried to persuade the emotional side that it was just words, just a story, no worse than *The Silence of the Lambs*, for example. But I still couldn't shake the chills that had begun as I'd read 'The Exhibitionist'.

The closer Monday's meeting got, the more anxious I got. I contacted Jenny on Sunday evening.

You ready to face psycho tomorrow?

Not really. Certainly be glad to get it over with.

Me too. Dreading it, to be honest. Is it just going to be the three of us: you, me and psycho Bertie?

Yes, 'fraid so.

Okay. Have you thought what you're going to say about the story.

I've tried. I think we just have to blag it in general terms like... I dunno... gruesome, grisly, dark, atmospheric...

Sick, twisted, psychotic... I finish the list for her.

We'll keep it as brief as possible. Say we're all so worried about Tom that we've decided to cancel the group.

Okay, good idea. Just let him think we thought the story was amazing and get rid of him asap.

That's the plan. I don't want him knowing we're just trying to get rid of him. I find the thought really unnerving.

I know. I do too. I shudder involuntarily.

Anyway, enough about Robert, let's talk about something a bit nicer... Coronavirus?

Oh yes, our old friend, CV. We're apparently past the peak now, at least.

Yep. Did you see they're trialling some contact tracing app on the Isle of Wight?

I did. It's started a whole new raft of Big Brother-style conspiracy theories.

God, if only the virus just attacked stupid people.

And psychopaths.

And Robert.

Yes, definitely Robert.

And then Tom wouldn't be in hospital.

I know. He does seem to be holding on though. I think the fact that he's not had to go on a ventilator is a really good sign.

Hope so. And once this is all over, we'll start a brand new writing group.

And write only about happy smiley things. And killing journalists, I thought to myself.

And cats.

Yes, and cats.

With that, we said our good byes. I felt a bit better about tomorrow's Zoom call as I got ready for bed that night. But still, I slept fitfully, disturbed by dreams of a young Russian woman suffocating to death inside a giant doll. The Sandman must've been holding the umbrella for naughty children over my head.

CHAPTER 28

Twisted

Monday May the fourth brought with it the first grey skies for a while. As I threw open the bedroom curtains, I couldn't help thinking how fitting the change in the weather was.

'May the fourth be with you, Amy Archer,' I muttered to myself as I trotted off downstairs to make coffee. I was feeling really anxious about the meeting now, and gave myself a bit of a talking to while the coffee machine burbled away. 'Pull yourself together. It's just a story. He's just a man. And after this you never have to see him again. And you thought he had nice blue eyes when you first met him.'

I took my coffee into the lounge and settled down to read over yesterday's chapters. I just needed to keep busy until ten o'clock. I found my concentration wandering though, and kept going over the same paragraph, still failing to spot a glaring typo. I kept yawning too. It felt like a combination of nerves and lack of sleep.

Finally, ten a.m. limped round and my laptop screen filled with three faces. Obviously the images were bigger than usual due to Pippa's and John's absence, and Robert's grinning visage made my stomach turn over. *How could I ever have thought he had nice eyes?* I wondered. He was wearing a Star Wars T-shirt. I'd half expected him to have on one that had 'Bring me a dream' printed on it.

I force a smile on my face. 'Morning.'

Two voices came back, 'Morning, Amy.'

Before I had a chance to say anything else, Robert dived in. 'So, what did you think?' He didn't even seem to have noticed that Pippa and John were missing.

'Wow, well, where do I start?' I say. 'Pretty powerful stuff.'

Robert nodded, grinning at me from the screen. 'Yeah! Right? Jenny? What did you think?'

I could feel Jenny's discomfort through the screen. 'Um, yeah, it was certainly very gruesome… and… atmospheric,' she said.

Robert kept nodding. 'I knew you'd like it.'

'It certainly felt like you got into character writing it,' I contributed next. 'Very convincing.'

'I'm glad you spotted that. I think I'm definitely growing as a writer,' he said.

'And a psychopath,' I muttered under my breath, before saying, 'Well, it was the first piece of your work we've read, but, like I said, it was very convincing which must say something about the writing.' *Yeah, that you're a psycho freak*, I thought.

He suddenly noticed the absence of Pippa and John then, obviously disappointed not to have a bigger audience. 'What about the others? Did they like it? I bet it gave Pippa nightmares!' He seemed to like that idea.

'Um… yes… they said it was very powerful and… er… dark,' Jenny said.

'Yes, and they were really sorry they couldn't be here today to tell you in person.' *To fuck off, you creep*.

'I'm so glad you all enjoyed it. I got a thrill out of writing it, that's for sure!'

I resisted the urge to say, *yeah, we know sicko*, and instead tried to bring the subject round to cancelling the group. Robert wasn't done though.

'Which was your favourite murder, out of all of them?'

Ooh, let me think? Was it the one where you pretty much had sex with a dead girl before dousing her in bleach and leaving her on the beach for some kids to find? Or when you cut the heart out of a poor innocent homeless man? And don't get me started on Daisy. Tough call. This was all going through my head in the few seconds it took me to come up with an answer. 'Well, it's difficult… they were all so good… um…' I was silently willing Jenny to jump in and save me, but she appeared to have become mute. And I don't mean she'd pushed the wrong Zoom button. I soldiered on. 'I don't think I can pick a favourite.' *They're all my least favourites.* 'To be honest, I think I liked the grand finale best – not necessarily the murder, but the idea of taking over the cinema to show the killer's own highlights. That was clever.'

Jenny thankfully pressed her mental unmute button at that point, and joined in again. 'Yeah, yeah, that was clever.' It was better than nothing. We just had to big him up a little bit more, and then go in for the kill. Of the group, that is.

Robert still wasn't done with us. 'So, you could see that it wasn't really about the killing, couldn't you? Or the victims? It was about the art installations themselves. You saw that, right?'

'Right, yes, yes, absolutely,' I nodded my agreement. Jenny had pressed her actual Zoom mute button this time. She didn't get out of it that easily. 'Er…Jenny, I think you've muted yourself accidentally,' I informed her.

Back in the Zoom. 'Oh, sorry, must've pressed it by accident,' she muttered.

'You saw it was about the art, didn't you?' I encouraged her.

'Oh, yeah, for sure. Um... yeah... it was all really clever... imaginative,' she said, bobbing her faded pink head up and down for emphasis. Or so we couldn't see her facial expression too clearly.

'And you didn't miss all the irony and twisting the social commentary?' Robert went on.

'Nope. Got all that. Very clever of you. Original.' I was running out of suitable adjectives. *Perverted, insane, certifiable, psychopathic, vile, repulsive, sickening, gross...* Okay, running out of adjectives I could actually use.

'And the way I use legend and folklore?' Robert. Still not done. 'With the Sandman and the Matryoshka doll?'

I nodded. 'Yep, got all that. Very good.' Good? Scraping the barrel now. I wondered if I could safely change the subject yet.

Apparently not. 'How about the end, where the killer is thinking about carrying on the killings in other towns? Did that work? Obviously, at some point he really wants the world to know his identity, so he can claim the killings as his own, and enjoy the fame, and notoriety... Maybe write a book from his prison cell. Have a movie made about him. All that sort of stuff.'

'Oh, I was convinced he had more killing in him. Absolutely,' I nodded.

Jenny's pink head bobbed up and down again.

'Excellent!' Robert said.

I grab my moment, while Robert has his head up his arse. 'So, anyway, Robert... I'm sad to say this is the last meeting of the group.' I'm not sure he's really listening. 'With everything that's happening, and Tom being in hospital, and so on...'

Jenny finally joins in, 'Yeah, we decided it was best to wind up 'Write Time, Write Place'.'

'So, today's the last meeting,' I add.

'Ever,' Jenny throws in for good measure.

He finally seems to register what we're saying. 'Oh!' He actually looks genuinely upset, which throws me and Jenny.

'Yeah, sorry, just doesn't feel right, you know… Tom… everything,' I shrug an apology.

'But you'll let me know when you start it up again?' he asks.

'Oh, yes, sure,' I say. '*If* we start it up again. Who knows what the future holds?' *Not you, that's for sure.*

Robert seems reassured. 'Well, I'm going to keep on writing my killer stories in the meantime. Got the bug now. Let's hope I don't end up in hospital like Tom, eh?'

I know what Jenny's thinking and feeling at this point, because I'm feeling exactly the same way. I grit my teeth and force myself to speak. 'Well, I guess that about wraps things up. It's been… er… fun. Take care, and… um… see you around.' *When hell freezes over.*

'Yep, you too. Bye,' Jenny waves and disappears from view.

I gabble a quick 'Bye' and hit Leave Meeting, holding a hand up and smiling grimly.

I've literally just stopped exhaling a sigh of relief when a WhatsApp video call comes through on my phone. Jenny.

'Thank fuck that's over,' she says, pressing her fingers into her temples. 'Gave me a splitting headache.'

'Still, it's done now, and we can forget we ever knew Robert-Psycho-Bloody-Seymour.'

Jenny giggles. 'I'll be very happy to see less of him,' she says, winking at me.

I cock my head on one side, letting my brain catch up with my ears. I replay what I said and the penny drops. 'Oh, very good. Seymour what you did there.'

'Best I could do at short notice. With a headache.'

'Well, the headache's been banished from the group now, so you can relax. After lockdown finally ends, we'll start over somewhere new.'

'But where else will we get that special Wetherspoons' ambience and hot chocolate for one thirty-five?'

'Not forgetting people drinking pints at ten a.m.,' I remind her.

'Yeah, okay, so I can live without them.'

'We'll find a nice coffee shop somewhere. It'll be fine.'

'Yes, it will. And Tom will be back with us, and all will be well,' Jenny adds with a smile.

'Notice freak-boy didn't even ask about Tom at the start of the meeting.'

'I know. I nearly said, Tom's still in hospital, thanks for asking. Chickened out though. Didn't want to find myself on a beach with a needle full of insulin in my arm!'

'Let's not waste any more energy thinking or talking about him. He's out of our lives.'

'Yippee! Good riddance!'

'Happy Star Wars Day, Jenny! May the fourth be with you.'

Jenny grinned. 'And with you, Amy!'

CHAPTER 29

Psycho killer

A week later and the country remains in lockdown, although the limit on going outside to exercise has been removed. I can now not go out and exercise as often as I want. The government has changed their slogan to: Stay Alert. Control the Virus. Save Lives, which everyone seems to find terribly confusing and has resulted in a new wave of funnies on the internet. We'd completed our seventh clap for the NHS, (I think they'd prefer a pay rise), and face coverings are now advised on public transport and in places where the social distancing rule of two metres can't be observed. Jenny's mask making business was turning into a nice little earner for her. I'd got my order in early and had two masks just in case. I'd seen a few people wearing them at the supermarket but, as I went late at night when there was hardly anyone there, I hadn't bothered with mine yet.

My book was progressing nicely, as was my tan, and I wasn't minding the solitary life too much on the whole. Like everyone, I had good days and bad days. The bad days just involved a lot more chocolate and sometimes a box of tissues. The strain was telling on my neighbours, whose annual row had become pretty much a weekly occurrence. They took it in turn to storm out now, with the other one yelling, 'If you walk out that door, don't bother coming back!' Whoever'd stormed out was usually back within the hour, and then they carried on as if nothing had happened. Until the next time. I'd gone from feeling embarrassed the first time it happened, to actually finding it quite amusing now. Lockdown was hard, whoever you were doing it with. Or not doing in my case. I couldn't remember the last time I'd been on a date, and there was no chance of that changing anytime soon. Cameron popped into my head and I hoped he and Richie were keeping in touch.

We were taking an actual break from the writing group – no one's heart seemed to be in it at the moment. We kept in touch via Facebook and Jenny and I chatted fairly often. We had fantastic news on May fourteenth when we heard that Tom was coming home from hospital. That night's clap for the NHS was especially poignant, and we all heaved a huge sigh of relief. I messaged Tom's wife; I could only imagine half of the emotions she was feeling. The other Tom, Captain Tom, who'd captured not just our hearts, but the nation's, was to be knighted after raising something like thirty-two million pounds. It was lovely to have some good news amongst all the doom and gloom.

Thankfully, neither Jenny nor I had heard from Robert. We assumed he was busy plotting the Exhibitionist's nationwide tour and thinking up sick new ways of displaying his victims.

It was about three weeks after our final meeting with Robert, that an item on the local news caught my attention. A body had been found in the harbour, next to the pink holiday home model. They didn't have any other information than that. A brief alarm bell rang in my head as I recalled Robert's grisly tale of Ambrus the Greek. I tried to shake off the thought, but it persisted, so I messaged Jenny.

Hey. Did you just see the news?

Yeah, I was actually just about to message you. Strange, huh?

Mmm… bit of an odd coincidence.

It is, but they didn't say anything about the body being chained to a chair or anything.

No, I s'pose. It could have been washed up there or something, couldn't it?

Yeah, defo. Could've fallen off a boat out in the Channel.

That's a point – there've been lots of dinghies with immigrants trying to get across.

There have. A record number this year apparently.

How desperate must the poor things be to try and get across in a tiny boat like that?

I know. And then wash up in bloody Folkestone! Poor buggers.

And, just like that, we'd talked ourselves out of the body being anything more sinister than a tragic accident.

When the body of a young woman was found by one of the 'Pent Houses' Jenny and I officially freaked out. We arranged to meet in person and I headed off to Folkestone later that day. It was the first time in ages I'd driven further than the local supermarket, and I didn't know whether to be scared or excited. Or if I'd need my passport. Strange times. The roads were oddly quiet as I drove the few miles to the meeting point at a local beauty spot. Jenny was already waiting when I made my way to the bench. She raised her arm in greeting as I approached. It was so lovely to see her in person. She was wearing one of her homemade masks. I wasn't surprised to see it had cats on. I waved back and sped up.

'Hey! It's so great to see you!' I said as we sat down at either end of the bench. We weren't quite two metres apart, but I wasn't too worried as I knew we'd both been sensible during lockdown. Jenny took off her mask and smiled at me.

'Good to see you too.' She waves her mask in the air. 'Just

wore it to show you. I've made dozens now. Nice to be out – this feels nearly normal. Ish.'

'Yes. Ish! I was starting to think life would only ever be virtual. You look really well,' I tell her.

'Thanks. I am well. Probably been exercising more than ever. And being a vegan means my diet's usually pretty healthy anyway.'

'Wish I could say the same,' I say. 'Although I have kept up the hula hooping, which is more than I did before.'

'Moved on to cheese and onion now?'

'Salt and vinegar actually.'

There's a moment's silence. I know we're each waiting for the other to mention the body police found. I dive in.

'So, the body… what do you make of it?'

'I have a really bad feeling, Amy. I mean, one body, okay, we can write that off as a coincidence. But two?' Jenny pulls a worried face.

'I know. I feel the same. As much as I don't want to believe it…'

'Christ, I know, it's unimaginable! Can Robert really be…' Jenny pauses, obviously reluctant to utter the words.

'A stone-cold killer?' I finish for her.

'Shit,' is all Jenny says in response.

We sit in silence again for a minute.

'Should we go to the police? Tell them about Robert? About his stories?'

'I s'pose so, yeah. Do you think they'll take us seriously?'

'They'd have to wouldn't they? With his stories to back us up.'

Jenny looks worried still. 'But what if they didn't believe us?

They could say that one of us could have copied Robert's ideas. After all, we've read his stories.'

I stop to think about what Jenny's said. 'What if we had proof? Before we went to the police?'

Jenny looks doubtful. 'Maybe… but how are we going to get proof? If he really is even the killer.'

'We could follow him?' I suggest.

'Bloody hell. The thought of tailing someone who's potentially a psycho killer doesn't fill me with joy,' Jenny says.

'What about going to his house? See if we can find any evidence of anything suspicious; anything relating to the murders.'

'That sounds just as terrifying as tailing him. Do we even know where he lives?'

I screw my face up. 'No. Could we find out somehow?' I think back to my earlier lack of success in digging up anything about Robert online. 'I don't think he has much of an internet presence, so he's probably ex-directory.'

'If he's actually the Exhibitionist then he'll soon have one hell of an internet presence,' Jenny says grimly.

'Jesus.'

Silence overtakes us again, both deep in thought.

Eventually, Jenny speaks. 'What if I found out his address on the pretext of sending out something to all the members of the writing group? Say… I dunno… I've had books made with our stories in or something, and I want to post them out to everyone?'

'That's a great idea. Then we can check out where he lives – at least we'll be doing something.'

'What if it really is him though? And he kills someone else

while we're fannying about?'

'Oh God, I really don't know! Let's just get his address asap and take it from there. I really don't fancy being dragged into the police station on suspicion of murder because we've read Robert's stories.'

'I wonder if he's shown them to anyone else? Someone outside the group.'

'Hm… could've done, I suppose. Anyway, I'll leave getting his address up to you and give me a shout when you've got it.'

Jenny nods. 'Why don't I do it now? Before I chicken out.' With that, she got her mobile out of her bag and composed a message to us all in the Facebook group, based on the idea we'd talked about.

My phone pinged almost immediately after she pressed send and I replied at once, figuring it would look more genuine and would get the others moving. I just hit reply and said I'd PM Jenny my address straight away. While I was doing that, Jenny messaged John and Pippa individually to tell them to play along and she'd explain when she next spoke to them. She added that they shouldn't reply with their addresses in the group message. It felt like a bad idea for Robert to know where any of us lived, murderer or not.

Jenny and I stayed and chatted a while longer. It was so nice to be outside, talking with someone in the flesh, instead of via a chat app. We talked about the pandemic, naturally, and how wonderful it was that Tom was back home with Cheryl. Eventually, we stood up to go, with Jenny promising to let me know when she heard from Robert. Assuming she did. If not, we'd have to go back to the drawing board.

CHAPTER 30

We know where you live

I finally heard back from Jenny just after ten p.m. that same night. She'd just received a message from Robert with his address. Apparently, he was excited at the prospect of seeing his words in print. Jenny was now worrying she might actually have to produce a short book.

'Don't worry,' I told her. 'We'll cross that bridge when, if, we come to it.'

'Hm… okay. Anyway, I looked up where he lives. It's on the outskirts of town – looks pretty rural, just a few cottages in a row. How are we going to do this? I don't have a car. We'd have to go in yours. But we wouldn't be socially distancing properly in a car.'

I understood Jenny's concerns, but no way was I doing this on my own. 'What if we both wear a mask? And I promise not to turn round to look at you. Unless I have to. For driving reasons,' I suggested.

'I s'pose that would be okay. In the circumstances,' she acceded.

'Great. When suits you?' I asked.

'Er… half past never o'clock on the nonteenth?'

'Sounds good to me. Seriously, though, we can't put this off.'

'No, I know, but I really just want to bury my head in the sand.'

'Therein lies the problem, my friend. So does our killer!' I couldn't help myself.

Jenny groaned. 'Oh my fucking God.'

'Sorry.' I was laughing now. With maybe just a touch of hysteria.

We eventually agreed that I would pick Jenny up at nine thirty the next morning. We'd agreed to go during daylight hours as we were both too scared to go after dark.

Jenny was waiting on her doorstep when I arrived. She had on a black hoodie over black jeans, and had swapped her cat mask for a plain dark grey one. I couldn't help giggling when I saw her.

'You look like a Ninja,' I said. 'Or a cat burglar.' I realised as the words were leaving my mouth that I didn't look too dissimilar in grey jeggings, hoodie and mask. We looked at each other and laughed. Anyone who saw us might actually think we were on our way to rob a bank.

'I'd prefer to nick a few cats than do what we're doing,' she said, as she got in beside me.

I made a point of looking straight ahead when I replied. 'I know. I can't say I'm looking forward to it much either.' I entered the address details into the sat. nav. and pulled away from the kerb.

'What's the plan then? What if he's at home?' Jenny asked.

'Um… I s'pose the first thing we need to do is look for a car at the address. If there's one there, we should probably abandon the plan and come back another time.'

'Definitely. I do NOT fancy being caught by Robert snooping round his gaff.'

'No, I know. Worst case scenario… if he appears, we could say we were out for a walk and realised we were close to where he lived and thought we'd pop by to say hello.' I realised how lame it sounded as I spoke, but I didn't have anything better. 'I think we'll just have to play it by ear.'

We drove in silence for the next ten minutes or so. When we were getting close, I pulled into a layby at the side of the road, and we got out of the car to walk the rest of the way. Jenny put her hood up which, to be honest, looked more suspicious until I thought about her pink hair. Nobody was going to remember my mousy-brown locks which I had tied back in a ponytail.

As we approached the row of cottages, we slowed down. My heart was beating so loudly I was surprised Jenny couldn't hear it. We knew from looking at the street view online that Robert's cottage was the last one in the row. There was no sign of a car outside the front of the end property, but as we arrived at the first house, we found a rough track, big enough for vehicles, leading round to the rear of the properties. I nudged Jenny. 'Do you think there's parking round the back?' I whispered.

'You what?' she said.

I realised that whispering didn't work so well with masks on, and repeated the question a bit louder.

'Yeah, maybe. Shall we check it out?'

I nodded, and we made our way up the track which did indeed lead behind the houses, turning left as we reached a row of garages and other outbuildings. We followed it to the far end, and were relieved to find no car parked there.

'What if it's in the garage?' Jenny hissed.

There was a garage and some sort of large shed or workshop, which hid the garden and the back of the house from view.

I shrugged, tiptoeing over to the garage window and peering in. It was hard to see inside, and I shielded my eyes as I tried to make out the interior. 'I can't see a car in there.'

'What about in there?' Jenny said, nodding towards the other building. We noticed that there was a pretty substantial-looking padlock on the door. To look in the window meant going round the side of the shed, and possibly being in sight of the house. Jenny seemed rooted to the spot, so I took a deep breath and covered the few feet around the corner. There was a metal gate between me and the back garden. I put my face up to the glass and peered in.

'Fuck! Oh my God,' I exclaimed, stumbling backwards. I could feel the colour draining from my face, which was now no doubt the same colour as my outfit. I grabbed Jenny by the arm – social distancing be damned – and pulled her away, back down the track, not stopping until we were safely in the car. I started the engine, turned the car round in the road and drove out of there and back to town.

'What?' Jenny kept saying. 'What is it, Amy? What did you see?'

I couldn't speak. I could barely breathe. I pulled my mask away from my mouth in an effort to get more oxygen to my brain. I just wanted to get to the safety of the town, and away from the risk of Robert catching us near his house. I just shook my head at Jenny. Only when we'd parked up once more did I turn to Jenny and tell her what I'd seen through the window of Robert's workshop.

'It was the Sandman.'

'What?'

'The Sandman. From Robert's story about the Russian girl on the beach. The model of himself he makes for the sandcastle competition.'

I can see horrified realisation dawning on Jenny's face. 'Oh my God, Amy. We have to go to the police! Now! Before he kills anyone else.'

I rest my face in my hands, waiting for the pounding in my chest to ease. I still can't believe what I saw. 'Could there be another explanation for it?' I ask, when I'm finally able to speak again. I already know the answer, and that I'm clutching at straws, but I desperately don't want to believe what I saw with my own two eyes.

Jenny shakes her head. 'I really don't see how there can be.'

'What if he just made it when he was researching the story? You know, to see if it was doable. Believable.'

'Maybe. If it wasn't for the bodies that've been found. I think we have to face facts, Amy. Robert is the Exhibitionist. Robert is a serial killer. And he's not going to stop unless we stop him.'

At this point, we abandon all pretence at social distancing and go to Jenny's house, where she makes tea for us both while I make a fuss of her cats.

Soon we're sitting in the lounge cradling mugs of tea – two sugars in mine, for the shock – and wondering what to do next.

'We should've gone straight to the police, shouldn't we?' I say finally.

'Yeah, we should,' Jenny agrees. 'Why didn't we?'

I stop to think for a minute. 'Honestly? I don't know.'

Silence again.

'I keep thinking about his story… about how the killer wants fame and notoriety and all that stuff…' Jenny says after a while.

I feel my eyebrows knit together, playing mental catch up with Jenny. It doesn't take long. We're usually on the same wavelength. I nod slowly, and take a sip of my hot, sweet tea.

*

A few days later, reports appear on the news that the body of a man believed to be responsible for three recent murders in the town has been found at his home. The man has been named as thirty-four-year-old Robert Seymour. Police say they are treating the death as suicide and are not seeking anyone else in connection with the matter.

*

A few days after that, I set off in the car to visit Jenny. The sun is shining again, and I drive with the windows down and the stereo up, singing along to 'Mr. Brightside'. I'm wearing denim shorts and a new T-shirt from Jenny that had arrived in the post yesterday. The song ends just as I pull up outside her house. I'm not wearing a mask – I figure with everything we'd been through together we're past masks.

Jenny grins at me as she opens the door – she too has decided to skip the mask. She sees what I'm wearing and her grin widens.

Her T-shirt matches mine.

Who knew we were both such big fans of The Killers?

EPILOGUE

That day at Jenny's, after we'd discovered the sand statue, we sat and talked for hours about what was happening and what we should do. There was still an element of disbelief that someone from our little local writing group could be a serial killer.

'I still can't get my head around it,' I said, shaking my head at Jenny.

'I know, me neither, but look at the evidence,' she said.

'But how can he be recreating the murders in his stories while we're in lockdown? It's not possible – the sandcastle competition is cancelled and the pubs are shut, for starters.'

'True, but the real killings don't have to be exactly the same as the stories, do they?'

'I s'pose not. And they do bear a horrible resemblance to the fictional ones, don't they?' I conceded reluctantly.

'Yep. I know the police haven't released many details, but the two locations can't be a coincidence.'

I still don't want to believe it. 'But what if he's shown the stories to someone else, and they're copying him?'

'Then how would you explain the Sandman sculpture in his shed?'

'Shit.' I'm running out of reasons not to accept the evidence.

'He'd still be able to find victims even during lockdown,' Jenny said.

'Yes, you're right. And in some ways, lockdown actually helps I suppose – seeing how quiet the streets are. Reduces the chances of being seen.'

'Exactly. Okay, so maybe he can't be as choosy with his victims and he can't match the storylines and the way the bodies are discovered, but he can still display them the same.'

'It really is him, isn't it?' I finally admit.

'I'm afraid so. And we're the only people that can stop him,' Jenny said grimly, nodding.

*

'We need a gun.' Jenny said it so matter-of-factly that I was more than a little stunned.

'What?! You want to shoot him? Have you ever even fired a gun? Are you sure we can't just go to the police?' I was having a major wobble about what we were considering.

Jenny shook her pink head. 'No. We have to do this, Amy. We can't let him be made known to the world. That's what he wants: the credit, the notoriety. Remember everything he said about his killer being like Jack the Ripper or someone like that. He doesn't deserve it. And we can prevent it from happening.'

I'd never seen this side of Jenny before; a gritty strength and determination. Mind you, I'd misjudged her before, all those months ago at the vet's. There was clearly still more to the depths of her personality that I hadn't plumbed. I didn't know what to say. Jenny spoke again.

'So, a gun. Any ideas how we could get one?'

'Er… no… funnily enough,' I replied. The whole conversation was becoming pretty surreal, but Jenny wasn't letting up.

She screwed her face up, obviously weighing something up in her mind. 'There is one possibility,' she said finally. 'My dodgy ex in London. He had some pretty shady connections. Probably wouldn't ask too many questions either.'

Another layer peeled away from Jenny's meek and mild exterior as I took in this new information.

'Onion,' I said. My mouth ejected the word before my brain could pull the plug on it.

'Onion? What are you on about?'

I cringed. 'You. You're like an onion. All these layers you keep peeling away, constantly surprising me with the person underneath.'

Jenny laughed. 'People do have a tendency to underestimate me,' she said.

'Yeah, I can see that.'

Eager to change the subject, I went back to the gun. 'I don't think I can shoot anyone. Not even Robert.'

Jenny shook her head. 'If it all goes to plan, we won't actually have to fire it.'

Blimey, there's a plan, I thought to myself. Jenny obviously read the confusion on my face and proceeded to outline 'the plan'. By the time she'd finished my mind was so boggled that I'd slipped into some weird dreamlike state which blurred reality and fiction.

I'm not quite sure how the next bit went, looking back now, but I found myself agreeing to Jenny contacting her dodgy ex in London about getting her a gun. I have to confess to having a moment where I wondered if she'd ever made him a cat food curry.

That night, as I lay in bed, unable to sleep and staring at the ceiling, I fully expected the Sandman to rock up at some point and open up an umbrella filled with a series of images Hieronymus Bosch or Salvador Dali would happily have taken credit for. By the time I finally drifted off to sleep, I'd managed to persuade myself that Jenny wouldn't go through with it. I woke the next morning, after what felt like a dreamless sleep, to a text message from Jenny.

Sorted. We need to meet him in Chatham later today.

My first thought, bizarrely, was Chatham? Why Chatham? I never go to Chatham. Or any other of the Medway Towns for the matter.

Okay I sent back meekly, whilst wondering what the fuck I was doing.

Pick me up at 7 came the instruction.

I sent back a thumbs up emoji, too stunned to come up with actual words. I still couldn't work out why I was going along with this madness but, at seven o'clock that night I found myself pulling up outside Jenny's.

She got in the car, looking entirely chilled about the fact that we were off to meet her ex to collect a lethal weapon. I'd wondered on the drive over if it would actually have bullets in. I was hoping not, as she said we weren't really going to fire it.

The roads were quiet between Folkestone and Chatham and I wondered if we were breaking lockdown rules by driving to another town. All we needed was to be stopped by the police and fined. I could just imagine being pulled over and asked what the purpose of our journey was.

'Er… exercise…' I heard my imaginary self saying.

And then imaginary Jenny chiming in with, 'Yeah, exercising our right to carry a gun', and laughing like a deranged person.

I was pretty sure at this point I must soon wake up and realise this was all a dream.

Jenny was in buoyant mood, however, and she turned up the stereo and sang along with The Killers' song 'Caution'. She'd opened the window and chucked it out from what I could see.

She directed me to a retail park on the outskirts of the town and, as I pulled into the car park, there was only one other car there.

'Great!' Jenny said. 'He's here already. Won't be a tick.' With that, she bounced out of the car and trotted over to the other one, looking as if she didn't have a care in the world. I could just about make out the driver of the car as he wound down his window: he had a skinhead and was smoking. He did indeed look pretty dodgy. Jenny leant down to the window – I assume they exchanged a few words, you know, How are you? How are the cats? Is your mum doing okay? What d'you want a gun for? – just small talk. Then I saw him hand her something and she turned back towards me, waving at him as she reached the car and got in, at which point I had visions of the gun going off. She banged her hands on the dashboard in front of her and I flinched again. 'Let's go!' she yelled, as if I was the getaway driver.

I pulled the car out of the car park and set off back the way we'd come. I was even more anxious about being stopped by the police now.

I could see the shape of the gun wrapped inside a cloth resting in Jenny's lap. I wondered again if it was loaded. And if it was pointed at my leg. I took a breath and asked:

'So… um… is it… er… is it loaded? The gun, I mean. Has it got bullets in?'

'Er…yeah…of course it has. Not much use, otherwise, is it?' Jenny informed me.

'I just thought, as we're not actually going to fire it…' I let the sentence hang.

'No, I know, but we might have to fire a warning shot. You know, a threat. Show we're serious.'

Fuck, I thought. 'Right. Okay,' I said. I was trying to convince myself that at some point Jenny would come to her senses. Or I'd wake up.

I dropped Jenny back at hers and drove home in a daze. I couldn't for the life of me work out how I'd let myself get drawn into this crazy plan. We should've just gone to the police.

When I woke the next morning after another restless night, that thought hit me again like a shot to the heart. Another body had been found. This time it was the body of a young girl and she'd been found next to the war memorial in the old Bradstone Baptist Burial Ground. Something flipped inside me. Robert had just signed his own death warrant.

*

I rang Jenny straight away.

'We have to do it tonight.'

'You've seen the news then?'

'Yes. And I feel like we have blood on our hands now. If we'd gone to the police, that girl might still be alive.'

'Maybe. You don't know that for sure though.'

'All I know is we have to stop him. Now. Before anyone else dies.'

'Except him,' Jenny added.

I felt a bit mental by now. 'Well, yes, except him.'

'Okay. Come round to mine tonight. I'll do dinner if you want?' Jenny said.

Mental. *Yeah, let's have a nice dinner before we go out and commit murder.* 'Um… no, no dinner, thanks. Be round about nine?'

'Righty-o, see you later.'

I hung up the phone and shook my head. Jenny sounded as though we were just making plans to go to a WI meeting instead of confronting a psycho killer. Mind you, I felt as if the plot, my marbles and I had well and truly parted company now too.

The rest of that day consisted mainly of pacing and listening to the news. I was almost relieved when it was time to go and collect Jenny. I just wanted this over with.

We waited until just after dark before setting off to drive to Robert's, leaving our mobiles switched on in Jenny's kitchen. Parking in the lay-by we'd found previously, we put on our anti-Corona masks and gloves and walked the short distance to his cottage. I felt sick. I told Jenny. She told me not to throw up as it would ruin the nice mask she'd made and mess up the crime scene. Who was this cool, calm and collected woman?

I took a deep breath, which didn't really help in the mask, as Jenny knocked on the front door. She had a small rucksack on her back and I knew that she had her hand on the gun in her jacket pocket.

A light came on in the hall and I saw the silhouette of a man approaching. The feeling of nausea rose in my throat as I breathed in the now warm and moist fabric covering my nose and mouth. The door opened and there he stood: Robert Seymour. The Exhibitionist. With his cold blue eyes.

He couldn't keep the surprise from showing on his face at seeing the two of us standing on his doorstep, masks and all, at almost ten o'clock at night. I swallowed, unable to speak.

'Hello!' Jenny said, brightly, in a most un-Jenny-like fashion. Who was this woman? She was unrecognisable from the meek little mouse who used to bring her cats to the vet.

I tried to smile, still unable to speak.

'Oh… er… hello you two. This is a surprise,' Robert said finally. *You don't know the half of it*, I thought to myself as he stood aside and gestured for us to go in.

I followed Jenny into the house, which was surprisingly cosy and welcoming. I don't know what I'd been expecting – some sort of Hammer House of Horror? As we turned right into the lounge, Jenny was babbling something along the lines of 'Sorry… know it's late… Amy and I were talking about the book and we just wanted to get your thoughts and input'.

By this time, I'd completely parted company with reality and just sat on the sofa like a lobotomised mute. So, when Jenny took out the gun and aimed it at Robert, I barely reacted.

Robert leapt up. 'What the fuck, Jenny! That's not funny!'

'Do I look like I'm laughing?' Jenny said, sounding deadly calm.

I think I giggled. Some sort of nervous reaction I had no control over. Wholly inappropriate, whatever it was.

Jenny looked daggers at me.

Who are you? I thought.

Robert and Jenny were both on their feet now and the gun was pointed straight at his chest. It was like a scene from a movie, not the real lives of two aspiring writers and an engineer from Folkestone.

Jenny spoke again. 'Amy, get the letter.'

I went blank for a minute, 'til I remembered 'the plan'. I rummaged in the rucksack and took out the folded sheet of A4. I held it out to her, but she nodded to Robert and I handed it to him.

'Sign it,' Jenny said.

I suddenly remembered the pen and scrabbled about in the bag again, handing Robert the black biro I produced. It was verging on the ridiculous. I was half expecting Cameron to flounce in at this point, and announce that we couldn't kill his lover, before pulling a gun on us. In my head it turned into a blackly comic Mexican standoff.

Robert's expression was a mixture of anger and confusion which darkened as he read the words. I didn't know exactly what Jenny had written, but I knew it was along the lines of him being the Exhibitionist and not being able to live with what he'd done.

'Sign the fucking letter,' Jenny said, waving the gun menacingly.

Robert hesitated, clearly weighing up his options, but whatever he saw on Jenny's face persuaded him she was serious, and he scrawled his signature at the bottom of the letter.

'Okay, you've had your fun, now let's stop with the sick joke,' he said, throwing paper and pen to the floor.

'The fun's just started, Robert, and the only sick joke here is you.'

I had to give Jenny credit, she was bloody brilliant. I couldn't have written this better myself. The thought that maybe we should join a drama group flitted into my head, and I giggled again. Jenny shot me another disapproving look.

'You crazy bitch!' Robert said. I think he was addressing Jenny. I was less crazy, more inept and slightly befuddled sidekick. I really felt like I was having some wacky out of body experience.

'Amy, go upstairs and find a belt,' Jenny said, without taking her eyes off Robert. I knew there was a rope in the rucksack, so I will admit to being a little confused. The plan had been to get him to hang himself at gun point, and Jenny had already tied the noose. Maybe she'd decided this was more poetic. I did as I was instructed anyway. I guess Jenny was adapting as she went. The planner had become a pantser. The pantser had become… well… just pants, really.

I went upstairs and found my way into what was obviously Robert's bedroom. I clicked on the light and looked around to get my bearings. I spotted a pair of jeans with a belt on draped over a chair in the corner. As I crossed the room to retrieve the belt I couldn't help noticing what was on the bedside table. It was a pile of photographs. I picked them up. A pair of terrified blue eyes stared back at me, from the face of an angelic-looking girl of about fourteen. She had a gag in her mouth. My hand flew to my mouth and a sob hit the back of my throat as I looked at the next couple of photos. When I saw her lifeless body laid out on the ground, the sob escaped and after it came a flood of icy rage.

I dropped the photographs and ran back downstairs, into the lounge, grabbed the gun out of Jenny's hands and, before either she or Robert could react, I shot him in the side of his head at close range.

There was a burst of red as Robert's head lurched away from the impact. I stumbled backwards at the unfamiliar recoil, dropping the gun, and for a moment everything was a blur. When I regained my focus, Robert was lying half on the sofa, obviously dead, and Jenny was staring at him in disbelief. Eventually, after what seemed like an age, she looked over at me.

'Fuck me,' she said, raising her eyebrows.

Jenny tells me I went into shock then and started shaking uncontrollably and gibbering incoherently about it not being a dream after all then. Thankfully, she went into take charge mode. She took me by the shoulders:

'Look at me, Amy,' she said. 'Look at me. He deserved to die. You've done the world a favour.'

'But…' I started.

'No buts. We can still make this work – make it look like a suicide. Hanging would've been my preference, but…' she shrugged.

'I… it was the photographs… upstairs… the girl…' I mumbled.

'Photographs? Show me.' I led Jenny back up to the bedroom and picked up the scattered pictures, handing them to her.

'Sick fuck,' she said angrily, storming back down the stairs. I think she would have shot Robert if I hadn't beaten her to it.

Jenny put the suicide note we'd made Robert sign on the floor next to him with the photographs. Hopefully they'd think looking at the images had sent him mad with remorse or something and he'd shot himself.

'Take off your gloves,' she instructed.

I did as I was told and watched as Jenny proceeded to rub them all over Robert's left hand and wrist, transferring gunshot residue to him. She then picked up the gun and put it in his hand.

'Lucky for you he's left-handed,' Jenny said as she stood back to look at the tableau.

I didn't answer her. I wasn't feeling terribly lucky right now.

'If he'd been right-handed, he wouldn't have been able to shoot himself in the left side of his head,' she continued. I just wanted her to stop talking. She seemed satisfied with the scene. 'Right, let's get out of here. Don't touch anything on the way out.'

I nodded like the dumb mute I'd become and followed Jenny out of the house. She turned off the hall light and pulled the door closed after us, leading me like a child back to the car.

I came round a bit then, back in the safe space of my car. I realised I had to drive, took a breath and got us safely back to Jenny's.

'Do you want to stay here tonight?' Jenny asked. 'Might be better not to be on your own.'

I thought for a moment and all I wanted was to get home and close the door on the world. 'Um… no, thanks. I think I need to go home.'

'Okay, if you're sure, but I'm phoning you first thing to make sure you're alright. Remember, he deserved to die, Amy.' She hugged me awkwardly in the confines of the car. Any pretence at social distancing was long gone between us by now. 'Drive carefully. Text me when you get in.'

'Yes. Okay. I will.'

I don't remember the drive home. I don't remember texting Jenny, or falling into bed fully clothed. When I woke the next morning, I wondered briefly if it had all been a horrible nightmare. Any hopes of that were dashed when I went into the bathroom and saw the blood spatter on my sleeve. I promptly threw up.

I stripped off all my clothes and put them in a hot wash, before climbing into the shower myself. As I was drying myself I heard my mobile going. It was Jenny, of course.

'Hey, morning. How are you?' she said.

'Um… I'm honestly not sure. I think I must be in shock or something.'

'You're bound to be after a traumatic incident like last night.'

'Yeah. I don't know what came over me. I just saw those photos of that girl and…'

'You don't need to explain it to me, Amy. I totally get it.'

'But I killed a man, I…'

'You killed a killer, there's a difference.'

'Is there? I don't know, Jenny… And what if they don't believe it was suicide? I can't go to prison.'

'You're not going to prison. There's no reason they'll suspect anyone else was involved. Trust me, it's going to be alright.'

And it was.

My agent always told me that as writers we must experience things in order to write about them and, to be honest, writing this book has been kind of cathartic.

THE END

Acknowledgements

Thank you for reading *The Write Way to Die.* I really hope you enjoyed reading it as much as I enjoyed writing it. I wrote it during the first few months of the Covid-19 pandemic, and this aspect of the story reflects my own experience of that strange time in all our lives. I think writing helped get me through the difficult days.

My grateful thanks go to James Essinger at The Conrad Press for always believing in me, and to Karla for her careful proof-reading. To Charlotte Mouncey for her brilliant cover design and typesetting, as ever. To Cathy White for inviting me to join her writing group in Folkestone, which spawned the idea for this book. I'm also grateful to Cathy for proofreading my work and telling me when I'm using 'that' too much! I'd also like to thank 'Mr. Lewisham' who briefly touched my life while I was writing this book, and for his early encouragement on the murder stories. I hope to read a book by him one day. My love and thanks go to two people whose friendship got me through 2020: Kathy Matthews and Gwynne Morgan. And last, but never least, I give thanks for my son, Sam, who is simply the best human being on the planet.

Addendum

This second edition of *The Write Way to Die* was published by my new publisher, Hut 22 Books. A great deal has changed in my personal and writing life since I wrote this book. I have moved to Folkestone, where the book is set, and it has become the first in a series. As I write this addendum, I am penning the fourth book. I have to add thanks to my partner, photographer Dirk Seyfried, who is incredibly supportive of my writing, and a rather brilliant sounding-board!

Amy and Jenny return in the next gripping instalment.

The Exhibitionist's back, and his summer collection's to die for ...

When more bodies start turning up at the art installations scattered around the seaside town of Folkestone, best friends Amy and Jenny panic. Can the Exhibitionist really be back? Did they get the wrong man the previous summer? There's only one way to find out, so the friends turn amateur detective once more as they bumble their way through stakeouts and stalking of a killer who is literally painting the town red with the blood of his victims.

Available in paperback and eBook

Having seen off two serial killers in as many years, Amy and Jenny are looking forward to a quiet life, but their hometown of Folkestone has other ideas ...

Throwing themselves into the local pub quiz scene, the friends are shocked when members of other teams start dropping dead at an alarming rate. Jenny's convinced they simply died of old age, but Amy's not so sure and sets out to investigate, hoping to find enough evidence to convince her friend there's more to it. When Amy gets too close to the truth, she puts a target on her own back. Will she be the next quizzer to meet a questionable end?

'A fun, action-packed crime romp set against the backdrop of the good ol' British pub-quiz scene. This story plays out so naturally you almost forget it's a novel. Hugely satisfying.'
Charlie Gallagher, Author of the Maddie Ives Books

Available in paperback and eBook

Amy and Jenny are back in *The Wrong Mind Murders*, and looking forward to getting back to normal after the ordeal of Amy's kidnapping. As ever, their seaside hometown of Folkestone has other ideas, and Amy's spidey senses are soon tingling once more.

Belinda has moved to Folkestone for a fresh start following the painful end of her marriage, and is quickly befriended by Amy and the others, who are drawn to her gentle nature. But, as the saying goes, still waters run deep: is Belinda hiding a murky secret? And are the seemingly random murders happening in the town actually connected?

Available in paperback and eBook